TRAILING WEST

TRAILING WEST

Louis L'Amour

LEISURE BOOKS NEW YORK CITY

A LEISURE BOOK®

August 2008

Published by special arrangement with Golden West Literary Agency.

Dorchester Publishing Co., Inc.
200 Madison Avenue
New York, NY 10016

ISBN 10: 0-8439-6067-1
ISBN 13: 978-0-8439-6067-9

The name "Leisure Books" and the stylized "L" with design are trademarks of Dorchester Publishing Co., Inc.

Printed in the United States of America.

10 9 8 7 6 5 4 3 2 1

TABLE OF CONTENTS

Introduction

by Jon Tuska

L ouis Dearborn LaMoore (1908–1988) was born in Jamestown, North Dakota. He left home at fifteen and subsequently held a wide variety of jobs although he worked mostly as a merchant seaman. From his earliest youth, L'Amour had a love of verse. His first published work was a poem, "The Chap Worth While," appearing when he was eighteen years old in his former hometown's newspaper, the *Jamestown Sun*. It is the only poem from his early years that he left out of *Smoke from This Altar*, which appeared in 1939 from Lusk Publishers in Oklahoma City, a book which L'Amour published himself; however, this poem is reproduced in *The Louis L'Amour Companion* (Andrews and McMeel, 1992) edited by Robert Weinberg. L'Amour wrote poems and articles for a number of small circulation arts magazines all through the early 1930s and, after hundreds of rejection slips, finally had his first story accepted, "Anything for a Pal" in *True Gang Life* (10/35). He returned in 1938 to live with his family where they had settled in Choctaw, Oklahoma, determined to make writing his career. He wrote a fight story bought by Standard Magazines that year and became acquainted with editor Leo Margulies who was to play an important rôle later in L'Amour's life. "The Town No Guns Could Tame" in *New Western* (3/40) was his first published Western story.

During the Second World War L'Amour was drafted and ultimately served with the U.S. Army Transportation Corps in Europe. However, in the two years before he was shipped out, he managed to write a great many adventure stories for Standard Magazines. The first story he published in 1946, the year of his discharge, was a Western, "Law of the Desert Born" in *Dime Western* (4/46). A call to Leo Margulies resulted in L'Amour's agreeing to write Western stories for the various Western pulp magazines published by Standard Magazines, a third of which appeared under the byline Jim Mayo, the name of a character in L'Amour's earlier adventure fiction. The proposal for L'Amour to write new Hopalong Cassidy novels came from Margulies who wanted to launch *Hopalong Cassidy's Western Magazine* to take advantage of the popularity William Boyd's old films and new television series were enjoying with a new generation. Doubleday & Company agreed to publish the pulp novelettes in hardcover books. L'Amour was paid $500 a story, no royalties, and he was assigned the house name Tex Burns. L'Amour read Clarence E. Mulford's books about the Bar-20 and based his Hopalong Cassidy on Mulford's original creation. Only two issues of the magazine appeared before it ceased publication. Doubleday felt that the Hopalong character had to appear exactly as William Boyd did in the films and on television and thus even the first two novels had to be revamped to meet with this requirement prior to publication in book form.

L'Amour's first Western novel under his own byline was *Westward the Tide* (World's Work, 1950). It
was rejected by every American publisher to which
it was submitted. World's Work paid a flat £75 without royalties for British Empire rights in perpetuity.
L'Amour sold his first Western short story to a slick
magazine a year later, "The Gift of Cochise" in *Col-
lier's* (7/5/52). Robert Fellows and John Wayne purchased screen rights to this story from L'Amour for
$4,000 and James Edward Grant, one of Wayne's
favorite screenwriters, developed a script from it,
changing L'Amour's Ches Lane to Hondo Lane.
L'Amour retained the right to novelize Grant's
screenplay, which differs substantially from his
short story, and he was able to get an endorsement
from Wayne to be used as a blurb, stating that *Hondo*
was the finest Western Wayne had ever read. *Hondo*
(Fawcett Gold Medal, 1953) by Louis L'Amour was
released on the same day as the film, *Hondo* (Warner,
1953), with a first printing of 320,000 copies.

With *Showdown at Yellow Butte* (Ace, 1953) by
Jim Mayo, L'Amour began a series of short Western novels for Don Wollheim that could be doubled with other short novels by other authors in
Ace Publishing's paperback two-fers. Advances
on these were $800 and usually the author never
earned any royalties. *Heller with a Gun* (Fawcett
Gold Medal, 1955) was the first of a series of original Westerns L'Amour had agreed to write under
his own name following the success for Fawcett of
Hondo. L'Amour wanted even this early to have
his Western novels published in hardcover edi-
tions. He expanded "Guns of the Timberland" by
Jim Mayo in *West* (9/50) for *Guns of the Timber-
lands* (Jason Press, 1955), a hardcover Western for

which he was paid an advance of $250. Another novel for Jason Press followed and then *Silver Cañon* (Avalon Books, 1956) for Thomas Bouregy & Company. These were basically lending library publishers and the books seldom earned much money above the small advances paid.

The great turn in L'Amour's fortunes came about because of problems Saul David was having with his original paperback Westerns program at Bantam Books. Fred Glidden had been signed to a contract to produce two original paperback Luke Short Western novels a year for an advance of $15,000 each. It was a long-term contract but, in the first ten years of it, Fred only wrote six novels. Literary agent Marguerite Harper then persuaded Bantam that Fred's brother, Jon, could help fulfill the contract and Jon was signed for eight Peter Dawson Western novels. When Jon died suddenly before completing even one book for Bantam, Harper managed to engage a ghostwriter at the Disney studios to write these eight "Peter Dawson" novels, beginning with *The Savages* (Bantam, 1959). They proved inferior to anything Jon had ever written and what sales they had seemed to be due only to the Peter Dawson name.

Saul David wanted to know from L'Amour if *he* could deliver two Western novels a year. L'Amour said he could, and he did. In fact, by 1962 this number was increased to three original paperback novels a year. The first L'Amour novel to appear under the Bantam contract was *Radigan* (Bantam, 1958).

A basic element to many a range war plot is the villain's means for crowding out the other ranchers in a district. He brings in a giant herd that requires all the available grass and forces all the smaller ranchers out of business. It was this same strategy Bantam used in marketing L'Amour. *All* of his Western titles were continuously kept in print. Independent distributors were required to buy titles in lots of 10,000 copies if they wanted access to other Bantam titles at significantly discounted prices. In time L'Amour's paperbacks forced almost everyone else off the racks in the Western sections. L'Amour himself comprised the other half of this successful strategy. He dressed up in cowboy outfits, traveled about the country in a motor home visiting with independent distributors, taking them to dinner and charming them, making them personal friends. He promoted himself at every available opportunity. L'Amour insisted that he was telling the stories of the people who had made America a great nation and he appealed to patriotism as much as to commercialism in his rhetoric.

Once when we were talking and Louis had showed me his topographical maps and his library of thousands of volumes that he claimed he used for research, he asserted that, if he claimed there was a rock in a road at a certain point in a story, his readers knew that if they went to that spot they would find the rock just as he described it. I told him that might be so but I personally was troubled by the many inconsistencies in his stories. Take *Last Stand at Papago Wells* (Fawcett Gold Medal, 1957). Five characters are killed during an Indian raid. One of the surviving characters emerges from seclusion after the attack and counts *six* corpses.

"I'll have to go back and count them again," L'Amour said, and smiled. "But, you know, I don't think the people who read my books would really care."

There are many fine, and some spectacular, moments in Louis L'Amour's Western fiction. I think he was at his best in the shorter forms, especially his magazine stories, and the two best stories he ever wrote appeared in the 1950s, "The Gift of Cochise" early in the decade and "War Party" in *The Saturday Evening Post* (6/59). The latter was later expanded by L'Amour to serve as the opening chapters for *Bendigo Shafter* (Dutton, 1979). "War Party" possesses several of the characteristics in purest form, which I suspect, no matter how diluted they ultimately would become, account in largest measure for the loyal following Louis L'Amour won from his readers: the young male narrator who is in the process of growing into manhood and who is evaluating other human beings and his own experiences; a resourceful frontier woman who has beauty as well as fortitude; a strong male character who is single and hence marriageable; and the powerful, romantic, strangely compelling vision of the American West that invests L'Amour's Western fiction and makes it such a delightful escape from the cares of a later time—in this author's words from this story, that "big country needing big men and women to live in it" and where there was no place for "the frightened or the mean."

Trap of Gold

Wetherton had been three months out of Horsehead before he found his first color. At first, it was a few scattered grains taken from the base of an alluvial fan where millions of tons of sand and silt had washed down from a chain of rugged peaks; yet the gold was ragged under the magnifying glass.

Gold that has carried any distance becomes worn and polished by the abrasive action of the accompanying rocks and sand, so this could not have been carried far. With caution born of harsh experience, he seated himself and lit his pipe, yet excitement was strong within him.

A contemplative man by nature, his experience had taught him how a man may be deluded by hope, yet all his instincts told him the source of the gold was somewhere on the mountain above. It could have come down the wash that skirted the base of the mountain, but the ragged condition of the gold made that improbable.

The base of the fan was a half mile across and hundreds of feet thick, built of silt and sand washed down by centuries of erosion among the higher peaks. The point of the wide V of the fan lay between two towering upthrusts of granite, but from where Wetherton sat, he could see that the actual source of the fan lay much higher.

Wetherton made camp near a tiny spring west of the fan, then picketed his burros and began his climb. When he was well over 2,000 feet higher, he stopped, resting again, and, while resting, he dry-panned some of the silt. Surprisingly there were more than a few grains of gold even in that first pan, so he continued his climb and passed at last between the towering portals of the granite columns.

Above this natural gate were three smaller alluvial fans that joined at the gate to pour into the greater fan below. Dry-panning two of these brought no results, but the third, even by the relatively poor method of dry-panning, showed a dozen colors, all of good size.

The head of this fan lay in a gigantic crack in a granite upthrust that resembled a fantastic ruin. Pausing to catch his breath, he let his gaze wander along the base of this upthrust, and right before him the crumbling granite was slashed with a vein of quartz that was literally laced with gold!

Struggling nearer through the loose sand, his heart pounding more from excitement than from altitude and exertion, he came to an abrupt stop. The band of quartz was six feet wide, and that six feet was cobwebbed with gold.

It was unbelievable, but there it was.

Yet even in this moment of success, something about the beetling cliff stopped him from going forward. His innate caution took hold, and he drew back to examine it at greater length. Wary of what he saw, he circled the batholith, and then climbed to the ridge behind it, from which he could look down upon the roof. What he saw from there left him dry-mouthed and jittery.

The granite upthrust was obviously a part of a much older range, one that had weathered and worn, suffered from shock and twisting, until finally this tower of granite had been violently upthrust, leaving it standing, a shaky ruin among younger and sturdier peaks. In the process, the rock had been shattered and riven by mighty forces until it had become a miner's horror. Wetherton stared, fascinated by the prospect. With enormous wealth there for the taking, every ounce must be taken at the risk of life.

One stick of powder might bring the whole crumbling mass down in a heap, and it loomed all of 300 feet above its base in the fan. The roof of the batholith was riven with gigantic cracks, literally seamed with breaks like the wall of an ancient building that has remained standing after heavy bombing. Walking back to the base of the tower, Wetherton found he could actually break loose chunks of the quartz with his fingers.

The vein itself lay on the downhill side and at the very base. The outer wall of the upthrust was sharply tilted so that a man working at the vein would be cutting his way into the very foundations of the tower, and any single blow of the pick might bring the whole mass down upon him. Furthermore, if the rock did fall, the vein would be hopelessly buried under thousands of tons of rock and lost without the expenditure of much more capital than he could command. And at this moment, Wetherton's total of money in hand amounted to slightly less than $40.

Thirty yards from the face, he seated himself

upon the sand and filled his pipe once more. A man might take tons out of there without trouble, and yet it might collapse at the first blow. He knew he had no choice. He needed money, and it lay there before him. Even if he were at first successful, there were two things he must avoid. The first was tolerance of danger that might bring carelessness; the second, that urge to go back for that little bit more that could kill him.

It was well into the afternoon, and he had not eaten, yet he was not hungry. He circled the batholith, studying it from every angle, only to reach the conclusion that his first estimate had been correct. The only way to get to the gold was to go into the very shadow of the leaning wall and attack it at its base, digging it out by main strength. From where he stood, it seemed ridiculous that a mere man with a pick could topple that mass of rock, yet he knew how delicate such a balance could be.

The tower was situated on what might be described as the military crest of the ridge, and the alluvial fan sloped steeply away from its lower side, steeper than a steep stairway. The top of the leaning wall overshadowed the top of the fan, and, if it started to crumble and a man had warning, he might run to the north with a bare chance of escape. The soft sand in which he must run would be an impediment, but that could be alleviated by making a walk from flat rocks sunken into the sand.

It was dusk when he returned to his camp. Deliberately he had not permitted himself to begin work, not by so much as a sample. He must be deliberate in all his actions, and never for a second should he forget the mass that towered above him. A split second of hesitation when the crash came—and he accepted it as inevitable—would mean burial under tons of crumbled rock.

The following morning, he picketed his burros on a small meadow near the spring, cleaned the spring itself, and prepared a lunch. Then he removed his shirt, drew on a pair of gloves, and walked to the face of the cliff. Yet even then he did not begin, knowing that upon this habit of care and deliberation might depend not only his success in the venture but life itself. He gathered flat stones and began building his walk. *When you start moving*, he told himself, *you'll have to be fast*.

Finally, and with infinite care, he began tapping at the quartz, enlarging cracks with the pick, removing fragments, then prying loose whole chunks. He did not swing the pick but used it as a lever. The quartz was rotten, and a man might obtain a considerable amount by this method of picking or even pulling with the hands. When he had a sack filled with the richest quartz, he carried it over his path to a safe place beyond the shadow of the tower. Returning, he tamped a few more flat rocks into his path and began on the second sack. He worked with greater care than was, perhaps, essential. He was not and had never been a gambling man.

In the present operation, he was taking a carefully calculated risk in which every eventuality had been weighed and judged. He needed the money, and he intended to have it; he had a good idea of his chances of success, but knew that his gravest danger was to become too greedy, too much engrossed in his task.

Dragging the two sacks down the hill, he found a flat block of stone and with a singlejack proceeded to break up the quartz. It was a slow and hard job, but he had no better means of extracting the gold. After breaking or crushing the quartz, much of the gold could be separated by a knife blade, for it was amazingly concentrated. With water from the spring, Wetherton panned the remainder until it was too dark to see.

Out of his blankets by daybreak, he ate breakfast and completed the extraction of the gold. At a rough estimate, his first day's work would run to $400. He made a cache for the gold sack and took the now-empty ore sacks and climbed back to the tower.

The air was clear and fresh, the sun warm after the chill of night, and he liked the feel of the pick in his hands.

Laura and Tommy awaited him back in Horsehead, and, if he was killed here, there was small chance they would ever know what had become of him. But he did not intend to be killed. The gold he was extracting from this rock was for them and not for himself.

It would mean an easier life in a larger town, a home of their own, and the things to make the home a woman desires. And it meant an education for Tommy. For himself all he needed was the thought of that home to return to, his wife and son—and the desert itself. And one was as necessary to him as the other.

The desert would be the death of him. He had been told that many times and did not need to be told, for few men knew the desert as he did. The

desert was to him what an orchestra is to a fine
conductor, what the human body is to a surgeon. It
was his work, his life, and the thing he knew best.
He always smiled when he looked first into the
desert as he started a new trip. Would this be it?

The morning drew on, and he continued to work
with an even-paced swing of the pick, a careful fill-
ing of the sack. The gold showed bright and beautiful in the crystalline quartz, which was so much
more beautiful than the gold itself. From time to
time as the morning drew on, he paused to rest
and to breathe deeply of the fresh, clear air. Deliberately he refused to hurry.

For nineteen days, he worked tirelessly, eight
hours a day at first, then lessening his hours to
seven, and then to six. Wetherton did not explain
to himself why he did this, but he realized it was
becoming increasingly difficult to stay on the job.
Again and again, he would walk away from the
rock face on one excuse or another, and each time
he would begin to feel his scalp prickle, his steps
grow quicker, and each time he returned more reluctantly.

Three times, beginning on the 13th, again on the
17th, and finally on the 19th day, he heard movement within the tower. Whether that whispering
in the rock was normal he did not know. Such a
natural movement might have been going on for
centuries. He only knew that it happened then,
and each time it happened, a cold chill went along
his spine.

His work had cut a deep notch at the base of the
tower, such a notch as a man might make in felling
a tree, but wider and deeper. The sacks of gold,

too, were increasing. They now numbered seven, and their total would, he believed, amount to more than $5,000—probably nearer to $6,000. As he cut deeper into the rock, the vein was growing richer.

He worked on his knees now. The vein had slanted downward as he cut into the base of the tower, and he was all of nine feet into the rock with the great mass of it above him. If that rock gave way while he was working, he would be crushed in an instant, with no chance of escape. Nevertheless, he continued.

The change in the rock tower was not the only change, for he had lost weight, and he no longer slept well. On the night of the 20th day, he decided he had $6,000 and his goal would be $10,000. And the following day, the rock was the richest ever! As if to tantalize him into working on and on, the deeper he cut, the richer the ore became. By nightfall of that day, he had taken out more than $1,000.

Now the lust for the gold was getting into him, taking him by the throat. He was fascinated by the danger of the tower as well as the desire for the gold. Three more days to go—could he leave it then? He looked again at the tower and felt a peculiar sense of foreboding, a feeling that here he was to die, that he would never escape. Was it his imagination, or had the outer wall leaned a little more?

On the morning of the 22nd day, he climbed the fan over a path that use had built into a series of continuous steps. He had never counted those steps, but there must have been over 1,000 of them. Dropping his canteen into a shaded hollow and pick in hand, he started for the tower.

The forward tilt *did* seem somewhat more than

before. Or was it the light? The crack that ran behind the outer wall seemed to have widened, and, when he examined it more closely, he found a small pile of freshly run silt near the bottom of the crack. So it had moved!

Wetherton hesitated, staring at the rock with wary attention. He was a fool to go back in there again. Seven thousand dollars was more than he had ever had in his life before, yet in the next few hours he could take out at least $1,000 more, and in the next three days he could easily have the $10,000 he had set for his goal.

He walked to the opening, dropped to his knees, and crawled into the narrowing, flat-roofed hole. No sooner was he inside than fear climbed up into his throat. He felt trapped, stifled, but he fought down the mounting panic and began to work. His first blows were so frightened and feeble that nothing came loose. Yet when he did get started, he began to work with a feverish intensity that was wholly unlike him.

When he slowed, and then stopped to fill his sack, he was gasping for breath, but despite his hurry, the sack was not quite full. Reluctantly he lifted his pick again, but before he could strike a blow, the gigantic mass above him seemed to *creak* like something tired and old. A deep shudder went through the colossal pile, and then a deep grinding that turned him sick with horror. All his plans for instant flight were frozen, and it was not until the groaning ceased that he realized he was lying on his back, breathless with fear and expectancy. Slowly he edged his way into the air and walked, fighting the desire to run away from the rock.

When he stopped near his canteen, he was wringing with cold sweat and trembling in every muscle. He sat down on the rock and fought for control. It was not until some twenty minutes had passed that he could trust himself to get to his feet.

Despite his experience, he knew that, if he did not go back now, he would never go. He had taken out but one sack for the day and wanted another. Circling the batholith, he examined the widening crack, endeavoring again, for the third time, to find another means of access to the vein.

The tilt of the outer wall was obvious, and it could stand no more without toppling. It was possible that by cutting into the wall of the column and striking down, he might tap the vein at a safer point. Yet this added blow at the foundation would bring the tower nearer to collapse and render his other hole untenable. Even this new attempt would not be safe, although immeasurably more secure than the hole he had left. Hesitating, he looked back at the hole.

Once more? The ore was now fabulously rich, and the few pounds he needed to complete the sack he could get in just a little while. He stared at the black and undoubtedly narrower hole, then looked up at the leaning wall. He picked up his pick and, his mouth dry, started back, drawn by a fascination that was beyond all reason.

His heart pounding, he dropped to his knees at the tunnel face. The air seemed stifling, and he could feel his scalp tingling, but once he started to crawl, it was better. The face where he now worked was at least sixteen feet from the tunnel mouth. Pick in hand, he began to wedge chunks from their seat. The going seemed harder now, and the chunks did not come loose so easily. Above him, the tower made no sound. The crushing weight was now something tangible. He could almost feel it growing, increasing with every move of his. The mountain seemed resting on his shoulder, crushing the air from his lungs.

Suddenly he stopped. His sack almost full, he stopped and lay very still, staring up at the bulk of the rock above him.

No.

He would go no farther. Now he would quit. Not another sackful. Not another pound. He would go out now. He would go down the mountain without a backward look, and he would keep going. His wife waiting at home, little Tommy, who would run gladly to meet him—these were too much to gamble.

With the decision came peace, came certainty. He sighed deeply and relaxed, and then it seemed to him that every muscle in his body had been knotted with strain. He turned on his side and with great deliberation gathered his lantern, his sack, his hand pick.

He had won. He had defeated the crumbling tower; he had defeated his own greed. He backed easily, without the caution that had marked his earlier movements in the cave. His blind, trusting foot found the projecting rock, a piece of quartz that stuck out from the rough-hewn wall.

The blow was too weak, too feeble to have brought forth the reaction that followed. The rock seemed to quiver like the flesh of a beast when stabbed; a queer vibration went through that ancient rock, then a deep, gasping sigh.

He had waited too long!

Fear came swiftly in upon him, crowding him,

while his body twisted, contracting into the smallest possible space. He tried to will his muscles to move beneath the growing sounds that vibrated through the passage. The whispers of the rock grew into a terrifying groan, and there was a *rattle* of pebbles. Then silence.

The silence was more horrifying than the sound. Somehow he was crawling, even as he expected the avalanche of gold to bury him. Abruptly his feet were in the open. He was out.

He ran without stopping, but behind him he heard a growing roar that he couldn't outrace. When he knew from the slope of the land that he must be safe from falling rock, he fell to his knees. He turned and looked back. The muted, roaring sound, like thunder beyond mountains, continued, but there was no visible change in the tower. Suddenly, as he watched, the whole rock formation seemed to shift and tip. The movement lasted only seconds, but before the tons of rock had found their new equilibrium, his tunnel and the area around it had utterly vanished from sight.

When he could finally stand, Wetherton gathered up his sack of ore and his canteen. The wind was cool upon his face as he walked away, and he did not look back again.

Keep Travelin', Rider

I

When Tack Gentry sighted the weather-beaten buildings of the G Bar, he touched spurs to the buckskin and the horse broke into a fast canter that carried the cowhand down the trail and around into the ranch yard. He swung down.

"Hey!" he yelled happily, grinning. "Is that all the welcome I get?"

The door pushed open and a man stepped out on the worn porch. The man had a stubble of beard and a drooping mustache. His blue eyes were small and narrow.

"Who are you?" he demanded. "And what do you want?"

"I'm Tack Gentry," Tack said. "Where's Uncle John?"

"I don't know you," the man said, "and I never heard of no Uncle John. I reckon you got onto the wrong spread, youngster."

"Wrong spread?" Tack laughed. "Quit your funnin'! I helped build that house there, and built the corrals by my lonesome, while Uncle John was sick. Where is everybody?"

The man looked at him carefully and then lifted

his eyes to a point beyond Tack. A voice spoke from behind the cowhand. "Reckon you been gone a while, ain't you?"

Gentry turned. The man behind him was short, stocky, and blond. He had a wide, flat face, a small broken nose, and cruel eyes.

"Gone? I reckon, yes. I've been gone most of a year. Went north with a trail herd to Ellsworth, then took me a job as *segundo* on a herd movin' to Wyoming."

Tack stared around, his eyes alert and curious. There was something wrong here, something very wrong. The neatness that had been typical of Uncle John Gentry was gone. The place looked run-down, the porch was untidy, the door hung loosely on its hinges, even the horses in the corral were different.

"Where's Uncle John?" Tack demanded again. "Quit stallin'!"

The blond man smiled, his lips parting over broken teeth and a hard, cynical light coming into his eyes. "If you mean John Gentry, who used to live on this place, he's gone. He drawed on the wrong man and got himself killed."

"What?" Tack's stomach felt like he had been kicked. He stood there, staring. "He *drew* on somebody? Uncle John?" Tack shook his head. "That's impossible. John Gentry was a Quaker. He never lifted a hand in violence against anybody or anything in his life. He never even wore a gun, never owned one."

"I only know what they tell me," the blond man said, "but we got work to do, and I reckon you better slope out of here. And," he added grimly, "if you're smart, you'll keep right on goin', clean out of the country!"

"What do you mean?" Tack's thoughts were in a turmoil, trying to accustom himself to this change, wondering what could have happened, what was behind it.

"I mean you'll find things considerably changed around here. If you decide not to leave," he added, "you might ride into Sunbonnet and look up Van Hardin or Dick Olney and tell him I said to give you all you had comin'. Tell 'em Soderman sent you."

"Who's Van Hardin?" Tack asked. The name was unfamiliar.

"You been away, all right," Soderman acknowledged. "Or you'd know who Van Hardin is. He runs this country. He's the ramrod, Hardin is. Olney's sheriff."

Tack Gentry rode away from his home ranch with his thoughts in confusion. Uncle John killed in a gunfight? Why, that was out of reason! The old man wouldn't fight. He never had and never would. And this Dick Olney was sheriff! What had become of Pete Liscomb? No election was due for another year, and Pete had been a good sheriff.

There was one way to solve the problem and get the whole story, and that was to circle around and ride by the London Ranch. Bill could give him the whole story, and, besides, he wanted to see Betty. It had been a long time.

The six miles to the headquarters of the London Ranch went by swiftly, yet, as Tack rode, he scanned the grassy levels along the Maravillas. There were cattle enough, more than he had ever seen on the old G Bar, and all of them wearing the G Bar brand.

He reined in sharply. What the . . . ? Why, if Uncle John was dead, the ranch belonged to him! But if that was so, who was Soderman? And what were they doing on his ranch?

Three men were loafing on the wide verandah of the London ranch house when Tack rode up. All their faces were unfamiliar. He glanced warily from one to the other.

"Where's Bill London?" he asked.

"London?" The man in the wide brown hat shrugged. "Reckon he's to home, over in Sunbonnet Pass. He ain't never over here."

"This is his ranch, isn't it?" Tack demanded.

All three men seemed to tense. "His ranch?" The man in the brown hat shook his head. "Reckon you're a stranger around here. This ranch belongs to Van Hardin. London ain't got a ranch. Nothin' but a few acres back against the creek over to Sunbonnet Pass. He and that girl of his live there. I reckon, though,"—he grinned suddenly—"she won't be there much longer. Hear tell she's goin' to work in the Longhorn dance hall."

"Betty London? In the Longhorn?" Tack exclaimed. "Don't make me laugh, partner! Betty's too nice a girl for that! She wouldn't. . . ."

"They got it advertised," the brown-hatted man said calmly.

An hour later a very thoughtful Tack Gentry rode up the dusty street of Sunbonnet. In that hour of riding he had been doing a lot of thinking, and he was remembering what Soderman had said. He was to tell Hardin or Olney that Soderman had sent him to get all that was coming to him. Suddenly that remark took on a new significance.

Tack swung down in front of the Longhorn. Emblazoned on the front of the saloon was a huge poster announcing that Betty London was the coming attraction, that she would sing and entertain at the Longhorn. Compressing his lips, Tack walked into the saloon.

Nothing was familiar except the bar and the tables. The man behind the bar was squat and fat, and his eyes peered at Tack from folds of flesh. "What's it fur you?" he demanded.

"Rye," Tack said. He let his eyes swing slowly around the room. Not a familiar face greeted him. Shorty Davis was gone. Nick Farmer was not around. These men were strangers, a tight-mouthed, hard-eyed crew.

Gentry glanced at the bartender. "Any ridin' jobs around here? Driftin' through, and thought I might like to tie in with one of the outfits around here."

"Keep driftin'," the bartender said, not glancing at him. "Everybody's got a full crew."

One door swung open and a tall, clean-cut man walked into the room, glancing around. He wore a neat gray suit and a dark hat. Tack saw the bartender's eyes harden and glanced thoughtfully at the newcomer. The man's face was very thin, and, when he removed his hat, his ash blond hair was neatly combed.

He glanced around, and his eyes lighted on Tack. "Stranger?" he asked pleasantly. "Then may I buy you a drink? I don't like to drink alone, but haven't sunk so low as to drink with these coyotes."

Tack stiffened, expecting a reaction from some of the seated men, but there was none. Puzzled, he glanced at the blond man and, seeing the cynical good humor in the man's eyes, nodded. "Sure, I'll drink with you."

"My name," the tall man added, "is Anson Childe, by profession a lawyer, by dint of circumstances a gambler, and by choice a student. You perhaps wonder," he added, "why these men do not resent my reference to them as coyotes. There are three reasons, I expect. The first is that some subconscious sense of truth makes them appreciate the justice of the term. Second, they know I am gifted with considerable dexterity in expounding the gospel of Judge Colt. Third, they know that I am dying of tuberculosis and as a result have no fear of bullets. It is not exactly fear that keeps them from drawing on me. Let us say it is a matter of mathematics, and a problem none of them has succeeded in solving with any degree of comfort is the result. It is . . . how many of them would die before I did? You can appreciate, my friend, the quandary in which this places them, and also the disagreeable realization that bullets are no respecters of persons, nor am I. The several out there who might draw know that I know who they are. The result is that they know they would be first to die." Childe looked at Tack thoughtfully. "I heard you ask about a riding job as I came in. You look like an honest man, and there is no place here for such."

Gentry hunted for the right words. Then he said: "This country looks like it was settled by honest men."

Anson Childe studied his glass. "Yes," he said, "but at the right moment they lacked a leader. One was too opposed to violence, another was too law-abiding, and the rest lacked resolution."

If there was a friend in the community, this man was it. Tack finished his drink and strode to the door. The bartender met his eyes as he glanced back.

"Keep on driftin'," the bartender said.

Tack Gentry smiled. "I like it here," he said, "and I'm stayin'."

He swung into the saddle and turned his buck-skin toward Sunbonnet Pass. He still had no idea exactly what had happened during the year of his absence, yet Childe's remark coupled with what the others had said told him a little. Apparently some strong, resolute men had moved in and taken over, and there had been no concerted fight against them, no organization, and no leadership.

Childe had said that one was opposed to violence. That would have been his uncle John. The one who was too law-abiding would be Bill London. London had always been strong for law and order and settling things in a legal way. The others had been honest men, but small ranchers and individually unable to oppose whatever was done to them. Yet whatever had happened, the incoming elements had apparently moved with speed and finesse. Had it been one ranch, it would have been different. But the ranches and the town seemed completely subjugated.

The buckskin took the trail at an easy canter, skirting the long red cliff of Horse Thief Mesa and wading the creek at Gunsight. Sunbonnet Pass opened before him like a gate in the mountains. To the left, in a grove of trees, was a small adobe house and a corral.

Two horses were standing at the corral as he

rode up. His eyes narrowed as he saw them. Button and Blackie! Two of his uncle's favorites and two horses he had raised from colts. He swung down and started toward them, when he saw the three people on the steps.

He turned to face them, and his heart jumped. Betty London had not changed.

Her eyes widened, and her face went dead white. "Tack!" she gasped. "Tack Gentry!"

Even as she spoke, Tack saw the sudden shock with which the two men turned to stare. "That's right, Betty," he said quietly. "I just got home."

"But . . . but . . . we heard you were dead!"

"I'm not." His eyes shifted to the two men—a thick-shouldered, deep-chested man with a square, swarthy face and a lean, raw-boned man wearing a star. The one with the star would be Dick Olney. The other must be Van Hardin.

Tack's eyes swung to Olney. "I heard my uncle John Gentry was killed. Did you investigate his death?"

Olney's eyes were careful. "Yeah," he said. "He was killed in a fair fight. Gun in his hand."

"My uncle," Tack replied, "was a Quaker. He never lifted a hand in violence in his life."

"He was a might slow, I reckon," Olney said coolly, "but he had the gun in his hand when I found him."

"Who shot him?"

"*Hombre* name of Soderman. But like I say, it was a fair fight."

"Like blazes!" Tack flashed. "You'll never make me believe Uncle John wore a gun! That gun was planted on him!"

"You're jumpin' to conclusions," Van Hardin

said smoothly. "I saw the gun myself. There were a dozen witnesses."

"Who saw the fight?" Gentry demanded.

"They saw the gun in his hand. In his right hand," Hardin said.

Tack laughed suddenly, harshly. "That does it. Uncle John's right hand has been useless ever since Shiloh, when it was shot to pieces tryin' to get to a wounded soldier. He couldn't hold a feather in those fingers, let alone a gun."

Hardin's face tightened, and Dick Olney's eyes shifted to Hardin's face.

"You'd be better off," Hardin said quietly, "to let sleepin' dogs lie. We ain't goin' to have you comin' in here stirrin' up a peaceful community."

"My uncle John was murdered," Gentry said quietly. "I mean to see his murderer punished. That ranch belongs to me. I intend to get it back."

Van Hardin smiled. "Evidently you aren't aware of what happened here," he said quietly. "Your uncle John was in a noncombatant outfit durin' the war, was he not? Well, while he was gone, the ranch he had claimed was abandoned. Soderman and I started to run cattle on that range and the land that was claimed by Bill London. No claim to the range was asserted by anyone. We made improvements, and then, durin' our temporary absence with a trail herd, John Gentry and Bill London returned and moved in. Naturally, when we returned, the case was taken to court. The court ruled the ranches belonged to Soderman and myself."

"And the cattle?" Tack asked. "What of the cattle my uncle owned?"

Hardin shrugged. "The brand had been taken over by the new owners and registered in their name. As I understand it, you left with a trail herd immediately after you came back to Texas. My claim was originally asserted during your uncle's absence. I could,"—he smiled—"lay claim to the money you got from that trail herd. Where is it?"

"Suppose you find out?" Tack replied. "I'm goin' to tell you one thing. I'm goin' to find who murdered my uncle, if it was Soderman or not. I'm also goin' to fight you in court. Now, if you'll excuse me,"—he turned his eyes to Betty who had stood, wide-eyed and silent—"I'd like to talk to Bill London."

"He can't see you," Hardin said. "He's asleep."

Gentry's eyes hardened. "You runnin' this place, too?"

"Betty London is going to work for me," Hardin replied. "We may be married later, so in a sense I'm speaking for her."

"Is that right?" Tack demanded, his eyes meeting Betty's.

Her face was miserable. "I'm afraid it is, Tack."

"You've forgotten your promise, then?" he demanded.

"Things . . . things changed, Tack," she faltered. "I . . . I can't talk about it."

"I reckon, Gentry," Olney interrupted, "it's time you rode on. There's nothin' in this neck of the woods for you. You've played out your hand here. Ride on, and you'll save yourself a lot of trouble. They're hirin' hands over on the Pecos."

"I'm stayin'," Gentry said flatly.

"Remember," Olney warned, "I'm the sheriff. At the first sign of trouble, I'll come lookin' for you."

Gentry swung into the saddle. His eyes shifted to Betty's face, and for an instant she seemed about to speak. Then he turned and rode away. He did not look back. It was not until after he was gone that he remembered Button and Blackie. To think they were in the possession of Hardin and Olney! The twin blacks he had reared and worked with, training them to do tricks, teaching them all the lore of the cow country horses and much more.

The picture was clear now. In the year in which he had been gone these men had come in, asserted their claims, taken them to carpetbag courts, and made them stick. Backing their legal claims with guns, they had taken over the country with speed and finesse. At every turn, he was blocked. Betty had turned against him. Bill London was either a prisoner in his own house or something else was wrong. Olney was sheriff, and probably they had their own judge.

He could quit. He could pull out and go on to the Pecos. It would be the easiest way. It was even what Uncle John might have wished him to do, for John Gentry was a peace-loving man. Tack Gentry was of another breed. His father had been killed fighting Comanches, and Tack had gone to war when a mere boy. Uncle John had found a place for himself in a noncombatant outfit, but Tack had fought long and well.

His ride north with the trail herd had been rough and bloody. Twice they had fought off Indians, and once they had mixed it with rustlers. In Ellsworth, a gunman named Paris had made trouble that ended with Paris dead on the floor. Tack had left town in a hurry, ridden to the new camp at Dodge, and then joined a trail herd headed for Wyoming. Indian fighting had been the order of the day, and once, rounding up a bunch of steers lost from the herd in a stampede, Tack had run into three rustlers after the same steers. Tack had downed two of them in the subsequent battle, and then shot it out with the other in a daylong rifle battle that covered a cedar- and boulder-strewn hillside. Finally, just before sundown, they met in a hand-to-hand battle with Bowie knives.

Tack remained long enough to see his old friend Major Powell, with whom he had participated in the Wagon Box fight, and then had wandered back to Kansas. On the Platte he had joined a bunch of buffalo hunters, stayed with them a couple of months, and then trailed back to Dodge.

II

Sunbonnet's Longhorn Saloon was ablaze with lights when he drifted into town that night. He stopped at the livery stable and put up his horse. He had taken a roundabout route, scouting the country, so he decided that Hardin and Olney were probably already in town. By now they would know of his call at the ranch and his meeting with Anson Childe.

He was laboring under no delusions about his future. Van Hardin would not hesitate to see him put out of the way if he attempted to regain his property. Hardin had brains, and Olney was no fool. There were things Gentry must know before anything could be done, and the one man in town who could and would tell him was Childe.

Leaving the livery stable, he started up the street. Turning, he glanced back to see the liveryman standing in the stable door. He dropped his hand quickly, but Gentry believed he had signaled someone across the street. Yet there was no one in sight, and the row of buildings seemed blank and empty.

Only three buildings were lighted. The Longhorn, a smaller, cheaper saloon, and the old general store. There was a light upstairs over the small saloon and several lights in the annex to the Longhorn, which passed as a hotel, the only one in Sunbonnet.

Tack walked along the street, his boot heels sounding loud in the still night air. Ahead of him was a space between the buildings, and, when he drew abreast of it, he did a quick sidestep off the street, flattening against the building.

He heard footsteps, hesitation, and then lightly running steps, and suddenly a man dived around the corner and grated to a stop on the gravel, staring down the alleyway between the buildings. He did not see Tack, who was flattened in the dense shadow against the building and behind a rain barrel.

The man started forward suddenly, and Tack reached out and grabbed his ankle. Caught in midstride, the fellow plunged over on his head, and then lay still. For an instant, Gentry hesitated, then struck and shielded a match with his left hand. It was the brown-hatted man he had talked to on the porch of London's ranch. His head had hit a stone, and he was out cold.

Swiftly Tack shucked the fellow's gun and emptied the shells from it, and then pushed it back in his holster. A folded paper had fallen from the unconscious man's pocket, and Tack picked it up. Then, moving fast, he went down the alley until he was in back of the small saloon. By the light from a back window, he read the note.

"This," he muttered, "may help."

Come to town quick. Trouble's brewing. We can't have anything happen now.

                                                            V.H.

Van Hardin. They didn't want trouble now. Why, *now*? Folding the note, he slipped it into his pocket and flattened against the side of the saloon, studying the interior. Only two men sat in the dim interior, two men who played cards at a small table. The bartender leaned on the bar and read a newspaper. When the bartender turned his head, Tack recognized him.

Red Furness had worked for his father. He had soldiered with him. He might still be friendly. Tack lifted his knuckles and tapped lightly on the window.

At the second tap, Red looked up. Tack lighted a match and moved it past the window. Neither of the cardplayers seemed to have noticed. Red straightened, folded his paper, and then, picking up a cup, walked back toward the window. When he got there, he dipped the cup into the water bucket with one hand and with the other lifted the window a few inches.

"This is Tack Gentry. Where does Childe hang out?"

Red's whisper was low. "Got him an office and sleepin' room upstairs. There's a back stairway. You watch yourself."

Tack stepped away from his window and made his way to the stairway he had already glimpsed. It might be a trap, but he believed Red was loyal. Also, he was not sure the word was out to kill him. They probably merely wanted him out of the way and hoped he could be warned to move on. The position of the Hardin group seemed secure enough.

Reaching the top of the stairs, he walked along the narrow catwalk to the door. He tapped softly.

After an instant, there was a voice. "What do you want?"

"This is Tack Gentry. You talked to me in the saloon." The door opened to darkness, and he stepped in. When it closed, he felt a pistol barrel against his spine.

"Hold still," Childe warned.

Behind him a match struck, and then a candle was lighted. The light still glowed in the other room, seen only by the crack under the door. Childe grinned at him. "Got to be careful," he said. "They have tried twice to dry-gulch me. I put flowers on their graves every Monday." He smiled. "And keep an extra one dug. Ever since I had that new grave dug, I've been left alone. Somehow it seems to have a very sobering influence on the local roughs." He sat down. "I tire quicker than I once did. So you're Gentry. Betty London told me about you. She thought you were dead. There was a rumor that you'd been killed by the Indians in Wyoming."

"No, I came out all right. What I want to know, rememberin' you said you were a lawyer, is what kind of a claim do they have on my ranch?"

"A good one, unfortunately. While you and your uncle were gone, and most of the other men in the locality, several of these men came in and began to brand cattle. After branding a good many, they left. They returned and began working around, about the time you left, and then they ordered your uncle off. He wouldn't go, and they took the case to court. There were no lawyers here then, and your uncle tried to handle it himself. The judge was their man, and suddenly a half dozen witnesses appeared and were sworn in. They testified that the land had been taken and held by Soderman,

Olney, and Hardin. They claimed their brands on the cattle asserted their claim to the land, to the home ranches of both London and Gentry. The free range was something else, but with the two big ranches in their hands and the bulk of the free range lying beyond their holdings, they were in a position to freeze out the smaller ranchers. They established a squatter's right to each of the big ranches."

"Can they do that?" Tack demanded. "It doesn't seem fair."

"The usual thing is to allow no claim unless they have occupied the land for twenty years without hindrance, but with a carpetbag court they do about as they please. Judge Weaver is completely in Van Hardin's hands, and your uncle John was on the losing side in this war."

"How did Uncle John get killed?" Tack asked.

Childe shrugged. "They said he called Soderman a liar and Soderman went for his gun. Your uncle had a gun on him when they found him. It was probably a cold-blooded killing because Gentry planned on a trip to Austin and was going to appeal the case."

"Have you seen Bill London lately?"

"Only once since the accident."

"Accident?"

"Yes, London was headed for home, dozing along in the buckboard as he always did, when his team ran away with him. The buckboard was overturned and London's back was injured. He can't ride anymore and can't sit up very long at a time."

"Was it really an accident?" Tack wanted to know.

Childe shrugged. "I doubt it. We couldn't prove

a thing. One of the horses had a bad cut on the hip. It looked as if someone with a steel-tipped bullwhip had hit the animal from beside the road."

"Thorough," Tack said. "They don't miss a bet."

Childe nodded. Leaning back in his chair, he put his feet on the desk. He studied Tack Gentry thoughtfully. "You know, you'll be next. They won't stand for you messing around. I think you already have them worried."

Tack explained about the man following him, and then handed the note to Childe. The lawyer's eyes narrowed. "*Hmm*, sounds like they had some reason to soft-pedal the whole thing for a while. Maybe it's an idea for us. Maybe somebody is coming down here to look around, or maybe somebody has grown suspicious."

Tack looked at Childe thoughtfully. "What's your position in all this?"

The tall man shrugged, and then laughed lightly. "I've no stake in it, Gentry. I didn't know London or your uncle John, either. But I heard rumors, and I didn't like the attitude of the local bosses, Hardin and Olney. I'm just a burr under the saddle with which they ride this community, no more. It amuses me to needle them, and they are afraid of me."

"Got any clients?"

"Clients?" Anson Childe chuckled. "Not a one. Not likely to have any, either. In a country so throttled by one man as this is, there isn't any litigation. Nobody can win against him, and they are too busy hating Hardin to want to have trouble with each other."

"Well, then," Tack said, "you've got a client now.

Go down to Austin. Demand an investigation. Lay the facts on the table for them. Maybe you can't do any good, but at least you can stir up a lot of trouble. The main thing will be to get people talking. They evidently want quiet, so we'll give them noise. Find out all you can. Get some detectives started on Hardin's trail. Find out who they are, who they were, and where they came from."

Childe sat up. "I'd like it," he said ruefully, "but I don't have that kind of money." He gestured at the room. "I'm behind on my rent here. Red owns the building, so he lets me stay."

Tack grinned and unbuttoned his shirt, drawing out a money belt. "I sold some cattle up north." He counted out $1,000. "Take that. Spend all or any part of it, but create a smell down there. Tell everybody about the situation here."

Childe got up, his face flushed with enthusiasm. "Man, nothing could please me more. I'll make it hot for them. I'll . . ." He went into a fit of coughing, and Tack watched him gravely. Finally Childe straightened. "You're putting your trust in a sick man, Gentry."

"I'm putting my trust in a fighter," Tack said dryly. "You'll do." He hesitated briefly. "Also, check the title on this land."

They shook hands silently, and Tack went to the door. Softly he opened it and stepped out into the cool night. Well, for better or worse the battle was opened now for the next step. He came down off the wooden stairs, and then walked to the street. There was no one it sight. Tack Gentry crossed the street and pushed through the swinging doors of the Longhorn.

The saloon and dance hall was crowded. A few

familiar faces, but they were sullen faces, lined and hard. The faces of bitter men, defeated, but not whipped. The others were new faces, the hard, tough faces of gun hands, the weather-beaten cowpunchers who had come in to take the new jobs. He pushed his way to the bar.

There were three bartenders now, and it wasn't until he ordered that the squat, fat man glanced down the bar and saw him. His jaw hardened and he spoke to the bartender who was getting a bottle to pour Gentry's rye.

The bartender, a lean, sallow-faced man, strolled back to him. "We're not servin' you," he said. "I got my orders."

Tack reached across the bar, his hand shooting out so fast the bartender had no chance to withdraw. Catching the man by his stiff collar, two fingers inside the collar and their knuckles jammed hard into the man's Adam's apple, he jerked him to the bar.

"Pour!" he said.

The man tried to speak, but Tack gripped harder and shoved back on the knuckles. Weakly, desperately, his face turning blue, the man poured. He slopped out twice what he got in the glass, but he poured. Then Tack shoved hard and the man brought up violently against the backbar.

Tack lifted his glass with his left hand, his eyes sweeping the crowd, all of whom had drawn back slightly. "To honest ranchers!" he said loudly and clearly and downed his drink.

A big, hard-faced man shoved through the crowd. "Maybe you're meanin' some of us ain't honest?" he suggested.

"That's right!" Tack Gentry let his voice ring out in the room, and he heard the *rattle* of chips cease, and the shuffling of feet died away. The crowd was listening. "That's exactly right! There were honest men here, but they were murdered or crippled. My uncle John Gentry was murdered. They tried to make it look like a fair and square killin' . . . they stuck a gun in his hand!"

"That's right!" A man broke in. "He had a gun! I seen it!"

Tack's eyes shifted. "What hand was it in?"

"His right hand!" the man stated positively, belligerently. "I seen it!"

"Thank you, pardner," Tack said politely. "The gun was in John Gentry's right hand . . . and John Gentry's right hand had been paralyzed ever since Shiloh!"

"Huh?" The man who had seen the gun stepped back, his face whitening a little.

Somebody back in the crowd shouted out: "That's right! You're durn' tootin' that's right! Never could use a rope 'count of it!"

Tack looked around at the crowd, and his eyes halted on the big man. He was going to break the power of Hardin, Olney, and Soderman, and he was going to start right here.

"There's goin' to be an investigation," he said loudly, "and it'll begin down in Austin. Any of you fellers bought property from Hardin, or Olney better get your money back."

"You're talkin' a lot!" The big man thrust toward him, his wide, heavy shoulders looking broad enough for two men. "You said some of us were thieves!"

"Thieves and murderers," Tack added. "If you're one of the worms that crawl in Hardin's tracks, that goes for you!"

The big man lunged.

"Get him, Starr!" somebody shouted loudly.

Tack Gentry suddenly felt a fierce surge of pure animal joy. He stepped back, and then stepped in suddenly, and his right swung, low and hard. It caught Starr as he was coming in, caught him in the pit of the stomach. He grunted and stopped dead in his tracks, but Tack set himself and swung wickedly with both hands. His left smashed into Starr's mouth, and his right split a cut over his cheekbone. Starr staggered and fell back into the crowd. He came out of the crowd, shook his head, and charged like a bull.

Tack weaved inside of the swinging fists and impaled the bigger man on a straight, hard left hand. Then he crossed a wicked right to the cut cheek, and gore cascaded down the man's face. Tack stepped in, smashing both hands to the man's body, and then, as Starr stabbed a thumb at his eye, Tack jerked his head aside and butted Starr in the face.

His nose broken, his cheek laid open to the bone, Starr staggered back, and Tack Gentry walked in, swinging with both hands. This was the beginning. This man worked for Hardin and he was going to be an example. When he left this room, Starr's face was going to be a sample of the crashing of Van Hardin's power. With left and right he cut and slashed at the big man's face, and Starr, overwhelmed by the attack, helpless after that first wicked body blow, crumpled under those smashing fists. He hit the floor suddenly and lay there, moaning softly.

A man shoved through the crowd, and then stopped. It was Van Hardin. He looked down at the man on the floor, then his eyes, dark with hate, lifted to meet Tack Gentry's eyes.

"Lookin' for trouble, are you?" he said.

"Only catchin' up with some that started while I was gone, Van," Tack said. He felt good. He was on the balls of his feet and ready. He had liked the jarring of blows, liked the feeling of combat. He was ready. "You should have made sure I was dead, Hardin, before you tried to steal property from a kindly old man."

"Nothing was stolen," Van Hardin said evenly, calmly. "We took only what was ours, and in a strictly legal manner."

"There will be an investigation," Gentry replied bluntly, "from Austin. Then we'll thrash the whole thing out."

Hardin's eyes sharpened and he was suddenly wary. "An investigation? What makes you think so?"

Tack was aware that Hardin was worried. "Because I'm startin' it. I'm askin' for it, and I'll get it. There was a lot you didn't know about that land you stole, Hardin. You were like most crooks. You could only see your side of the question and it looked very simple and easy, but there's always the thing you overlook, and *you* overlooked somethin'."

The doors swung wide and Olney pushed into the room. He stopped, glancing from Hardin to Gentry. "What goes on here?" he demanded.

"Gentry is accusin' us of bein' thieves," Hardin said carelessly.

Olney turned and faced Tack. "He's in no position

to accuse anybody of anything," he said. "I'm arrestin' him for murder!"

There was a stir in the room, and Tack Gentry felt the sudden sickness of fear. "Murder? Are you crazy?" he demanded.

"I'm not, but you may be," the sheriff said. "I've just come from the office of Anson Childe. He's been murdered. You were his last visitor. You were observed sneaking into his place by the back stairs. You were observed sneaking out of it. I'm arresting you for murder."

The room was suddenly still, and Tack Gentry felt the rise of hostility toward him. Many men had admired the courage of Anson Childe; many men had been helped by him. Frightened themselves, they had enjoyed his flouting of Hardin and Olney. Now he was dead, murdered.

"Childe was my friend," Tack protested. "He was goin' to Austin for me."

Hardin laughed sarcastically. "You mean he knew you had no case and refused to go, and in a fit of rage you killed him. You shot him."

"You'll have to come with me," Olney said grimly. "You'll get a fair trial."

Silently Tack looked at him. Swiftly thoughts raced through his mind. There was no chance for escape. The crowd was too thick, and he had no idea if there was a horse out front, although there no doubt was, but his own horse was in the livery stable. Olney relieved him of his gun belt and they started toward the door. Starr, leaning against the doorpost, his face raw as chewed beef, glared at him evilly.

"I'll be seein' you," he said softly. "Soon."

Soderman and Hardin had fallen in around

him, and behind them were two of Hardin's roughs.

The jail was small, just four cells and an outer office. The door of one of the cells was opened and he was shoved inside. Hardin grinned at him. "This should settle the matter for Austin," he said. "Childe had friends down there."

Anson Childe murdered! Tack Gentry, numbed by the blow, stared at the stone wall. He had counted on Childe, counted on his stirring up an investigation. Once an investigation was started, he possessed two aces in the hole he could use to defeat Hardin in court, but it demanded a court not controlled by Hardin. With Childe's death he had no friends on the outside. Betty had barely spoken to him when they met, and, if she was going to work for Hardin in his dance hall, she must have changed much. Bill London was a cripple and unable to get around. Red Furness, for all his friendship, wouldn't come out in the open. Tack had no illusions about the murder. By the time the case came to trial, they would have found ample evidence. They had his guns and they could fire two or three shots from them, whatever had been used on Childe. It would be a simple thing to frame him. Hardin would have no trouble in finding witnesses.

He was standing, staring out the small window, its lower sill just on the level of his eyes, when he heard a distant rumble of thunder and a jagged streak of lightning brightened the sky, followed by more thunder. The rains came slowly, softly, and then in steadily increasing volume. The jail was still and empty. Sounds of music and occasional shouts sounded from the Longhorn, then the roar of rain drowned them out. He threw himself down on the cot in the corner of the room and, lulled by the falling rain, was soon asleep.

A long time later, he awakened. The rain was still falling, but above it was another sound. Listening, he suddenly realized what it was. The dry wash behind the town was running, probably bank full. Lying there in the darkness, he became aware of still another sound, of the nearer rushing of water. Lifting his head, he listened. Then he got to his feet and crossed the small cell.

Water was running under the corner of the jail. There had been a good deal of rain lately, and he had noted that the barrel at the corner of the jail had been full. It was overflowing, and the water had evidently washed under the corner of the building.

He walked back and sat down on the bed, and, as he listened to the water, an idea came to him suddenly. Tack got up and went to the corner of the cell. Striking a match, he studied the wall and floor. Both were damp. He stamped on the stone flags of the floor, but they were solid. He kicked at the wall. It was also solid.

How thick were those walls? Judging by what he remembered of the door, the walls were all of eight inches thick, but how about the floor? Kneeling on the floor, he struck another match, studying the mortar around the corner flagstone.

Then he felt in his pockets. There was nothing there he could use to dig that mortar. His pocket knife, his Bowie knife, his keys—all were gone. Suddenly he had an inspiration. Slipping off his wide leather belt, he began to dig at the mortar with the edge of his heavy brass belt buckle.

The mortar was damp, but he worked steadily. His hands slipped on the sweaty buckle and he skinned his fingers and knuckles on the rough stone floor, yet he persevered, scraping, scratching, digging out tiny fragments of mortar. From time to time he straightened up and stamped on the stone. It was solid as Gibraltar.

Five hours he scraped and scratched, digging until his belt buckle was no longer of use. He had scraped out almost two inches of mortar. Sweeping up the scattered grains of mortar, and digging some of the mud off his boots, he filled in the cracks as best he could. Then he walked to his bunk and sprawled out and was instantly asleep.

III

Early in the morning, he heard someone stirring around outside. Then Olney walked back to his cell and looked in at him. Starr followed in a few minutes, carrying a plate of food and a pot of coffee. His face was badly bruised and swollen, and his eyes were hot with hate. He put the food down, and then walked away. Olney loitered.

"Gentry," he said suddenly, "I hate to see a good hand in this spot."

Tack looked up. "I'll bet you do," he said sarcastically.

"No use takin' that attitude," Olney protested, "after all, you made trouble for us. Why couldn't you leave well enough alone? You were in the clear, you had a few dollars apparently, and you could do all right. Hardin took possession of those ranches legally. He can hold 'em, too."

"We'll see."

"No, I mean it. He can. Why don't you drop the whole thing?"

"Drop it?" Tack laughed. "How can I drop it? I'm in jail for murder now, and you know as well as I do I never killed Anson Childe. This trial will smoke the whole story out of its hole. I mean to see that it does."

Olney winced, and Tack could see he had touched a tender spot. That was what they were afraid of. They had him now, but they didn't want him. They wanted nothing so much as to be completely rid of him.

"Only make trouble for folks," Olney protested. "You won't get nowhere. You can bet that, if you go to trial, we'll have all the evidence we need."

"Sure. I know I'll be framed."

"What can you expect?" Olney shrugged. "You're askin' for it. Why don't you play smart? If you'd leave the country, we could sort of arrange maybe to turn you loose."

Tack looked up at him. "You mean that?" *Like blazes*, he told himself. *I can see you turnin' me loose! And when I walked out, you'd have somebody there to smoke me down, shot escaping jail. Yeah, I know.* "If I thought you'd let me go . . . ." He hesitated, angling to get Olney's reaction.

The sheriff put his head close to the bars. "You know me, Tack," he whispered. "I don't want to see you stick your head in a noose. Sure, you spoke out of turn, and you tried to scare up trouble for us, but if you'd leave, I think I could arrange it."

"Just give me the chance," Tack assured him. "Once I get out of here, I'll really start movin'." *And that's no lie*, he added to himself.

Olney went away, and the morning dragged slowly. They would let him go. He was praying now they would wait until the next day. Yet even if they did permit him to escape, even if they did not have him shot as he was leaving, what could he do? Childe, his best means of assistance, was dead. At every turn he was stopped. They had the law, and they had the guns.

His talk the night before would have implanted doubts. His whipping of Starr would have pleased many, and some of them would realize that his arrest for the murder of Childe was a frame. Yet none of these people would do anything about it without leadership. None of them wanted his own neck in a noose.

Olney dropped in later and leaned close to the bars. "I'll have something arranged by tomorrow," he said.

Tack lay back on the bunk and fell asleep. All day the rain had continued without interruption except for a few minutes at a time. The hills would be soggy now, the trails bad. He could hear the wash running strongly, running like a river not thirty yards behind the jail.

Darkness fell, and he ate again, and then returned to his bunk. With a good lawyer and a fair judge he could beat them in court. He had an ace in the hole that would help, and another that might do the job.

He waited until the jail was silent and he could hear the usual sounds from the Longhorn. Then he got up and walked over to the corner. All day water had been running under the corner of the jail and must have excavated a fair-size hole by now. Tack knelt down and took from his pocket the fork he had secreted after his meal.

Olney, preoccupied with plans to allow Tack Gentry to escape and sure that Tack was accepting the plan, had paid little attention to the returned plate.

On his knees, Tack dug out the loosely filled in

dust and dirt, and then began digging frantically at the hole. He worked steadily for an hour, and then crossed to the bucket for a drink of water and to stretch, and then he returned to work.

Another hour passed. He got up and stamped on the stone. It seemed to sink under his feet. He bent his knees and jumped, coming down hard on his heels. The stone gave way so suddenly he almost went through. He caught himself, withdrew his feet from the hole, and bent over, striking a match. It was no more than six inches to the surface of the water, and even a glance told him it must be much deeper than he had believed.

He took another look, waited an instant, and then lowered his feet into the water. The current jerked at them, and then he lowered his body through the hole and let go. Instantly he was jerked away and literally thrown downstream. He caught a quick glimpse of a light from a window, and then he was whirling over and over. He grabbed frantically, hoping to get his hands on something, but they clutched only empty air. Frantically he fought toward where there must be a bank, realizing he was in a roaring stream all of six feet deep. He struck nothing and was thrown, almost hurtled, downstream with what seemed to be overwhelming speed. Something black loomed near him, and at the same instant the water caught at him, rushing with even greater power. He grabbed again at the blob of blackness, and his hand caught a root.

Yet it was nothing secure, merely a huge cottonwood log rushing downstream. Working his way along it, he managed to get a leg over and crawled atop it. Fortunately the log did not roll over.

Lying there in the blackness, he realized what must have happened. Behind the row of buildings that fronted on the street, of which the jail was one, was a shallow, sandy ditch. At one end of it the bluff reared up. The dry wash skirted one side of the triangle firmed by the bluff, and the ditch formed the other. Water flowing off the bluff and off the roofs of the buildings and from the street of the town and the rise beyond it had flooded into the ditch, washing it deeper. Yet now he knew he was in the current of the wash itself, now running bank full, a raging torrent.

A brief flash of lightning revealed the stream down which he was shooting like a chip in a mill-race. Below, he knew, was Cathedral Gorge, a narrow boulder-strewn gash in the mountain down which this wash would thunder like an express train. Tack had seen logs go down it, smashing into boulders, hurled against the rocky walls, and then shooting at last out into the open flat below the gorge. And he knew instantly that no living thing could hope to ride a charging log through the black, roaring depths of the gorge and come out anything but a mangled, lifeless pulp.

The log he was bestriding hit a wave, and water drenched him. Then the log whirled dizzily around a bend in the wash. Before him and around another bend he could hear the roar of the gorge. The log swung, and then the driving roots ripped into a heap of débris at the bend of the wash, and the log swung wickedly across the current. Scrambling like a madman, Tack fought his way toward the roots, and then, even as the log ripped loose, he hurled himself at the heap of débris.

He landed in a heap of broken boughs, and felt

something gouge him, and then, scrambling, he made the rocks and clambered up into their shelter, lying there on a flat rock, gasping for breath.

A long time later he got up. Something was wrong with his right leg. It felt numb and sore. He crawled over the rocks and stumbled over the muddy earth toward the partial shelter of a clump of trees.

He needed shelter, and he needed a gun. Tack Gentry knew that now that he was free they would scour the country for him. They might believe him dead, but they would want to be certain. What he needed now was shelter, rest, and food. He needed to examine himself to see how badly he was injured, yet where could he turn?

Betty? She was too far away and he had no horse. Red Furness? Possibly, but how much the man would or could help he did not know. Yet thinking of Red made him think of Childe. There was a place for him. If he could only get to Childe's quarters over the saloon!

Luckily he had landed on the same side of the wash as the town. He was stiff and sore, and his leg was paining him grievously. Yet there was no time to be lost. What the hour was he had no idea, but he knew his progress would be slow, and he must be careful. The rain was pounding down, but he was so wet now that it made no difference.

How long it took him he never knew. He could have been no more than a mile from town, perhaps less, and he walked, crawled, and pulled himself to the edge of town, and then behind the buildings until he reached the dark back stairway to Anson Childe's room. Step by step he crawled up. Fortunately the door was unlocked.

Once inside, he stood there in the darkness, listening. There was no sound. This room was windowless but for one very small and tightly curtained window at the top of the wall. Tack felt for the candle, found it, and fumbled for a match. When he had the candle alight, he started pulling off his clothes.

Naked, he dried himself with a towel, avoiding the injured leg. Then he found a bottle and poured himself a drink. He tossed it off, and then sat down on the edge of the bed and looked at his leg.

It almost made him sick to look at it. Hurled against a root or something in the dark, he had torn a great, mangled wound in the calf of his leg. No artery appeared to have been injured, but in places his shinbone was visible through the ripped flesh. The wound in the calf was deeper. Cleansing it as best he could, he found a white shirt belonging to Childe and bandaged his leg.

Exhausted, he fell asleep—when, he never recalled. Only hours later he awakened suddenly to find sunlight streaming through the door into the front room. His leg was stiff and sore, and, when he moved, it throbbed with pain. Using a cane he found hanging in the room, he pulled himself up and staggered to the door.

The curtains in the front room were up and sunlight streamed in. The rain seemed to be gone. From where he stood he could see into the street, and almost the first person he saw was Van Hardin. He was standing in front of the Longhorn talking to Soderman and the mustached man Tack had first seen at his own ranch.

The sight reminded him, and Tack hunted around for a gun. He found a pair of beautifully matched Colts, silver-plated and ivory-handled. He strapped them on with their ornate belt and holsters. Then, standing in a corner, he found a riot gun and a Henry rifle. He checked the loads in all the guns, found several boxes of ammunition for each of them, and emptied a box of .45s into the pockets of a pair of Childe's pants he pulled on. Then he put a double handful of shotgun shells into the pockets of a leather jacket he found. He sat down then, for he was weak and trembling.

IV

His time was short. Sooner or later someone would come to this room. Either someone would think of it, or someone would come to claim the room for himself. Red Furness had no idea he was there, so would probably not hesitate to let anyone come up.

He locked the door, and then dug around and found a stale loaf of bread and some cheese. Then he lay down to rest. His leg was throbbing with pain, and he knew it needed care, and badly.

When he awakened, he studied the street from a vantage point well inside the room and to one side of the window. Several knots of men were standing around talking, more men than should have been in town at that hour. He recognized one or two of them as being old-timers around. Twice he saw Olney ride by, and the sheriff was carrying a riot gun.

Starr and the mustached man were loafing in front of the Longhorn, and two other men Tack recognized as coming from the old London Ranch were there.

He ate some more bread and cheese. He was just finishing his sandwich when a buckboard turned into the street, and his heart jumped when he saw Betty London was driving. Beside her in the seat was her father, Bill, worn and old, his hair white now, but he was wearing a gun!

Something was stirring down below. It began to look as if the lid was about to blow off. Yet Tack had no idea of his own status. He was an escaped prisoner and as such could be shot on sight legally by Olney or Starr, who seemed to be a deputy. From the wary attitude of the Van Hardin men he knew that they were disturbed by their lack of knowledge of him.

Yet the day passed without incident, and finally he returned to the bunk and lay down after checking his guns once more. The time for the payoff was near, he knew. It could come at any moment. He was lying there, thinking about that and looking up at the rough plank ceiling when he heard steps on the stairs.

He arose so suddenly that a twinge of pain shot through the weight that had become his leg. The steps were on the front stairs, not the back. A quick glance from the window told him it was Betty London. What did she want here?

Her hand fell on the knob and it turned. He eased off the bed and turned the key in the lock. She hesitated just an instant, and then stepped in. When their eyes met, hers went wide, and her face went white to the lips.

"You!" she gasped. "Oh, Tack! What have you been doing? Where have you been?"

She started toward him, but he backed up and sat down on the bed. "Wait. Do they know I'm up here?" he demanded harshly.

"No, Tack. I came up to see if some papers were

here, some papers I gave to Anson Childe before he was . . . murdered."

"You think I did that?" he demanded.

"No, of course not." Her eyes held a question. "Tack, what's the matter? Don't you like me anymore?"

"Don't I like you?" His lips twisted with bitterness. "Lady, you've got a nerve to ask that. I come back and find my girl about to go dancin' in a cheap saloon dance hall, and . . ."

"I needed money, Tack," Betty said quietly. "Dad needed care. We didn't have any money. Everything we had was lost when we lost the ranch. Hardin offered me the job. He said he wouldn't let anybody molest me."

"What about him?"

"I could take care of him." She looked at him, puzzled. "Tack, what's the matter? Why are you sitting down? Are you hurt?"

"My leg." He shook his head as she started forward. "Don't bother about it. There's no time. What are they saying down there? What's all the crowd in town? Give it to me, quick."

"Some of them think you were drowned in escaping from jail. I don't think Van Hardin thinks that, nor Olney. They seem very disturbed. The crowd is in town for Childe's funeral and because some of them think you were murdered once Olney got you in jail. Some of our old friends."

"Betty!" The call came from the street below. It was Van Hardin's voice.

"Don't answer." Tack Gentry got up. His dark green eyes were hard. "I want him to come up."

Betty waited, her eyes wide, listening. Footsteps sounded on the stairway, and then the door shoved open. "Bet . . ." Van Hardin's voice died out and he stood there, one hand on the doorknob, staring at Tack.

"Howdy, Hardin," Tack said, "I was hopin' you'd come."

Van Hardin said nothing. His powerful shoulders filled the open door, his eyes were set, and the shock was fading from them now.

"Got a few things to tell you, Hardin," Tack continued gently. "Before you go out of this feet first, I want you to know what a sucker you've been."

"A sucker I've been?" Hardin laughed. "What chance have you got? The street down there is full of my men. You've friends there, too, but they lack leadership. They don't know what to do. My men have their orders. And then I won't have any trouble with you, Gentry. Your old friends around here told me all about you. Soft, like that uncle of yours."

"Ever hear of Black Jack Paris, Hardin?"

"The gunman? Of course, but what's he got to do with you?"

"Nothin', now. He did once, up in Ellsworth, Kansas. They dug a bed for him next mornin', Hardin. He was too slow. You said I was soft? Well, maybe I was once. Maybe in spots I still am, but you see, since the folks around here have seen me, I've been over the cattle trails, been doin' some Injun fightin', and rustler killin'. It makes a sight of change in a man, Hardin. But that ain't what I wanted you to know. I wanted you to know what a fool you were, tryin' to steal this ranch. You see, the land in our home ranch wasn't like the rest of this land, Hardin."

"What do you mean?" Hardin demanded suspiciously.

"Why, you're the smart boy," Tack drawled easily. "You should have checked before takin' so much for granted. You see, the Gentry Ranch was a land grant. My grandmother, she was a Basque, see? The land came to us through her family, and the will she left was that it would belong to us as long as any of us lived, that it couldn't be sold or traded, and in case we all died, it was to go to the state of Texas."

Van Hardin stared. "What?" he gasped. "What kind of fool deal is this you're givin' me?"

"Fool deal is right." Tack said quietly. "You see, the state of Texas knows no Gentry would sell or trade, knowin' we couldn't, so if somebody else showed up with the land, they were bound to ask a sight of questions. Sooner or later they'd have got around to askin' you how come."

Hardin seemed stunned. From the street below, there was a sound of horses' hoofs.

Then a voice said from Tack's left: "You better get out, Van. There's talkin' to be done in the street. I want Tack Gentry."

Tack's head jerked around. It was Soderman. The short, squinty-eyed man was staring at him, gun in hand. He heard Hardin turn and bolt out of the room, saw resolution in Soderman's eyes. Hurling himself toward the wall, Gentry's hand flashed for his pistol.

A gun blasted in the room with a roar like a cannon, and Gentry felt the angry whip of the bullet, and then he fired twice, low down. Soderman fell back against the doorjamb, both hands grabbing at his stomach, just below his belt buckle. "You shot me!" he gasped, round-eyed. "You shot . . . me!"

"Like you did my uncle," Tack said coolly.

"Only you had better than an even break, and he had no break at all."

Gentry could feel blood from the opened wound trickling down his leg. He glanced at Betty. "I've got to get down there," he said. "He's a slick talker."

Van Hardin was standing down in the street. Beside him was Olney and nearby was Starr. Other men, a half dozen of them, loitered nearby.

Slowly Tack Gentry began stumping down the stairs. All eyes looked up. Red Furness saw him and spoke out: "Tack, these three men are Rangers come down from Austin to make some inquiries."

Hardin pointed at Gentry. "He's wanted for murdering Anson Childe! Also for jailbreaking, and unless I'm much mistaken he has killed another man up there in Childe's office!"

The Rangers looked at him curiously, and then one of them glanced at Hardin. "You-all the *hombre* what lays claim to the Gentry place?"

Hardin swallowed quickly, and then his eyes shifted. "No, that was Soderman. The man who was upstairs."

Hardin looked at Tack Gentry. With the Rangers here he knew his game was played out. He smiled suddenly. "You've nothin' on me at all, gents," he said coolly. "Soderman killed John Gentry and laid claim to his ranch. I don't know nothin' about it."

"You engineered it!" Bill London burst out. "Same as you did the stealin' of my ranch!"

"You've no proof," Hardin sneered. "Not a particle. My name is on no papers, and you have no evidence."

Coolly he strode across to his black horse and swung into the saddle. He was smiling gently, but there was sneering triumph behind the smile. "You've nothin' on me, not a thing."

"Don't let him get away!" Bill London shouted. "He's the wust one of the whole kit and kaboodle of 'em!"

"But he's right," the Ranger protested. "In all the papers we've found, there's not a single item to tie him up. If he's in it, he's been almighty smart."

"Then arrest him for horse stealin'," Tack Gentry said. "That's my black horse he's on."

Hardin's face went cold, and then he smiled. "Why, that's crazy! That's foolish," he said. "This is my horse. I reared him from a colt. Anybody could be mistaken, 'cause one black horse is like another. My brand's on him, and you can all see it's an old brand."

Tack Gentry stepped out in front of the black horse. "Button!" he said sharply. "Button!"

At the familiar voice, the black horse's head jerked up.

"Button!" Tack called. "Hut! Hut!"

As the name and the sharp command rolled out, Button reacted like an explosion of dynamite. He jumped straight up in the air and came down hard. Then he sunfished wildly, and Van Hardin hit the dirt in a heap.

"Button!" Tack commanded. "Go get Blackie!"

Instantly the horse wheeled and trotted to the hitching rail where Blackie stood ground-hitched as Olney had left him. Button caught the reins in his teeth and led the other black horse back.

The Ranger grinned. "Reckon, mister," he said, "you done proved your case. The man's a horse thief."

Hardin climbed to his feet, his face dark with fury. "You think you'll get away with that?" His hand flashed for his gun.

Tack Gentry had been watching him, and now his own hand moved down and then up. The two guns barked as one. A chip flew from the stair post beside Tack, but Van Hardin turned slowly and went to his knees in the dust.

At almost the same instant, a sharp voice rang out. "Olney! Starr!"

Olney's face went white and he wheeled, hand flashing for his gun. "Anson Childe," he gasped.

Childe stood on the platform in front of his room and fired once, twice, three times. Sheriff Olney went down, coughing and muttering. Starr backed through the swinging doors of the saloon and sat down hard in the sawdust.

Tack stared at him. "What the . . . ?"

The tall young lawyer came down the steps. "Fooled them, didn't I? They tried to get me once too often. I got their man with a shotgun in the face. Then I changed clothes with him and lit out for Austin. I came in with the Rangers, and then left them on the edge of town. They told me they'd let us have it our way unless they were needed."

"Saves the state of Texas a sight of money," one of the Rangers drawled. "Anyway, we been checkin' on this here Hardin. On Olney, too. That's why they wanted to keep things quiet around here. They knowed we was checkin' on 'em."

The Rangers moved in and with the help of a few of the townspeople rounded up Hardin's other followers.

Tack grinned at the lawyer. "Lived up to your

name, pardner," he said. "You sure did! All your sheep in the fold, now."

"What do you mean? Lived up to my name?" Anson Childe looked around.

Gentry grinned. "And a little Childe shall lead them," he said.

Dutchman's Flat

The dust of Dutchman's Flat had settled in a gray film upon their faces, and Neill could see the streaks made by the sweat on their cheeks and brows and knew his own must be the same. No man of them was smiling and they rode with their rifles in their hands, six grim and purposeful men upon the trail of a single rider.

They were men shaped and tempered to the harsh ways of a harsh land, strong in their sense of justice, ruthless in their demand for punishment, relentless in pursuit. From the desert they had carved their homes, and from the desert they drew their courage and their code, and the desert knows no mercy.

"Where's he headin', you reckon?"

"Home, most likely. He'll need grub an' a rifle. He's been livin' on the old Sorenson place."

Kimmel spat. "He's welcome to it. That place starved out four men I know of." He stared at the hoof tracks ahead. "He's got a good horse."

"Big buckskin. Reckon we'll catch him, Hardin?"

"Sure. Not this side of his place, though. There ain't no shortcuts we can take to head him off, and he's pointin' for home straight as a horse can travel."

"Ain't tryin' to cover his trail none."

"No use tryin'." Hardin squinted his eyes against the glare of the sun. "He knows we figure he'll head for his ranch."

"He's no tenderfoot." Kesney expressed the thought that had been dawning upon them all in the last two hours. "He knows how to save a horse, an' he knows a trail."

They rode on in near silence. Hardin scratched his unshaven jaw. The dust lifted from the hoofs of the horses as they weaved their way through the catclaw and mesquite. It was a parched and sun-baked land, with only dancing heat waves and the blue distance of the mountains to draw them on. The trail they followed led straight as a man could ride across the country. Only at draws or nests of rocks did it swerve, where they noticed the rider always gave his horse the best of it.

No rider of the desert must see a man to know him, for it is enough to follow his trail. In these things are the ways of a man made plain, his kindness or cruelty, his ignorance or cunning, his strength and his weakness. There are indications that cannot escape a man who has followed trails, and in the two hours since they had ridden out of Freedom the six had already learned much of the man they followed. And they would learn more.

"What started it?"

The words sounded empty and alone in the vast stillness of the basin.

Hardin turned his head slightly so the words could drift back. It was the manner of a man who rides much in the wind or rain. He shifted the rifle to his left hand and wiped his sweaty right palm on his coarse pants leg.

"Some loose talk. He was in the Bon Ton buyin' grub an' such. Johnny said somethin' at which he took offense, an' they had some words. Johnny was wearin' a gun, but this Lock wasn't, so he gets him a gun an' goes over to the Longhorn. He pushes open the door an' shoots Johnny twice through the body. In the back." Hardin spat. "He fired a third shot, but that missed Johnny and busted a bottle of whiskey."

There was a moment's silence while they digested this, and then Neill looked up.

"We lynchin' him for the killin' or bustin' the whiskey?"

It was a good question, but drew no reply. The dignity of the five other riders was not to be touched by humor. They were riders on a mission. Neill let his eyes drift over the dusty copper of the desert. He had no liking for the idea of lynching any man, and he did not know the squatter from the Sorenson place. Living there should be punishment enough for any man. Besides . . . "Who saw the shooting?" he asked.

"Nobody seen it, actually. Only he never gave Johnny a fair shake. Sam was behind the bar, but he was down to the other end and it happened too fast."

"What's his name? Somebody call him Lock?" Neill asked. There was something incongruous in lynching a man whose name you did not know. He shifted in the saddle, squinting his eyes toward the distant lakes dancing in the mirage of heat waves.

"What's it matter? Lock, his name is. Chat Lock."

"Funny name."

The comment drew no response. The dust was thicker now and Neill pulled his bandanna over his nose and mouth. His eyes were drawn back to the distant blue of the lakes. They were enticingly cool and beautiful, lying across the way ahead and in the basin off to the right. This was the mirage that lured many a man from his trail to pursue the always retreating shoreline of the lake. It looked like water, it really did.

Maybe there was water in the heat waves. Maybe if a man knew how, he could extract it and drink. The thought drew his hand to his canteen, but he took it away without drinking. The *sloshing* water in the canteen was no longer enticing, for it was warm, brackish, and unsatisfying.

"You know him, Kimmel?" Kesney asked. He was a wiry little man, hard as a whipstock with bits of sharp steel for eyes and brown muscle-corded hands. "I wouldn't know him if I saw him."

"Sure, I know him. Big feller, strong made, rusty-like hair an' maybe forty year old. Looks plumb salty, too, an' from what I hear he's no friendly sort of man. Squattin' on that Sorenson place looks plumb suspicious, for no man can make him a livin' on that dry-as-a-bone place. No fit place for man nor beast. Ever'body figures no honest man would squat on such a place."

It seemed a strange thing, to be searching out a man who none of them really knew. Of course, they had all known Johnny Webb. He was a handsome, popular young man, a daredevil and a hellion, but a very attractive one, and a top hand to boot. They had all known him and had all liked him. Then, one of the things that made them so sure that this had been a wrong killing, even aside from the shots in the back, was the fact that Johnny Webb had been the fastest man in the Spring Valley country. Fast, and a dead shot.

Johnny had worked with all these men, and they were good men—hard men, but good. Kimmel, Hardin, and Kesney had all made something of their ranches, as had the others, only somewhat less so. They had come West when the going was rough, fought Indians and rustlers, and then battled drought, dust, and hot, hard winds. It took a strong man to survive in this country, and they had survived. He, Neill, was the youngest of them all and the newest in the country. He was still looked upon with some reserve. He had been here only five years.

Neill could see the tracks of the buckskin, and it gave him a strange feeling to realize that the man who rode that horse would soon be dead, hanging from a noose in one of those ropes attached to a saddle horn of Hardin or Kimmel. Neill had never killed a man or seen one killed by another man, and the thought made him uncomfortable.

Yet Johnny was gone, and his laughter and his jokes were things past. They had brightened more than one roundup, more than one bitter day of heartbreaking labor on the range. Not that he had been an angel. He had been a proper hand with a gun and could throw one. And in his time he had had his troubles.

"He's walkin' his horse," Kesney said, "leadin' him."

"He's a heavy man," Hardin agreed, "an' he figures to give us a long chase."

"Gone lame on him, maybe," Kimmel suggested. "No, that horse isn't limpin'. This Lock is a smart one."

They had walked out of the ankle-deep dust now and were crossing a parched, dry plain of crusted earth. Hardin reined in suddenly and pointed.

"Look there. He indicated a couple of flecks on the face of the earth crust where something had spilled. "Water splashed."

"Careless," Neill said. "He'll need that water."

"No," Kesney said. "He was pourin' water in a cloth to wipe out his horse's nostrils. Bet you a dollar."

"Sure," Hardin agreed, "that's it. Horse breathes a lot better. A man runnin' could kill a good horse on this flat. He knows that."

They rode on, and for almost a half hour no one spoke. Neill frowned at the sun. It had been on his left a few minutes ago, and now they rode straight into it.

"What's he doin'?" Kesney said wonderingly. "This ain't the way to his place!" The trail had turned again, and now the sun was on their right. Then it turned again and was at their backs. Hardin was in the lead, and he drew up and swore wickedly.

They ranged alongside him, and rode down into a draw that cracked the face of the desert alongside the trail they had followed. Below them was a place where a horse had stood, and across the bank something white fluttered from the parched clump of greasewood.

Kesney slid from the saddle and crossed the wash. When he had the slip of white, he stared at it, and then they heard him swear. He walked back and handed it to Hardin. They crowded near.

Neill took the slip from Hardin's fingers after he had read it. It was torn from some sort of book and the words were plain enough, scrawled with a flat rock for a rest.

> *That was a fair shutin anyways six aint nowhars enuf, go fetch more men. Man on the gray better titen his girth or heel have him a sorebacked hoss.*

"Why, that . . . !" Short swore softly. "He was lyin' within fifty yards of us when we come by. Had him a rifle, too. I seen it in a saddle scabbard on that buckskin in town. He could have got one of us, anyway!"

"Two or three most likely," Kimmel commented. The men stared at the paper, and then looked back into the wash. The sand showed a trail, but cattle had walked here, too. It would make the going a little slower.

Neill, his face flushed and his ears red, was tightening his saddle girth. The others avoided his eyes. The insult to him, even if the advice was good, was an insult to them all. Their jaws tightened. The squatter was playing Indian with them, and none of them liked it.

"Fair shootin', yeah!" Sutter exploded. "Right in the back!"

The trail led down the wash now, and it was slower going. The occasional puffs of wind they had left on the desert above were gone and the heat in the bottom of the wash was ovenlike. They rode into it, almost seeming to push their way through flames that seared. Sweat dripped into their eyes until they smarted, and trickled in tiny rivulets through their dust-caked beards, making their faces itch maddeningly.

The wash spilled out into a wide, flat bed of sand left by the rains of bygone years, and the tracks were plainer now. Neill tightened his bandanna and rode on, sodden with heat and weariness. The trail seemed deliberately to lead them into the worst regions, for now he was riding straight toward an alkali lake that loomed ahead.

At the edge of the water, the trail vanished. Lock had ridden right into the lake. They drew up and stared at it, unbelieving.

"He can't cross," Hardin stated flatly. "That's deep out to the middle. Durned treacherous, too. A horse could get bogged down mighty easy."

They skirted the lake, taking it carefully, three going one way, and three the other. Finally, glancing back, Neill caught sight of Kesney's uplifted arm.

"They found it," he said. "Let's go back." Yet, as he rode, he was thinking what they all knew. This was a delay, for Lock knew they would have to scout the shores both ways to find his trail, and there would be a delay while the last three rejoined the first. A small thing, but in such a chase it was important.

"Why not ride right on to the ranch?" Short suggested.

"We might," Hardin speculated. "On the other hand he might fool us an' never go nigh it. Then we could lose him."

The trail became easier, for now Lock was heading straight into the mountains.

"Where's he goin'?" Kesney demanded irritably. "This don't make sense, nohow!"

There was no reply, the horsemen stretching out in single file, riding up the draw into the mountains. Suddenly Kimmel, who was now in the lead, drew up. Before him a thread of water trickled from the rock and spilled into a basin of stones.

"Huh!" Hardin stared. "I never knowed about this spring afore. Might's well have a drink." He swung down.

They all got down, and Neill rolled a smoke.

"Somebody sure fixed her up nice," he said. "That wall of stone makin' that basin ain't so old."

"No, it ain't."

Short watched them drink and grinned.

"He's a fox, right enough. He's an old *ladino*, this one. A reg'lar mossyhorn. It don't take time for one man to drink, an' one hoss. But here we got six men an' six horses to drink an' we lose more time."

"You really think he planned it that way?" Neill was skeptical.

Hardin looked around at him. "Sure. This Lock knows his way around."

When they were riding on, Neill thought about that. Lock *was* shrewd. He was desert wise. And he was leading them a chase. If not even Hardin knew of this spring, and he had been twenty years in the Spring Valley country, then Lock must know a good deal about the country. Of course, this range of mountains was singularly desolate, and there was nothing in them to draw a man.

So they knew this about their quarry. He was a man wise in the ways of desert and trail, and one who knew the country. Also, Neill reflected, it was probable he had built that basin himself. Nobody lived over this way but Lock, for it was not far to the Sorenson place.

Now they climbed a single horse trail across the starkly eroded foothills, sprinkled with clumps of Joshua and Spanish bayonet. It was a weird and broken land, where long fingers of black lava stretched down the hills and out into the desert as though clawing toward the alkali lake they had left behind. The trail mounted steadily and a little breeze touched their cheeks. Neill lifted his hand and wiped dust from his brow and it came away in flakes, plastered by sweat.

The trail doubled and changed, now across the rock face of the burned red sandstone, then into the lava itself, skirting hills where the exposed ledges mounted in layers like a vast cake of many colors. Then the way dipped down, and they wound among huge boulders, smooth as so many water-worn pebbles. Neill sagged in the saddle, for the hours were growing long, and the trail showed no sign of ending.

"Lucky he ain't waitin' to shoot," Kimmel commented, voicing the first remark in over an hour. "He could pick us off like flies."

As if in reply to his comment, there was an angry whine above them, and then the *crack* of a rifle.

As one man they scattered for shelter, whipping rifles from their scabbards, for all but two had replaced them when they reached the lake. Hardin swore, and Kimmel wormed his way to a better view of the country ahead.

Short had left the saddle in his scramble for shelter, and his horse stood in the open, the canteen making a large lump behind the saddle. Suddenly the horse leaped to the solid *thud* of a striking bullet, and then followed the *crack* of the rifle, echoing over the mountainside.

Short swore viciously. "If he killed that horse . . .!" But the horse, while shifting nervously, seemed uninjured.

"Hell!" Kesney yelled. "He shot your canteen!"

It was true enough. Water was pouring onto the ground, and, swearing, Short started to get up. Sutter grabbed his arm.

"Hold it! If he could get that canteen, he could get you!"

They waited, and the trickle of water slowed, then faded to a drip. All of them stared angrily at the unrewarding rocks ahead of them. One canteen the less. Still they had all filled up at the spring and should have enough. Uncomfortably, however, they realized that the object of their chase, the man called Chat Lock, knew where he was taking them, and he had not emptied that canteen by chance. Now they understood the nature of the man they followed. He did nothing without object.

Lying on the sand or rocks they waited, peering ahead.

"He's probably ridin' off now!" Sutter barked.

Nobody showed any disposition to move. The idea appealed to none of them, for the shot into the canteen showed plainly enough the man they followed was no child with a rifle. Kimmel finally put his hat on a rifle muzzle and lifted it. There was no response. Then he tried sticking it around a corner.

Nothing happened, and he withdrew it. Almost at once, a shot hit the trail not far from where the hat had been. The indication was plain. Lock was warning them not only that he was still there, but that he was not to be fooled by so obvious a trick.

They waited, and Hardin suddenly slid over a rock and began a flanking movement. He crawled, and they waited, watching his progress. The cover he had was good, and he could crawl almost to where the hidden marksman must be. Finally he disappeared from their sight, and they waited. Neill tasted the water in his canteen and dozed.

At last they heard a long yell, and, looking up, they saw Hardin standing on a rock far up the trail, waving them on. Mounting, they led Hardin's horse and rode on up the trail. He met them at the trail side, and his eyes were angry.

"Gone!" he said, thrusting out a hard palm. In it lay three brass cartridge shells. "Found 'em standing up in a line on a rock. An' look here." He pointed, and they stared down at the trail where he indicated. A neat arrow made of stones pointed down the trail ahead of them, and scratches on the face of the sandstone above it were the words:

FOLLER THE SIGNS

Kesney jerked his hat from his head and hurled it to the ground.

"Why, that dirty . . . !" He stopped, beside himself with anger. The contempt of the man they pursued was obvious. He was making fools of them, deliberately teasing them, indicating his trail as to a child or a tenderfoot.

"That ratty back-shootin' killer!" Short said. "I'll take pleasure in usin' a rope on him! Thinks he's smart!"

They started on, and the horse ahead of them

left a plain trail, but a quarter of a mile farther along three dried pieces of mesquite had been laid in the trail to form another arrow.

Neill stared at it. This was becoming a personal matter now. He was deliberately playing with them, and he must know how that would set with men such as Kimmel and Hardin. It was a deliberate challenge; more, it was a sign of the utmost contempt.

The vast emptiness of the basin they skirted now was becoming lost in the misty purple light of late afternoon. On the right, the wall of the mountain grew steeper and turned a deeper red. The burned red of the earlier hours was now a bright rust red, and here and there long fingers of quartz shot their white arrows down into the face of the cliff.

They all saw the next message, but all read and averted their eyes. It was written on a blank face of the cliff. First, there was an arrow, pointing ahead, and then the words:

SHADE, SO YOU DON'T GIT SUNSTROK

They rode on, and for several miles, as the shadows drew down, they followed the markers their quarry left at intervals along the trail. All six of the men were tired and beaten. Their horses moved slowly, and the desert air was growing chill. It had been a long chase.

Suddenly Kimmel and Kesney, who rode side by side, reined in. A small wall of rock was across the trail, and an arrow pointed downward into a deep cleft.

"What do you think, Hardin? He could pick us off man by man."

Hardin studied the situation with misgivings and hesitated, lighting a smoke.

"He ain't done it yet."

Neill's remark fell into the still air like a rock into a calm pool of water. As the rings of ripples spread wider into the thoughts of the other five, he waited.

Lock could have killed one or two of them, perhaps all of them by now. Why had he not? Was he waiting for darkness and an easy getaway? Or was he leading them into a trap?

"The devil with it!" Hardin exclaimed impatiently. He wheeled his horse and, pistol in hand, started down into the narrow rift in the dark. One by one, they followed. The darkness closed around them, and the air was damp and chill. They rode on, and then the trail mounted steeply toward a grayness ahead of them, and they came out in a small basin. Ahead of them they heard a trickle of running water and saw the darkness of trees.

Cautiously they approached. Suddenly they saw the light of a fire. Hardin drew up sharply and slid from his horse. The others followed. In a widening circle, they crept toward the fire. Kesney was the first to reach it, and the sound of his swearing rent the stillness and shattered it like thin glass. They swarmed in around him.

The fire was built close beside a small running stream, and nearby was a neat pile of dry sticks. On a paper, laid out carefully on a rock, was a small mound of coffee, and another of sugar. Nobody said anything for a minute, staring at the fire and the coffee. The taunt was obvious, and they were bitter men. It was bad enough to have a stranger make such fools of them on a trail, to treat them like tenderfeet, but to prepare a camp for them . . .

"I'll be cussed if I will!" Short said violently. "I'll go sleep on the desert first!"

"Well . . ." Hardin was philosophical. "Might's well make the most of it. We can't trail him at night, no way."

Kimmel had dug a coffeepot out of his pack and was getting water from the stream that flowed from a basin just above the camp. Several of the others began to dig out grub, and Kesney sat down glumly, staring into the fire. He started to pick a stick off the pile left for them, and then jerked his hand as though he had seen a snake. Getting up, he stalked back into the trees, and, after a minute, he returned.

Sutter was looking around, and suddenly he spoke. "Boys, I know this place! Only I never knew about that crack in the wall. This here's the Mormon Well!"

Hardin sat up and looked around. "Durned if it ain't," he said. "I ain't been in here for six or seven years."

Sutter squatted on his haunches. "Look!" He was excited and eager, sketching with a stick in the sand. "Here's Mormon Well, where we are. Right over here to the northwest there's an old sawmill an' a tank just above it. I'll bet a side of beef that durned killer is holed up for the night in that sawmill!"

Kesney, who had taken most to heart the taunting of the man they pursued, was on his knees, staring at the diagram drawn in the damp sand. He was nodding thoughtfully.

"He's right! He sure is. I remember that old mill! I holed up there one time in a bad storm. Spent two days in it. If that sidewinder stays there to-night, we can get him!"

As they ate, they talked over their plan. Traveling over the rugged mountains ahead of them was almost impossible in the darkness, and, besides, even if Lock could go the night without stopping, his horse could not. The buckskin must have a rest. Moreover, with all the time Lock had been losing along the trail, he could not be far ahead. It stood to reason that he must have planned just this, for them to stop here, and to hole up in the sawmill himself.

"We'd better surprise him," Hardin suggested. "That sawmill is heavy timber, an' a man in there with a rifle an' plenty of ammunition could stand us off for a week."

"Has he got plenty?"

"Sure he has," Neill told them. "I was in the Bon Ton when he bought his stuff. He's got grub and he's got plenty of forty-fours. They do for either his Colt or his Winchester."

Unspoken as yet, but present in the mind of each man, was a growing respect for their quarry, a respect and an element of doubt. Would such a man as this shoot another in the back? The evidence against him was plain enough, or seemed plain enough.

Yet beyond the respect there was something else, for it was no longer simply a matter of justice to be done, but a personal thing. Each of them felt in some measure that his reputation was at stake. It had not been enough for Lock to leave an obvi-ous trail, but he must leave markers, the sort to be used for any tenderfoot. There were men in this group who could trail a wood tick through a pine forest.

"Well," Kimmel said reluctantly and somewhat grimly, "he left us good coffee, anyway."

They tried the coffee and agreed. Few things in this world are so comforting and so warming to the heart as hot coffee on a chilly night over a campfire when the day has been long and weary. They drank, and they relaxed. And as they relaxed, the seeds of doubt began to sprout and put forth branches of speculation.

"He could have got more'n one of us today," Sutter hazarded. "This one is brush wise."

"I'll pull that rope on him!" Short stated positively. "No man makes a fool out of me." But in his voice there was something lacking.

"You know," Kesney suggested, "if he knows these hills like he seems to, an' if he really wanted to lose us, we'd have to burn the stump and sift the ashes before we found him."

There was no reply. Hardin drew back and eased the leg of his pants away from the skin, for the cloth had grown too hot for comfort.

Short tossed a stick from the neat pile into the fire. "That mill ain't so far away," he suggested. "Shall we give her a try?"

"Later." Hardin leaned back against a log and yawned. "She's been a hard day."

"Both them bullets go in Johnny's back?"

The question moved among them like a ghost. Short stirred uneasily, and Kesney looked up and glared around. "Sure they did! Didn't they, Hardin?"

"Sure." He paused thoughtfully. "Well, no. One

of them was under his left arm. Right between the ribs. Looked like a heart shot to me. The other one went through near his spine."

"The hell with it," Kesney declared. "No slick, rustlin' squatter can come into this country and shoot one of our boys. He was shot in the back, an' I seen both holes. Johnny got that one nigh the spine, an' he must have turned and tried to draw, then got that bullet through the heart."

Nobody had seen it. Neill remembered that, and the thought rankled. Were they doing an injustice? He felt like a traitor at the thought, but secretly he had acquired a strong tinge of respect for the man they followed.

The fire flickered and the shadows danced a slow, rhythmic quadrille against the dark background of trees. He peeled bark from the log beside him and fed it into the fire. It caught, sparked brightly, and popped once or twice. Hardin leaned over and pushed the coffeepot nearer the coals. Kesney checked the loads in his Winchester.

"How far to that sawmill, Hardin?"

"About six miles, the way we go."

"Let's get started." Short got to his feet and brushed off the sand. "I want to get home. Got my boys buildin' fence. You either keep a close watch or they are off gal hootin' over the hills."

They tightened their saddle girths, doused the fire, and mounted up. With Hardin in the lead once more, they moved off into the darkness.

Neill brought up the rear. It was damp and chill among the cliffs and felt like the inside of a cavern. Overhead the stars were very bright. Mary was going to be worried, for he was never home so late.

Nor did he like leaving her alone. He wanted to be home, eating a warm supper and going to bed in the old four-poster with the patchwork quilt Mary's grandmother had made pulled over him. What enthusiasm he had had for the chase was gone. The warm fire, the coffee, his own weariness, and the growing respect for Lock had changed him.

Now they all knew he was not the manner of man they had supposed. Justice can be a harsh taskmaster, but Western men know their kind, and the lines were strongly drawn. When you have slept beside a man on the trail, worked with him and with others like him, you come to know your kind. In the trail of the man Chat Lock, each rider of the posse was seeing the sort of man he knew, the sort he could respect. The thought was nagging and insubstantial, but each of them felt a growing doubt, even Short and Kesney, who were most obdurate and resentful.

They knew how a back-shooter lived and worked. He had his brand on everything he did. The mark of this man was the mark of a man who did things, who stood upon his own two feet, and who, if he died, died facing his enemy. To the unknowing, such conclusions might seem doubtful, but the men of the desert knew their kind.

The mill was dark and silent, a great looming hulk beside the stream and the still pool of the millpond. They dismounted and eased close. Then, according to a prearranged plan, they scattered and surrounded it. From behind a lodgepole pine, Hardin called out.

"We're comin' in, Lock! We want you!"

The challenge was harsh and ringing. Now that

the moment had come, something of the old suspense returned. They listened to the water babbling as it trickled over the old dam, and then they moved. At their first step, they heard Lock's voice.

"Don't you come in here, boys! I don't want to kill none of you, but you come an' I will! That was a fair shootin'! You've got no call to come after me!"

Hardin hesitated, chewing his mustache. "You shot him in the back!" he yelled.

"No such thing! He was a-facin' the bar when I come in. He seen I was heeled, an' he drawed as he turned. I beat him to it. My first shot took him in the side an' he was knocked back against the bar. My second hit him in the back, an' the third missed as he was a-fallin'. You *hombres* didn't see that fight."

The sound of his voice trailed off, and the water chuckled over the stones and then sighed to a murmur among the trees. The logic of Lock's statement struck them all. It *could* have been that way.

A long moment passed, and then Hardin spoke up again.

"You come in and we'll give you a trial. Fair an' square."

"How?" Lock's voice was a challenge. "You ain't got no witness. Neither have I. Ain't nobody to say what happened there but me, as Johnny ain't alive."

"Johnny was a mighty good man, an' he was our friend!" Short shouted. "No murderin' squatter is goin' to move into this country an' start shootin' folks up!"

There was no reply to that, and they waited, hesitating a little. Neill leaned disconsolately against the tree where he stood. After all, Lock might be telling the truth. How did they know? There was no use hanging a man unless you were sure.

"Gab!" Short's comment was explosive. "Let's move in, Hardin! Let's get him! He's lyin'! Nobody could beat Johnny, we know that!"

"Webb was a good man in his own country!" Lock shouted in reply. The momentary silence that followed held them, and then, almost as a man they began moving in. Neill did not know exactly when or why he started. Inside, he felt sick and empty. He was fed up on the whole business, and every instinct told him this man was no back-shooter.

Carefully they moved, for they knew this man was handy with a gun. Suddenly Hardin's voice rang out.

"Hold it, men! Stay where you are until daybreak! Keep your eyes open an' your ears. If he gets out of here, he'll be lucky, an' in the daylight we can get him, or fire the mill!"

Neill sank to a sitting position behind a log. Relief was a great warmth that swept over him. There wouldn't be any killing tonight. Not tonight, at least.

Yet, as the hours passed, his ears grew more and more attuned to the darkness. A rabbit rustled, a pinecone dropped from a tree, the wind stirred high in the pine tops, and the few stars winked through, lonesomely peering down upon the silent men.

With daylight they moved in and they went through the doors and up to the windows of the old mill, and it was empty and still. They stared at each other, and Short swore viciously, the sound booming in the echoing, empty room.

"Let's go down to the Sorenson place," Kimmel said. "He'll be there."

And somehow they were all very sure he would be. They knew he would be because they knew him for their kind of man. He would retreat no farther than his own ranch, his own hearth. There, if they were to have him and hang him, they would have to burn him out, and men would die in the process. Yet with these men there was no fear. They felt the drive of duty, the need for maintaining some law in this lonely desert and mountain land. There was only doubt that had grown until each man was shaken with it. Even Short, who the markers by the trail had angered, and Kesney, who was the best tracker among them, even better than Hardin, had been irritated by it, too.

The sun was up and warming them when they rode over the brow of the hill and looked down into the parched basin where the Sorenson place lay.

But it was no parched basin. Hardin drew up so suddenly his startled horse almost reared. It was no longer the Sorenson place.

The house had been patched and rebuilt. The roof had spots of new lumber upon it, and the old pole barn had been made watertight and strong. A new corral had been built, and to the right of the house was a fenced-in garden of vegetables, green and pretty after the desert of the day before.

Thoughtfully, and in a tight cavalcade, they rode down the hill. The stock they saw was fat and healthy, and the corral was filled with horses.

"Been a lot of work done here," Kimmel said. And he knew how much work it took to make such a place attractive.

"Don't look like no killer's place!" Neill burst out. Then he flushed and drew back, embarrassed by his statement. He was the youngest of these men and the newest in the country.

No response was forthcoming. He had but stated what they all believed. There was something stable and lasting and something real and genuine in this place.

"I been waitin' for you."

The remark from behind them stiffened every spine. Chat Lock was here, behind them. And he would have a gun on them, and, if one of them moved, he could die.

"My wife's down there fixin' breakfast. I told her I had some friends comin' in. A posse huntin' a killer. I've told her nothin' about this trouble. You ride down there now, you keep your guns. You eat your breakfast, and then, if you feel bound and determined to get somebody for a fair shootin', I'll come out with anyone of you or all of you, but I ain't goin' to hang. I ain't namin' no one man because I don't want to force no fight on anybody. You ride down there now."

They rode, and in the dooryard they dismounted. Neill turned then, and for the first time he saw Chat Lock.

He was a big man, compact and strong. His rusty brown hair topped a brown, sun-hardened face, but with the warmth in his eyes it was a friendly sort of face. Not at all what he expected.

Hardin looked at him. "You made some changes here."

"I reckon." Lock gestured toward the well. "Dug by hand. My wife worked the windlass." He looked around at them, taking them in with one sweep of his eyes. "I've got the grandest woman in the world."

Neill felt hot tears in his eyes suddenly and busied himself loosening his saddle girth to keep the others from seeing. That was the way he felt about Mary.

The door opened suddenly, and they turned. The sight of a woman in this desert country was enough to make any man turn. What they saw was not what they expected. She was young, perhaps in her middle twenties, and she was pretty, with brown wavy hair and gray eyes and a few freckles on her nose. "Won't you come in? Chat told me he had some friends coming for breakfast, and it isn't often we have anybody in."

Heavy-footed and shamefaced they walked up on the porch. Kesney saw the care and neatness with which the hard-hewn planks had been fitted. Here, too, was the same evidence of lasting, of permanence, of strength. This was the sort of man a country needed. He thought the thought before he fixed his attention on it, and then he flushed.

Inside, the room was as neat as the girl herself. How did she get the floors so clean? Before he thought, he phrased the question. She smiled.

"Oh, that was Chat's idea. He made a frame and fastened a piece of pumice stone to a stick. It cuts into all the cracks and keeps them very clean."

The food smelled good, and, when Hardin looked at his hands, Chat motioned to the door.

"There's water an' towels if you want to wash up."

Neill rolled up his sleeves and dipped his hands in the basin. The water was soft, and that was rare in this country, and the soap felt good on his hands. When he had dried his hands, he walked in. Hardin and Kesney had already seated themselves, and Lock's wife was pouring coffee.

"Men," Lock said, "this is Mary. You'll have to tell her your names. I reckon I missed them."

Mary. Neill looked up. She was Mary, too. He looked down at his plate again and ate a few bites. When he looked up, she was smiling at him.

"My wife's name is Mary," he said. "She's a fine girl."

"She would be. But why don't you bring her over? I haven't talked with a woman in so long I wouldn't know how it seemed. Chat, why haven't you invited them over?"

Chat mumbled something, and Neill stared at his coffee. The men ate in uncomfortable silence. Hardin's eyes kept shifting around the room. That pumice stone. He'd have to fix up a deal like that for Jane. She was always fussing about the work of keeping a board floor clean. That washstand inside, too, with pipes made of hollow logs to carry the water out so she wouldn't have to be running back and forth. That was an idea, too.

They finished their meal reluctantly. One by one they trooped outside, avoiding each other's eyes. Chat Lock did not keep them waiting. He walked down among them.

"If there's to be shootin'," he said quietly, "let's get away from the house."

Hardin looked up. "Lock, was that right, what you said at the mill? Was it a fair shootin'?"

Lock nodded. "It was. Johnny Webb prodded me. I didn't want trouble, nor did I want to hide behind the fact I wasn't packin' an iron. I walked over to the saloon, not aimin' for trouble. I aimed to give him a chance if he wanted it. He drawed, an' I beat him. It was a fair shootin'."

"All right." Hardin nodded. "That's good enough for me. I reckon you're a different sort of man than any of us figured."

"Let's mount up," Short said. "I got fence to build."

Chat Lock put his hand on Hardin's saddle. "You folks come over sometime. She gets right lonesome. I don't mind it so much, but you know how womenfolks are."

"Sure," Hardin said, "sure thing."

"An' you bring your Mary over," he told Neill.

Neill nodded, his throat full. As they mounted the hill, he glanced back. Mary Lock was standing in the doorway, waving to them, and the sunlight was very bright in the clean-swept dooryard.

The Trail to
Crazy Man

I

In the dark, odorous forecastle a big man with wide shoulders sat at a scarred mess table, his feet spread to brace himself against the roll of the ship. A brass hurricane lantern, its light turned low, swung from a beam overhead, and in the vague light the big man studied a worn and sweat-stained chart. There was no sound in the forecastle but the distant rustle of the bow wash about the hull, the lazy creak of the square rigger's timbers, a few snores from sleeping men, and the hoarse, rasping breath of a man who was dying in the lower bunk.

The big man who bent over the chart wore a slipover jersey with alternate red and white stripes, a broad leather belt with a brass buckle, and coarse jeans. On his feet were woven leather sandals of soft, much-oiled leather. His hair was shaggy and uncut, but he was clean-shaven except for a mustache and burnsides. The chart he studied showed the coast of northern California. He marked a point on it with the tip of his knife, then checked the time with a heavy gold watch. After a swift calculation, he folded the chart and replaced it in an oilskin packet with other papers, and tucked the packet under his jersey above his belt.

Rising, he stood for an instant, canting to the roll of the ship, staring down at the white-haired man in the lower bunk. There was that about the big man to make him stand out in any crowd. He was a man born to command, not only because of his splendid physique and the strength of his character, but because of his personality. He knelt beside the bunk and touched the dying man's wrist. The pulse was feeble. Rafe Caradec crouched there, waiting, watching, thinking.

In a few hours at most, possibly even in a few minutes, this man would die. In the long year at sea his health had broken down under forced labor and constant beatings, and this last one had broken him up internally. When Charles Rodney was dead he, Rafe Caradec, would do what he must.

The ship rolled slightly, and the older man sighed and his lids opened suddenly. For a moment he stared upward into the ill-smelling darkness, then his head turned. He saw the big man crouched beside him. He smiled. His hand fumbled for Rafe's.

"Yuh . . . yuh've got the papers? Yuh won't forget?"

"I won't forget."

"Yuh must be careful."

"I know."

"See my wife, Carol. Explain to her that I didn't run away, that I wasn't afraid. Tell her I had the money, was comin' back. I'm worried about the mortgage I paid. I don't trust Barkow." Then the man lay silently, breathing deeply, hoarsely. For the first time in three days he was conscious and aware. "Take care of 'em, Rafe," he continued, rising up slightly. "I've got to trust yuh! Yuh're the only chance I have! Dyin' ain't bad, except for them. And to think . . . a whole year has gone by. Anything may have happened."

"You'd better rest," Rafe said gently.

"It's late for that. He's done me in this time. Why did this happen to me, Rafe? To us?"

Caradec shrugged his powerful shoulders. "I don't know. No reason, I guess. We were just there at the wrong time. We took a drink we shouldn't have taken."

The old man's voice lowered. "Yuh're goin' to try . . . tonight?"

Rafe smiled then. "Try? Tonight we're goin' ashore, Rodney. This is our only chance. I'm goin' to see the captain first."

Rodney smiled, and lay back, his face a shade whiter, his breathing more gentle.

A year they had been together, a brutal, ugly, awful year of labor, blood, and bitterness. It had begun, that year, one night in San Francisco in Hongkong Bohl's place on the Barbary Coast. Rafe Caradec was just back from Central America with a pocketful of money, his latest revolution cleaned up, and the proceeds in his pocket, and some of it in the bank. The months just past had been jungle months, dripping jungle, fever-ridden and stifling with heat and humidity. It had been a period of raids and battles, but finally it was over, and Rafe had taken his payment in cash and moved on. He had been on the town, making up for lost time—Rafe Caradec, gambler, soldier of fortune, wanderer of the far places.

Somewhere along the route that night he had met Charles Rodney, a sun-browned cattleman who had come to San Francisco to raise money for his ranch in Wyoming. They had had a couple of drinks and dropped in at Hongkong Bohl's dive. They'd had a drink there, too, and, when they awakened, it had been to the slow, long roll of the sea and the brutal voice of Bully Borger, skipper of the *Mary S.* Rafe had cursed himself for a tenderfoot and a fool. To have been shanghaied like any drunken farmer! He had shrugged it off, knowing the uselessness of resistance. After all, it was not his first trip to sea. Rodney had been wild. He had rushed to the captain and demanded to be put ashore, and Bully Borger had knocked him down and booted him senseless while the mate stood by with a pistol. That had happened twice more until Rodney returned to work almost a cripple, and frantic with worry over his wife and daughter.

As always, the crew had split into cliques. One of these consisted of Rafe, Rodney, Roy Penn, Rock Mullaney, and Tex Brisco. Penn had been a law student and occasional prospector. Mullaney was an able-bodied seaman, hardrock miner, and cowhand. They had been shanghaied in San Francisco in the same lot with Rafe and Rodney. Tex Brisco was a Texas cowhand who had been shanghaied from a waterfront dive in Galveston where he had gone to look at the sea.

Finding a friend in Rafe, Rodney had told him the whole story of his coming to Wyoming with his wife and daughter, of what drought and Indians had done to his herd, and how finally he had mortgaged his ranch to a man named Barkow. Rustlers had invaded the country, and he had lost cattle. Finally reaching the end of his rope, he had gone to San Francisco to get a loan from an old friend. In San Francisco, surprisingly, he had met

Barkow and some others, and paid off the mortgage. A few hours later, wandering into Hongkong Bohl's place, which had been recommended to him by Barkow's friends, he had been doped, robbed, and shanghaied.

When the ship returned to San Francisco after a year, Rodney had demanded to be put ashore, and Borger had laughed at him. Then Charles Rodney had tackled the big man again, and that time the beating had been final. With Rodney dying, the *Mary S.* had finished her loading and slipped out of port so he could be conveniently "lost at sea."

The cattleman's breathing had grown gentler, and Rafe leaned his head on the edge of the bunk, dozing. Rodney had given him the deed to the ranch, a deed that gave him half a share, the other half belonging to Rodney's wife and daughter. Caradec had promised to save the ranch if he possibly could. Rodney had also given him Barkow's signed receipt for the money.

Rafe's head came up with a jerk. How long he had slept he did not know. He stiffened as he glanced at Charles Rodney. The hoarse, rasping breath was gone; the even, gentle breath was no more. Rodney was dead.

For an instant, Rafe held the old man's wrist, then drew the blanket over Rodney's face. Abruptly then, he got up. A quick glance at his watch told him they had only a few minutes until they would sight Cape Mendocino. Grabbing a small bag of things off the upper bunk, he turned quickly to the companionway.

Two big feet and two hairy ankles were visible on the top step. They moved, and step by step a man came down the ladder. He was a big man, bigger than Rafe, and his small, cruel eyes stared at him, then at Rodney's bunk.

"Dead?"

"Yes."

The big man rubbed a fist along his unshaven jowl. He grinned at Rafe. "I heerd him speak aboot the ranch. It could be a nice thing, that. I heerd aboot them ranches. Money in 'em." His eyes brightened with cupidity and cunning. "We share an' share alike, eh?"

"No." Caradec's voice was flat. "The deed is made out to his daughter and me. His wife is to share, also. I aim to keep nothin' for myself."

The big man chuckled hoarsely. "I can see that," he said. "Josh Briggs is no fool, Caradec! You're intendin' to get it *all* for yourself. I want mine." He leaned on the handrail of the ladder. "We can have a nice thing, Caradec. They said there was trouble over there, huh? I guess we can handle any trouble, an' make some ourselves."

"The Rodneys get it all," Rafe said. "Stand aside. I'm in a hurry."

Briggs's face was ugly. "Don't get high an' mighty with me!" he said roughly. "Unless you split even with me, you don't get away. I know aboot the boat you've got ready. I can stop you there, or here."

Rafe Caradec knew the futility of words. There are some natures to whom only violence is an argument. His left hand shot up suddenly, his stiffened fingers and thumb making a V that caught Briggs where his jawbone joined his throat. The blow was short, vicious, unexpected. Briggs's head jerked back, and Rafe hooked short and hard with his right, then followed through with a smashing elbow that flattened Briggs's nose and showered him with blood.

Rafe dropped his bag, then struck, left and right to the body, then left and right to the chin. The last two blows cracked like pistol shots. Josh Briggs hit the foot of the ladder in a heap, rolled over, and lay still, his head partly under the table. Rafe picked up his bag and went up the ladder without so much as a backward glance.

II

On the dark deck Rafe Caradec moved aft along the starboard side. A shadow moved out from the mainmast.

"You ready?"

"Ready, Rock."

Two more men got up from the darkness near the foot of the mast, and all four hauled the boat from its place and got it to the side.

"This the right place?" Penn asked.

"Almost." Caradec straightened. "Get her ready. I'm going to call on the Old Man."

In the darkness he could feel their eyes on him. "You think that's wise?"

"No, but he killed Rodney. I've got to see him."

"You goin' to kill Borger?"

It was like them that they did not doubt he could if he wished. Somehow he had always impressed men so that what he wanted to accomplish, he would accomplish. "No, just a good beatin'. He's had it comin' for a long time."

Mullaney spat. He was a stocky, muscular man. "Yuh cusséd right he has! I'd like to help."

"No, there'll be no help for either of us. Stand by and watch for the mate."

Penn chuckled. "He's tied up aft, by the wheel."

Rafe Caradec turned and walked forward. His soft leather sandals made no noise on the hardwood deck, or on the companionway as he descended. He moved like a shadow along the bulkhead, and saw the door of the captain's cabin standing open. He was inside and had taken two steps before the captain looked up.

Bully Borger was big, almost a giant. He had a red beard around his jawbone under his chin. He squinted from cold, gray eyes at Rafe. "What's wrong?" he demanded. "Trouble on deck?"

"No, Captain," Rafe said shortly, "there's trouble here. I've come to beat you within an inch of your life, Captain. Charles Rodney is dead. You ruined his life, Captain, and then you killed him."

Borger was on his feet, catlike. Somehow he had always known this moment would come. A dozen times he had told himself he should kill Caradec, but the man was a seaman, and in the lot of shanghaied crews there were few. So he had delayed.

He lunged at the drawer for his brass knuckles. Rafe had been waiting for that, poised on the balls of his feet. His left hand dropped to the captain's wrist in a grip like steel, and his right hand sank to the wrist in the captain's middle. It stopped Borger, that punch did, stopped him flat-footed for only an instant, but that instant was enough. Rafe's head darted forward, butting the bigger man in the face, as Rafe felt the bones crunch under his hard skull.

Yet the agony gave Borger a burst of strength, and he tore the hand with the knuckles loose and got his fingers through their holes. He lunged, swinging a roundhouse blow that would have dropped a bull elephant. Rafe went under the swing, his movements timed perfectly, his actions almost negligent. He smashed left and right to the wind, and the punches drove hard at Borger's stomach, and he doubled up, gasping. Rafe dropped a palm to the back of the man's head and shoved him down, hard. At the same instant, his knee came up, smashing Borger's face into a gory pulp.

Bully Borger, the dirtiest fighter on many a waterfront, staggered back, moaning with pain. His face expressionless, Rafe Caradec stepped in and threw punches with both hands, driving, wicked punches that had the power of those broad shoulders behind them, and timed with the rolling of the ship. Left, right, left, right, blows that cut and chopped like meat cleavers. Borger tottered and fell back across the settee.

Rafe wheeled to see Penn's blond head in the doorway. Roy Penn stared at the bloody hulk, then at Rafe. "Better come on. The cape's showing off the starb'rd bow."

When they had the boat in the water, they slid down the rope one after the other, then Rafe slashed it with his belt knife, and the boat dropped back. The black hulk of the ship swept by them. Her stern lifted, then sank, and Rafe, at the tiller, turned the bow of the boat toward the monstrous blackness of the cape.

Mullaney and Penn got the sail up, when the mast was stepped, then Penn looked around at Rafe.

"That was mutiny, you know."

"It was," Rafe said calmly. "I didn't ask to go

aboard, and knockout drops in a Barbary Coast dive ain't my way of askin' for a year's job!"

"A year?" Penn swore. "Two years and more for me. For Tex, too."

"Yuh know this coast?" Mullaney asked.

Rafe nodded. "Not well, but there's a place just north of the cape where we can run in. To the south the sunken ledges and rocks might tear our bottom out, but I think we can make this other place. Can you all swim?"

The mountainous headland loomed black against the gray-turning sky of the hours before daybreak. The seaward face of the cape was rocky and water-worn along the shoreline. Rafe, studying the currents and the rocks, brought the boat neatly in among them and headed for a boulder-strewn gray beach where water curled and left a white ruffle of surf. They scrambled out of the boat and threw their gear on the narrow beach.

"How about the boat?" Texas demanded. "Do we leave it?"

"Shove her off, cut a hole in the bottom, and let her sink," Rafe said.

When the hole had been cut, they let the sea take the boat offshore a little, watching it fill and sink. Then they picked up their gear, and Rafe Caradec led them inland, working along the shoulder of the mountain. The northern slope was covered with brush and trees and afforded some concealment. Fog was rolling in from the sea, and soon the gray, cottony shroud of it settled over the countryside.

When they had several miles behind them, Rafe drew to a halt. Penn opened the sack he was carrying and got out some bread, figs, coffee, and a pot.

"Stole 'em out of the captain's stores," he said. "Figured we might as well eat."

"Got anything to drink?" Mullaney rubbed the dark stubble on his wide jaws.

"Uhn-huh. Two bottles of rum. Good stuff from Jamaica."

"Yuh'll do to ride the river with," Tex said, squatting on his heels. He glanced up at Rafe. "What comes now?"

"Wyomin', for me." Rafe broke some sticks and put them into the fire Rock was kindling. "I made my promise to Rodney, and I'll keep it."

"He trusted yuh." Tex studied him thoughtfully.

"Yes. I'm not goin' to let him down. Anyway," he added, smiling, "Wyomin's a long way from here, and we should be as far away as we can. They may try to find us. Mutiny's a hangin' offense."

"Ever run any cattle?" Tex wanted to know.

"Not since I was a kid. I was born in New Orleans, grew up near San Antonio. Rodney tried to tell me all he could."

"I been over the trail to Dodge twice," Tex said, "and to Wyomin' once. I'll be needin' a job."

"You're hired," Rafe said, "if we ever get the money to pay you."

"I'll chance it," Tex Brisco agreed. "I like the way yuh do things."

"Me for the gold fields in Nevady," Rock said.

"That's good for me," Penn said. "If me and Rock don't strike it rich, we may come huntin' a feed."

There was no trail through the tall grass but the one the mind could make, or the instinct of the cattle moving toward water, yet as the long-legged zebra dun moved along the flank of the little herd, Rafe Caradec thought he was coming home. This was a land for a man to love, a long, beautiful land of rolling grass and trees, of towering mountains pushing their dark peaks against the sky and the straight, slim beauty of lodgepole pines.

He sat easy in the saddle, more at home than in many months, for almost half his life had been lived astride a horse, and he liked the dun, which had an easy, space-eating stride. He had won the horse in a poker game in Ogden, and won the saddle and bridle in the same game. The new Winchester '73, newest and finest gun on the market, he had bought in San Francisco.

A breeze whispered in the grass, turning it to green and shifting silver as the wind stirred along the bottomland. Rafe heard the gallop of a horse behind him and reined in, turning. Tex Brisco rode up alongside.

"We should be about there, Rafe," he said, digging in his pocket for the makings. "Tell me about that business again, will yuh?"

Rafe nodded. "Rodney's brand was one he bought from an *hombre* named Shafter Mason. It was the Bar M. He had two thousand acres in Long Valley that he bought from Red Cloud, paid him good for it, and he was runnin' cattle on that, and some four thousand acres outside the valley. His cabin was built in the entrance to Crazy Man Cañon. He borrowed money, and mortgaged the land to a man named Bruce Barkow. Barkow's a big cattleman there, tied in with three or four others. He has several gunmen workin' for him, but he was the only man around who could loan him the money he needed."

"What's yore plan?" Brisco asked, his eyes following the cattle.

"Tex, I haven't got one. I couldn't plan until I saw the lay of the land. The first thing will be to find Missus Rodney and her daughter and, from them, learn what the situation is. Then we can go to work. In the meantime, I aim to sell these cattle and hunt up Red Cloud."

"That'll be tough," Tex suggested. "There's been some Injun trouble, and he's a Sioux. Mostly, they're on the prod right now."

"I can't help it, Tex," Rafe said. "I've got to see him, tell him I have the deed, and explain so's he'll understand. He might turn out to be a good friend, and he would certainly make a bad enemy."

"There may be some question about these cattle," Tex suggested dryly.

"What of it?" Rafe shrugged. "They are all strays, and we culled them out of cañons where no white man has been in years, and slapped our own brand on 'em. We've driven them two hundred miles, so nobody here has any claim on them. Whoever started cattle where we found these left the country a long time ago. You remember what that old trapper told us?"

"Yeah," Tex agreed, "our claim's good enough." He glanced again at the brand, then looked curiously at Rafe. "Man, why didn't yuh tell me yore old man owned the C Bar? My uncle rode for 'em a while! I heard a lot about 'em! When yuh said to put the C Bar on these cattle, yuh could have knocked me over with a axe! Why, Uncle Joe used to tell me all about the C Bar outfit. The old man had a son who was a ring-tailed terror as a kid.

Slick with a gun . . . say!" Tex Brisco stared at Rafe. "You wouldn't be the same one, would yuh?"

"I'm afraid I am," Rafe said. "For a kid I was too slick with a gun. Had a run-in with some old enemies of Dad's, and, when it was over, I hightailed for Mexico."

"Heard about it."

Tex turned his sorrel out in a tight circle to cut a steer back into the herd, and they moved on. Rafe Caradec rode warily, with an eye on the country. This was all Indian country, and the Sioux and Cheyennes had been hunting trouble ever since Custer had ridden into the Black Hills, which was the heart of the Indian country and almost sacred to the plains tribes. This was the near end of Long Valley where Rodney's range had begun, and it could be no more than a few miles to Crazy Man Cañon and his cabin.

Rafe touched a spur to the dun and cantered toward the head of the drive. There were three hundred head of cattle in this bunch, and, when the old trapper had told him about them, curiosity had impelled him to have a look. In the green bottom of several adjoining cañons these cattle, remnants of a herd brought into the country several years before, had looked fat and fine. It had been brutal, bitter work, but he and Tex had rounded up and branded the cattle, then hired two drifting cowhands to help them with the drive.

He passed the man riding point and headed for the strip of trees where Crazy Man Creek curved out of the cañon and turned in a long, sweeping semicircle out to the middle of the valley, then down its center, irrigating some of the finest grassland he had ever seen. Much of it, he noted, was sub-irrigated from the mountains that lifted on both sides of the valley. The air was fresh and cool after the long, hot drive over the mountains and desert. The heavy fragrance of the pines and the smell of the long grass shimmering with dew lifted to his nostrils. He moved the dun down to the stream, and sat his saddle while the horse dipped its muzzle into the clear, cold water of the Crazy Man. When the gelding lifted its head, Rafe waded him across the stream and climbed the opposite bank, then turned upstream toward the cañon.

III

The bench beside the stream, backed by its stand of lodgepole pines, looked just as Rodney had described it. Yet, as the cabin came into sight, Rafe's lips tightened with apprehension, for there was no sign of life. The dun, feeling his anxiety, broke into a canter. One glance sufficed. The cabin was empty, and evidently had been so for a long time.

Rafe was standing in the door when Tex rode up. Brisco glanced around, then at Rafe. "Well," he said, "looks like we've had a long ride for nothin'."

The other two hands rode up—Johnny Gill and Bo Marsh, both Texans. With restless saddles, they had finished a drive in the Wyoming country, then headed west and had ridden clear to Salt Lake. On their return they had run into Rafe and Tex, and hired on to work the herd east to Long Valley.

Gill, a short, leather-faced man of thirty, stared around. "I know this place," he said. "Used to be the Rodney Ranch. Feller name of Dan Shute took over. Rancher."

"Shute, eh?" Tex glanced at Caradec. "Not Barkow?"

Gill shook his head. "Barkow made out to be

helpin' Rodney's womenfolks, but he didn't do much good. Personal, I never figgered he cut no great swath a-tryin'. Anyway, this here Dan Shute is a bad *hombre*."

"Well," Rafe said casually, "mebbe we'll find out how bad. I aim to settle right here."

Gill looked at him thoughtfully. "Yuh're buyin' yoreself a piece of trouble, mister," he said. "But I never cottoned to Dan Shute myself. Yuh got any rightful claim to this range? This is where yuh was headed, ain't it?"

"That's right," Rafe said, "and I have a claim."

"Well, Bo," Gill said, hooking a leg over the saddle horn, "want to drift on, or do we stay and see how this gent stacks up with Dan Shute?"

Marsh grinned. He had a reckless, infectious grin. "Shore, Johnny," he said. "I'm for stayin' on. Shute's got him a big, redheaded hand ridin' for him that I never liked, no ways."

"Thanks, boys," Rafe said. "Looks like I've got an outfit. Keep the cattle in pretty close the next few days. I'm ridin' in to Painted Rock."

"That town belongs to Barkow," Gill advised. "Might pay yuh to kind of check up on Barkow and Shute. Some of the boys talkin' around the chuck wagon sort of figgered there was more to that than met the eye. That Bruce Barkow is a right important gent around here, but when yuh read his sign, it don't always add up."

"Mebbe," Rafe suggested thoughtfully, "you'd better come along. Let Tex and Marsh worry with the cattle."

Rafe Caradec turned the dun toward Painted Rock. Despite himself, he was worried. His liking for the little cattleman, Rodney, had been very real, and he had come to know and respect the man while aboard the *Mary S*. In the weeks that had followed the flight from the ship, he had been considering the problem of Rodney's ranch so much that it had become much his own problem. Now, Rodney's worst fears seemed to have been realized. The family had evidently been run off their ranch, and Dan Shute had taken possession. Whether there was any connection between Shute and Barkow remained to be seen, but Caradec knew that chuck wagon gossip can often come close to the truth, and that cowhands could many times see men more clearly than people who saw them only on their good behavior or when in town.

As he rode through the country toward Painted Rock, he studied it curiously and listened to Johnny Gill's comments. The little Texan had punched cattle in here two seasons, and knew the area better than most.

Painted Rock was the usual cow town. A double row of weather-beaten, false-fronted buildings, most of which had never been painted, and a few scattered dwellings, some of logs, most of stone. There was a two-story hotel, and a stone building, squat and solid, whose sign identified it as the PAINTED ROCK BANK.

Two buckboards and a spring wagon stood on the street, and a dozen saddle horses stood three-hoofed at hitching rails. A sign ahead of them and catercornered across from the stage station told them that here was the NATIONAL BAR.

Gill swung his horse in toward the hitching rail and dropped to the ground. He glanced across his saddle at Caradec. "The big *hombre* lookin' us over is the redhead Bo didn't like," he said in a low voice.

Rafe did not look around until he had tied his own horse with a slipknot. Then he hitched his guns into place on his hips. He was wearing two walnut-stocked pistols, purchased in San Francisco. He wore jeans, star boots, and a buckskin jacket. Stepping up on the boardwalk, Rafe glanced at the burly redhead. The man was studying them with frank curiosity.

"Howdy, Gill!" he said. "Long time no see."

"Is that bad?" Gill said, and shoved through the doors into the dim, cool interior of the National.

At the bar, Rafe glanced around. Two men stood nearby, drinking. Several others were scattered around at tables.

"Red-eye," Gill said, then in a lower tone: "Bruce Barkow is the big man with the black mustache, wearin' black and playin' poker. The Mexican-lookin' *hombre* across from him is Dan Shute's gun-slingin' *segundo*, Gee Bonaro."

Rafe nodded, and lifted his glass. Suddenly he grinned. "To Charles Rodney!" he said clearly.

Barkow jerked sharply and looked up, his face a shade paler. Bonaro turned his head slowly, like a lizard watching a fly. Gill and Rafe both tossed off their drinks and ignored the stares.

"Man," Gill said, grinning, his eyes dancing, "yuh don't waste no time, do yuh?"

Rafe Caradec turned. "By the way, Barkow," he said, "where can I find Missus Rodney and her daughter?"

Bruce Barkow put down his cards. "If yuh've

got any business," he said smoothly, "I'll handle it for 'em."

"Thanks," Rafe said. "My business is personal, and with them."

"Then," Barkow said, his eyes hardening, "yuh'll have trouble. Missus Rodney is dead. Died three months ago."

Rafe's lips tightened. "And her daughter?"

"Ann Rodney," Barkow said carefully, "is here in town. She is to be my wife soon. If yuh've got any business . . ."

"I'll transact it with her!" Rafe said sharply.

Turning abruptly, he walked out the door, Gill following. The little cowhand grinned, his leathery face folding into wrinkles that belied his thirty-odd years. "Like I say, boss," he chuckled, "yuh shore throw the hooks into 'em." He nodded toward a building across the street. "Let's try the Emporium. Rodney used to trade there, and Gene Baker who runs it was a friend of his."

The Emporium smelled of leather, dry goods, and all the varied and exciting smells of the general store. Rafe rounded a bale of jeans and walked back to the long counter, backed by shelves holding everything from pepper to rifle shells.

"Where am I to find Ann Rodney?" he asked.

The white-haired proprietor gave him a quick glance, then nodded to his right. Rafe turned and found himself looking into the large, soft dark eyes of a slender, yet beautifully shaped, girl in a print dress. Her lips were delicately lovely; her dark hair was gathered in a loose knot at the nape of her neck. She was so lovely that it left him a little breathless.

She smiled, and her eyes were questioning. "I'm Ann Rodney," she said. "What is it you want?"

"My name is Rafe Caradec," he said gently. "Your father sent me."

Her face went white to the lips, and she stepped back suddenly, dropping one hand to the counter as though for support. "You come . . . from my *father*? Why, I . . ."

Bruce Barkow, who had apparently followed them from the saloon, stepped in front of Rafe, his face flushed with anger. "Yuh've scared her to death," he snapped. "What do yuh mean, comin' in here with such a story? Charles Rodney has been dead for almost a year."

Rafe's eyes measured Barkow, his thoughts racing. "He has? How did he die?"

"He was killed," Barkow said, "for the money he was carryin', it looked like." Barkow's eyes suddenly turned triumphant. "Did you kill him?"

Rafe was suddenly aware that Johnny Gill was staring at him, his brows drawn together, puzzled and wondering. Gill, he realized, knew him but slightly and might easily become suspicious of his motives. Gene Baker, also, was studying him coldly, his eyes alive with suspicion. Ann Rodney stared at him, as if stunned by what he had said, and somehow uncertain.

"No," Rafe said coolly, "I didn't kill him, but I'd be plumb interested to know who made yuh believe he was dead."

"Believe he was dead?" Barkow laughed harshly. "I was with him when he died. We found him beside the trail, shot through the body by bandits. I brought back his belongings to Miss Rodney."

"Miss Rodney," Rafe began, "if I could talk to you a few minutes . . ."

"No," she whispered. "I don't want to talk to you. What can you be thinking of? Coming to me with such a story? What is it you want from me?"

"Somehow," Rafe said quietly, "you've got hold of some false information. Your father has been dead for no more than two months."

"Get out of here!" Barkow ordered, his hand on his gun. "Yuh're torturin' that poor young lady! Get out, I say! I don't know what scheme yuh've cooked up, but it won't work! If yuh know what's good for yuh, yuh'll leave this town while the goin' is good!"

Ann Rodney turned sharply around and ran from the store, heading for the storekeeper's living quarters.

"Yuh'd better get out, mister," Gene Baker said harshly. "We know how Rodney died. Yuh can't work no underhanded schemes on that young lady. Her pa died, and he talked before he died. Three men heard him."

Rafe Caradec turned and walked outside, standing on the boardwalk, frowning at the skyline. He was aware that Gill had moved up beside him.

"Boss," Gill said, "I ain't no lily, but neither am I takin' part in no deal to skin a young lady out of what is hers by rights. Yuh'd better throw a leg over yore saddle and get."

"Don't jump to conclusions, Johnny," Rafe advised, "and before you make any change in your plans, suppose you talk to Tex about this? He was with me, an' he knows all about Rodney's death as well as I do. If they brought any belongin's of his back here, there's somethin' more to this than we believed."

Gill kicked his boot toe against a loose board. "Tex was with yuh? Damn it, man! What of that yarn of theirs? It don't make sense."

"That's right," Caradec replied, "it don't, and before it will, we've got to do some diggin'." He added: "Suppose I told you that Barkow back there held a mortgage on the Rodney Ranch, and Rodney went to Frisco, got the money, and paid it in Frisco . . . then never got home?"

Gill stared at Rafe, his mouth tightening. "Then nobody here would know he ever paid that mortgage but Barkow? The man he paid it to?"

"That's right."

"Then I'd say this Barkow was a sneakin' polecat," Gill said harshly. "Let's brace him!"

"Not yet, Johnny. Not yet!"

A horrible thought had occurred to him. He had anticipated no such trouble, yet if he explained the circumstances of Rodney's death and was compelled to prove them, he would be arrested for mutiny on the high seas—a hanging offense! Not only his own life depended on silence, but the lives of Brisco, Penn, and Mullaney. There must be a way out. There had to be.

IV

s Rafe Caradec stood there in the bright sunlight, he began to understand a lot of things and wonder about them. If some of the possessions of Charles Rodney had been returned to Painted Rock, it implied that those who returned them knew something of the shanghaiing of Rodney. How else could they have come by his belongings? Bully Borger had shanghaied his own crew with the connivance of Hongkong Bohl. Had he taken Rodney by suggestion? Had the man been marked for him? Certainly it would not be the first time somebody had got rid of a man in such a manner. If that was the true story, it would account for some of Borger's animosity when he had beaten Rodney.

No doubt they had all been part of a plan to make sure that Charles Rodney never returned to San Francisco alive, or to Painted Rock. Yet believing such a thing and proving it were two vastly different things. Also, it presented a problem of motive. Land was not scarce in the West, and much of it could be had for the taking. Why, then, people would ask, would Barkow go to such efforts to get one piece of land? Rafe had Barkow's signature on the receipt, but that could be claimed to be a forgery. First, a motive beyond the mere value of two thousand acres of land and the money paid on the debt must be established. That might be all, and certainly men had been killed for less, but Bruce Barkow was no fool, nor was he a man who played for small stakes.

Rafe lit a cigarette and stared down the street. He must face another fact. Barkow was warned. Whatever he was gambling for, including the girl, was in danger now and would remain in peril as long as Rafe Caradec remained alive or in the country. That fact stood out cold and clear. Barkow knew by now that he must kill Rafe Caradec.

Rafe understood the situation perfectly. His life had been lived among men who played ruthlessly for the highest stakes. It was no shock to him that men would stoop to killing, or a dozen killings, if they could gain a desired end. From now on he must ride with cat eyes, always aware, and always ready.

Sending Gill to find and buy two packhorses, Rafe turned on his heel and went into the store. Barkow was gone, and Ann Rodney was still out of sight.

Baker looked up and his eyes held no welcome. "If yuh've got any business here," he said, "state it and get out. Charles Rodney was a friend of mine."

"He needed some smarter friends," Rafe replied shortly. "I came here to buy supplies, but if you want to, start askin' yourself some questions. Who profits by Rodney's death? What evidence have you got besides a few of his belongings, that might have been stolen, that he was killed a year ago? How reliable were the three men who were with him? If he went to San Francisco for the money, what were Barkow and the others doin' on the trail?"

"That's neither here nor there," Baker said roughly. "What do yuh want? I'll refuse no man food."

Coolly Caradec ordered what he wanted, aware that Baker was studying him. The man seemed puzzled.

"Where yuh livin'?" Baker asked suddenly. Some of the animosity seemed to have gone from his voice.

"At the Rodney cabin on the Crazy Man," Caradec said. "I'm stayin', too, till I get the straight of this. If Ann Rodney is wise, she won't get married or get rid of any rights to her property till this is cleared up."

"Shute won't let yuh stay there."

"I'll stay." Rafe gathered up the boxes of shells and stowed them in his pockets. "I'll be right there. While you're askin' yourself questions, ask why Barkow, who holds a mortgage that he claims is unpaid on the Rodney place, lets Dan Shute take over?"

"He didn't want trouble because of Ann," Baker said defensively. "He was right nice about it. He wouldn't foreclose. Givin' her a chance to pay up."

"As long as he's goin' to marry her, why should he foreclose?" Rafe turned away from the counter. "If Ann Rodney wants to see me, I'll tell her all about it, any time. I promised her father I'd take care of her, and I will, whether she likes it or not! Also," he added, "any man who says he talked to Rodney as he was dyin' *lies*!"

The door closed at the front of the store, and

Rafe Caradec turned to see the dark, Mexican-looking gunman Gill had indicated in the National Saloon, the man known as Gee Bonaro. The gunman came toward him, smiling and showing even white teeth under a thread of mustache.

"Would you repeat that to me, *señor*?" he asked pleasantly, a thumb hooked in his belt.

"Why not?" Rafe said sharply. He let his eyes, their contempt unveiled, go over the man slowly from head to foot, then back. "If you was one of 'em that said that, you're a liar. And if you touch that gun, I'll kill you."

Gee Bonaro's spread fingers hovered over the gun butt, and he stood flat-footed, an uncomfortable realization breaking over him. This big stranger was not frightened. In the green eyes was a coldness that turned Bonaro a little sick inside. He was uncomfortably aware that he stood, perilously, on the brink of death.

"Were you one of 'em?" Rafe demanded.

"*Sí, señor.*" Bonaro's tongue touched his lips.

"Where was this supposed to be?"

"Where he died, near Pilot Peak, on the trail."

"You're a white-livered liar, Bonaro. Rodney never got back to Pilot Peak. You're bein' trapped for somebody else's gain, and, if I were you, I'd back up and look the trail over again." Rafe's eyes held the man. "You say you saw him. How was he dressed?"

"Dressed?" Bonaro was startled and confused. Nobody had asked such a thing. He had no idea what to say. Suppose the same question was answered in a different way by one of the others? He wavered and was lost. "I . . . I don't know. I . . ."

He looked from Baker to Caradec and took a

step back, his tongue at his lips, his eyes like those of a trapped animal. He was confused. The big man facing him somehow robbed him of his sureness, his poise, and he had come here to kill him.

"Rodney talked to me only a few weeks ago, Bonaro," Rafe said coldly. "Think! How many others did he talk to? You're bein' mixed up in a cold-blooded killin', Bonaro! Now turn around and get out! And get out fast!"

Bonaro backed up, and Rafe took a forward step. Wheeling, the man scrambled for the door.

Rafe turned and glanced at Baker. "Think that over," he said coolly. "You'll take the word of a coyote like that about an honest man! Somebody's tryin' to rob Miss Rodney, and because you're believin' that cock-and-bull story, you're helpin' it along."

Gene Baker stood stock-still, his hands flat on the counter. What he had seen he would not have believed. Gee Bonaro had slain two men since coming to Painted Rock, and here a stranger had backed him down without lifting a hand or moving toward a gun. Baker rubbed his ear thoughtfully.

Johnny Gill met Rafe in front of the store with two packhorses. A glance told Caradec that the little cowhand had bought well.

Gill glanced questioningly at Rafe. "Did I miss somethin'? I seen that gun hand *segundo* of Shute's come out of that store like he was chased by the devil. You and him have a run-in?"

"I called him, and he backed down," Rafe told Gill. "He said he was one of the three who heard Rodney's last words. I told him he was a liar."

Johnny drew the rope tighter. He glanced out of

the corner of his eye at Rafe. This man had come into town and put himself on record for what he was and what he planned faster than anybody he had ever seen. *Shucks*, Johnny thought, grinning at the horse, *why go back to Texas? There'll be ruckus enough here, ridin' for that* hombre.

The town of Painted Rock numbered exactly eighty-nine inhabitants, and by sundown the arrival of Rafe Caradec and his challenge to Gee Bonaro was the talk of all of them. It was a behind-the-hand talking, but the story was going the rounds. Also, that Charles Rodney was alive—or had been alive until recently.

By nightfall Dan Shute heard that Caradec had moved into the Rodney house on Crazy Man, and an hour later he had stormed furiously into his bunkhouse and given Bonaro a tongue-lashing that turned the gunman livid with anger. Bruce Barkow was worried, and he made no pretense about it in his conference with Shute. The only hopeful note was that Caradec had said that Rodney was dead.

Gene Baker, sitting in his easy chair in his living quarters behind the store, was uneasy. He was aware that his silence was worrying his wife. He was also aware that Ann was silent herself, an unusual thing, for the girl was usually gay and full of fun and laughter. The idea that there could have been anything wrong about the story told by Barkow, Weber, and Bonaro had never entered the storekeeper's head. He had accepted the story as others had, for many men had been killed along the trails or had died in fights with Indians. It was another tragedy of the westward march, and he had done what he could—he and his wife had taken Ann Rodney into their home and loved her as their own child.

Now this stranger had come with his questions. Despite Baker's irritation that the matter had come up at all, and despite his outward denials of truth in what Caradec had said, he was aware of an inner doubt that gnawed at the walls of his confidence in Bruce Barkow. Whatever else he might be, Gene Baker was a fair man. He was forced to admit that Bonaro was not a man in whom reliance could be placed. He was a known gunman, and a suspected outlaw. That Shute hired him was bad enough in itself, yet when he thought of Shute, Baker was again uneasy. The twin ranches of Barkow and Shute surrounded the town on three sides. Their purchases represented no less than fifty percent of the storekeeper's business, and that did not include what the hands bought on their own. The drinking of the hands from the ranches supported the National Saloon, too, and Gene Baker, who for all his willingness to live and let live was a good citizen, or believed himself to be, found himself examining a situation he did not like. It was not a new situation in Painted Rock, and he had been unconsciously aware of it for some time, yet, while aware of it, he had tacitly accepted it. Now there seemed to be someone in the woodpile, or several of them.

As Baker smoked his pipe, he found himself realizing with some discomfort and growing doubt that Painted Rock was completely subservient to Barkow and Shute. Pod Gomer, who was town marshal, had been nominated for the job by Barkow at the council meeting. Joe Benson of the

National had seconded the motion, and Dan Shute had calmly suggested that the nomination be closed, and Gomer was voted in. Gene Baker had never liked Gomer, but the man was a good gun hand and certainly unafraid. Baker had voted with the others, as had Pat Higley, another responsible citizen of the town. In the same manner, Benson had been elected mayor of the town, and Roy Gargan had been made judge.

Remembering that the town was actually in the hands of Barkow and Shute, Baker also recalled that at first the tactics of the two big ranchers had caused grumbling among the smaller holders of land. Nothing had ever been done, largely because one of them, Stu Martin, who talked the loudest, had been killed in a fall from a cliff. A few weeks later another small rancher, Al Chase, had mistakenly tried to draw against Bonaro, and had died. Looked at in that light, the situation made Baker uneasy. Little things began to occur to him that had remained unconsidered, and he began to wonder just what could be done about it, even if he knew for sure that Rodney had been killed. Not only was he dependent on Shute and Barkow for business, but Benson, their partner and friend, owned the freight line that brought in his supplies.

Law was still largely a local matter. The Army maintained a fort not too far away, but the soldiers were busy keeping an eye on the Sioux and their allies who were becoming increasingly restive, what with the blooming gold camps at Bannock and Alder Gulch, Custer's invasion of the Black Hills, and the steady roll of wagon trains over the Bozeman and Laramie trails. If there were trouble here, Baker realized with a sudden, sickening fear, it would be settled locally, and that meant it would be settled by Dan Shute and Bruce Barkow. Yet, even as he thought of that, Baker recalled the tall man in the black, flat-crowned hat and buckskin jacket. There was something about Rafe Caradec that was convincing, something that made a man doubt he would be controlled by anybody or anything, at any time, or anywhere.

V

Rafe Caradec rode silently alongside Johnny Gill when they moved out of Painted Rock, trailing the two packhorses. The trail turned west by south and crossed the north fork of Clear Creek. They turned then along a narrow path that skirted the huge boulders fringing the mountains.

Gill turned his head slightly. "Might not be a bad idea to take to the hills, boss," he said carelessly. "There's a trail up that-a-way ... ain't much used, either."

Caradec glanced quickly at the little 'puncher, then nodded. "All right," he said, "lead off, if you want."

Johnny was riding with his rifle across his saddle, and his eyes were alert. That, Rafe decided, was not a bad idea. He jerked his head back toward Painted Rock. "What you think Barkow will do?"

Gill shrugged. "No tellin', but Dan Shute will know what to do. He'll be gunnin' for yuh, if yuh've shore enough got the straight of this. What yuh figger happened?"

Rafe hesitated, then he said carefully: "What happened to Charles Rodney wasn't any accident. It was planned and carried out mighty smooth."

He waited while the horse took a half dozen steps, then looked up suddenly. "Gill, you size up like a man to ride the river with. Here's the story, and if you ever tell it, you'll hang four good men."

Briefly and concisely, he outlined the shanghaiing of Rodney and himself, the events aboard ship, the escape.

"See?" he added. "It must have looked foolproof to them. Rodney goes away to sea and never comes back. Nobody but Barkow knows that mortgage was paid, and what did happen was somethin' they couldn't plan for, and probably didn't even think about."

Gill nodded. "Rodney must have been tougher'n anybody figgered," he said admiringly. "He never quit tryin', yuh say?"

"Right. He had only one idea, it looked like, and that was to live to get home to his wife and daughter. If," Rafe added, "the wife was anything like the daughter, I don't blame him."

The cowhand chuckled. "Yeah, I know what yuh mean. She's purty as a papoose in a red hat."

"You know, Gill," Rafe said speculatively, "there's one thing that bothers me. Why do they want that ranch so bad?"

"That's got me wonderin', too," Gill agreed. "It's a good ranch, mostly, except for that land at the mouth of the valley. Rises there to a sort of a dome, and the Crazy Man swings around it. Nothin' much grows there. The rest of it's a good ranch."

"Say anything about Tex or Bo?" Caradec asked.

"No," Gill said. "It figgers like war, now. No use lettin' the enemy know what you're holdin'."

The trail they followed left the grasslands of the

creek bottom and turned back up into the hills to a long plateau. They rode on among the tall pines, scattered here and there with birch or aspen along the slopes. A cool breeze stirred among the pines, and the horses walked along slowly, taking their time, their hoofbeats soundless on the cushion of pine needles. Once the trail wound down the steep side of a shadowy cañon, weaving back and forth, finally to reach bottom in a brawling, swift-running stream. Willows skirted the banks, and, while the horses were drinking, Rafe saw a trout leap in a pool above the rapids. A brown thrasher swept like a darting red-brown arrow past his head, and he could hear yellow warblers gossiping among the willows.

He himself was drinking when he saw the sand crumble from a spot on the bank and fall with a tiny splash into the creek. Carefully he got to his feet. His rifle was in his saddle boot, but his pistols were good enough for anything he could see in this narrow place. He glanced casually at Gill, and the cowhand was tightening his cinch, all unawares.

Caradec drew a long breath and hitched up his trousers, then hooked his thumbs in his belt near the gun butts. He had no idea who was there, but that sand did not fall without a reason. In his own mind he was sure that someone was standing in the willow thicket across and downstream, above where the sand had fallen. Someone was watching them.

"Ready?" Johnny suggested, looking at him curiously.

"Almost," Rafe drawled casually. "Sort of like this little place. It's cool and pleasant. Sort of place a man might like to rest a while, and where a body could watch his back trail, too." He was talking at random, hoping Gill would catch on. The 'puncher was looking at him intently now. "At least," Rafe added, "it would be nice here if a man *was* alone. He could think better."

It was then that his eye caught the color in the willows. It was a tiny corner of red, a bright, flaming crimson, and it lay where no such color should be. That was not likely to be a cowhand unless he was a Mexican or a dude, and they were scarce in this country. It could be an Indian. If whoever it was had planned to fire, a good chance had been missed while he and Gill drank. Two well-placed shots would have done for them both. Therefore, it was logical to discount the person in the willows as an enemy, or, if so, a patient enemy. To all appearances whoever lay in the willows preferred to remain unseen. It had all the earmarks of being someone or something trying to avoid trouble.

Gill was quiet and puzzled. Catlike, he watched Rafe for some sign to indicate what the trouble was. A quick scanning of the brush had revealed nothing, but Caradec was not the man to be spooked by a shadow.

"You speak Sioux?" Rafe asked casually.

Gill's mouth tightened. "A mite. Not so good, mebbe."

"Speak loud and say we are friends."

Johnny Gill's eyes were wary as he spoke. There was no sound, no reply.

"Try it again," Rafe suggested. "Tell him we want to talk. Tell him we want to talk to Red Cloud, the great chief."

Gill complied, and there was still no sound.

Rafe looked up at him. "I'm goin' to go over into those willows," he said softly. "Something's wrong."

"You watch yoreself!" Gill warned. "The Sioux are plenty smart."

Moving slowly, so as to excite no hostility, Rafe Caradec walked his horse across the stream, then swung down. There was neither sound nor movement from the willows. He walked back among the slender trees, glancing around, yet even then, close as he was, he might not have seen her had it not been for the red stripes. Her clothing blended perfectly with the willows and flowers along the stream bank.

She was a young squaw, slender and dark, with large, intelligent eyes. One look told Rafe that she was frightened speechless, and, knowing what had happened to squaws found by some of the white men, he could understand. Her legs were outstretched, and from the marks on the grass and the bank of the stream he could see she had been dragging herself. The reason was plain to see. One leg was broken just below the knee.

"Johnny," he said, not too loudly, "here's a young squaw. She's got a busted leg."

"Better get away quick!" Gill advised. "The Sioux are pretty mean where squaws are concerned."

"Not till I set that leg," Rafe said.

"Boss," Gill advised worriedly, "don't do it. She's liable to yell like blazes if yuh lay a hand on her. Our lives won't be worth a nickel. We've got troubles enough, without askin' for more."

Rafe walked a step nearer, and smiled at the girl. "I want to fix your leg," he said gently, motioning to it. "Don't be afraid."

She said nothing, staring at him, yet he walked up and knelt down. She drew back from his touch, and he saw then she had a knife. He smiled and touched the break with gentle fingers.

"Better cut some splints, Gill," he said. "She's got a bad break. Just a little jolt and it might pop right through the skin."

Working carefully, he set the leg. There was no sound from the girl, no sign of pain. Gill shook his head wonderingly.

"Nervy, ain't she?" Rafe suggested.

Taking the splints Gill had cut, he bound them on her leg.

"Better take the pack off that paint and split it between the two of us and the other hoss," he said. "We'll put her up on the hoss."

When they had her on the paint's back, Gill asked her, in Sioux: "How far to Indian camp?"

She looked at him, then at Rafe. Then she spoke quickly to him.

Gill grinned. "She says she talks to the chief. That means you. Her camp is about an hour south and west, in the hills."

"Tell her we'll take her most of the way."

Rafe swung into saddle, and they turned their horses back into the trail. Rafe rode ahead, the squaw and the packhorse following, and Johnny Gill, rifle still across the saddlebows, bringing up the rear.

They had gone no more than a mile when they heard voices, then three riders swung around a bend in the trail, reining in sharply. Tough-looking, bearded men, they stared from Rafe to the Indian girl. She gasped suddenly, and Rafe's eyes narrowed a little.

"See yuh got our pigeon!" A red-bearded man rode toward them, grinning. "We been a-chasin' her for a couple of hours. Purty thing, ain't she?"

"Yeah." A slim, wiry man with a hatchet face and a cigarette dangling from his lips was speaking. "Glad yuh found her. We'll take her off yore hands now."

"That's all right," Rafe said quietly. "We're taking her back to her village. She's got a broken leg."

"Takin' her back to the village?" the red-bearded man exclaimed. "Why, we cut that squaw out for ourselves, and we're slappin' our own brand on her. You get yore own squaws." He nodded toward the hatchet-faced man. "Get that lead rope, Boyne."

"Keep your hands off that rope!" Rafe's voice was cold. "You blasted fools will get us all killed. This girl's tribe would be down on your ears before night."

"We'll take care of that," Red persisted. "Get her, Boyne!"

Rafe smiled suddenly. "If you boys are lookin' for trouble, I reckon you've found it. I don't know how many of you want to die for this squaw, but any time you figger to take her away from us, some of you'd better start sizing up grave space."

Boyne's eyes narrowed wickedly. "Why, he's askin' for a ruckus, Red! Which eye shall I shoot him through?"

Rafe Caradec sat his horse calmly, smiling a little. "I reckon," he said, "you boys ain't any too battle-wise. You're bunched too much. Now, from where I sit, all three of you are dead in range and grouped nice for even one gun shootin', and I'm figurin' to use two." He spoke to Gill. "Johnny," he said quietly, "suppose these *hombres* start smokin' it, you take that fat one. Leave the redhead and this Boyne for me."

The fat cowhand shifted in his saddle uncomfortably. He was unpleasantly aware that he had turned his horse so he was sideward to Gill and, while presenting a fair target himself, would have to turn half around in the saddle to fire.

Boyne's eyes were hard and reckless. Rafe knew he was the one to watch. He wore his gun slung low, and that he fancied himself as a gun hand was obvious. Suddenly Rafe knew the man was going to draw.

"Hold it!" The voice cut sharply across the air like the crack of a whip. "Boyne, keep yore hand shoulder high! You, too, Red! Now turn yore horses with yore knees and start down the trail. If one of yuh even looks like yuh wanted to use a gun, I'll open up with this Henry and cut yuh into little pieces."

Boyne cursed wickedly. "Yuh're gettin' out of it easy this time!" he said viciously. "I'll see yuh again!"

Rafe smiled. "Why, shore, Boyne! Only next time you'd better take the rawhide lashin' off the butt of your Colt. Mighty handy when ridin' over rough country, but mighty unhandy when you need your gun in a hurry."

With a startled gasp, Boyne glanced down. The rawhide thong was tied over his gun to hold it in place. His face two shades whiter than a snake's belly, he turned his horse with his knees and started the trek down trail.

Bo Marsh stepped out of the brush with his rifle in his hands. He was grinning.

"Hey, boss! If I'd known that six-gun was tied down, I'd 'a' let yuh mow him down! That skunk needs it. That's Lem Boyne. He's a gunslinger for Dan Shute."

Gill laughed. "Man! Will our ears burn tonight! Rafe's run two of Shute's boys into the ground today!"

Marsh grinned. "Figgered yuh'd be headed home soon, and I was out after deer." He glanced at the squaw with the broken leg. "Got more trouble?"

"No," Rafe said. "Those *hombres* had been runnin' this girl down. She busted her leg gettin' away, so we fixed it up. Let's ride."

VI

The trail was smoother now and drifted casually from one cañon to another. Obviously it had been a game trail that had been found and used by Indians, trappers, and wandering buffalo hunters before the coming of the cowhands and trail drivers.

When they were still several miles from the cabin on the Crazy Man, the squaw spoke up suddenly. Gill looked over at Rafe.

"Her camp's just over that rise in a draw," he said.

Caradec nodded. Then he turned to the girl. She was looking at him, expecting him to speak.

"Tell her," he said, "that we share the land Rodney bought from Red Cloud. That we share it with the daughter of Rodney. Get her to tell Red Cloud we will live on the Crazy Man, and we are friends to the Sioux, that their women are safe with us, their horses will not be stolen, that we are friends to the warriors of Red Cloud and the great chiefs of the Sioux people."

Gill spoke slowly, emphatically, and the girl nodded. Then she turned her horse and rode up through the trees.

"Boss," Johnny said, "she's got our best hoss. That's the one I give the most money for!"

Rafe grinned. "Forget it. The girl was scared silly but wouldn't show it for anything. It's a cheap price to pay to get her home safe. Like I said, the Sioux make better friends than enemies."

When the three men rode up, Tex Brisco was carrying two buckets of water to the house. He grinned at them. "That grub looks good," he told them. "I've eaten so much antelope meat, the next thing you know I'll be boundin' along over the prairie myself."

While Marsh got busy with the grub, Johnny told Tex about the events of the trip.

"Nobody been around here," Brisco said. "I seen three Injuns, but they was off a couple of miles and didn't come this way. There hasn't been nobody else around."

During the three days that followed the trip to Painted Rock, Rafe Caradec scouted the range. There were a lot of Bar M cattle around, and most of them were in fairly good shape. His own cattle were mingling freely with them. The range would support many more head than it carried, and the upper end of Long Valley was almost untouched. There was much good grass in the mountain meadows, also, and in several cañons south of the Crazy Man.

Johnny Gill and Bo Marsh explained the lay of the land as they knew it.

"North of here," Gill said, "back of Painted Rock, and mostly west of there, the mountains rise up nigh onto nine thousand feet. Good huntin' country, some of the best I ever seen. South, toward the end of the valley, the mountains thin out. There's a pass through to the head of Otter Creek, and that country west of the mountains is good grazin' land, and nobody much in there yet. Injuns got a big powwow grounds over there. Still farther south there's a long road wall, runnin' purty much north and south. Only one entrance in thirty-five miles. Regular hole in the wall. A few men could get into that hole and stand off an army, and, if they wanted to hightail it, they could lose themselves in that backcountry."

Rafe scouted the crossing toward the head of Otter Creek, and rode down the creek to the grasslands below. This would be good grazing land, and mentally he made a note to make some plans for it.

He rode back to the ranch that night, and, when he was sitting on the stoop after the sun was down, he looked around at Tex Brisco. "You been over the trail from Texas?" he asked.

"Uhn-huh."

"Once aboard ship you were tellin' me about a stampede you had. Only got back about sixteen hundred head of a two-thousand-head herd. That sort of thing happen often?"

Tex laughed. "Shucks, yes! Stampedes are regular things along the trail. Yuh lose some cattle, yuh mebbe get more back, but there's plenty of maverick stock runnin' on the plains south of the Platte . . . all the way to the Canadian, as far as that goes."

"Reckon a few men could slip over there and round up some of that stock?"

Brisco sat up and glanced at Rafe. "Shore could.

Wild stuff, though, and it would be a man-sized job."

"Mebbe," Caradec suggested, "we'll try and do it. It would be one way of gettin' a herd pretty fast, or turnin' some quick money."

There followed days of hard, driving labor. Always one man stayed at the cabin keeping a sharp lookout for any of the Shute or Barkow riders. Caradec knew they would come and, when they did, they would be riding with only one idea in mind—to get rid of him.

In the visit to Painted Rock he had laid his cards on the table, and they had no idea how much he knew, or what his story of Charles Rodney could be. Rafe Caradec knew Barkow was worried, and that pleased him. Yet while the delayed attack was a concern, it was also a help.

There was some grumbling from the hands, but he kept them busy, cutting hay in the meadows and stacking it. Winter in this country was going to be bad—he needed no weather prophet to tell him that—and he had no intention of losing a lot of stock.

In a cañon that branched off from the head of Crazy Man, he had found a warm spring. There was small chance of it freezing, yet the water was not too hot to drink. In severe cold it would freeze, but otherwise it would offer an excellent watering place for his stock. They made no effort to bring hay back to the ranch, but arranged it in huge stacks back in the cañons and meadows.

There had been no sign of Indians, and Rafe avoided their camp, yet once, when he did pass nearby, there was no sign of them. It seemed as if they had moved out and left the country.

Then one night he heard a noise at the corral, and the snorting of a horse. Instantly he was out of bed and had his boots on when he heard Brisco swearing in the next room. They got outside in a hurry, fearing someone was rustling their stock. In the corral they could see the horses, and there was no one nearby.

Bo Marsh had walked over to the corral, and suddenly he called out.

"Boss! Look it here!"

They all trooped over, then stopped. Instead of five horses in the corral there were ten! One of them was the paint they had loaned the young squaw, but the others were strange horses, and every one was a picked animal.

"Well, I'll be damned!" Gill exploded. "Brung our own hoss and an extra for each of us. Reckon that big black is for you, boss."

By daylight, when they could examine the horses, Tex Brisco walked around them admiringly.

"Man," he said, "that was the best horse trade I ever heard of! There's four of the purtiest horses I ever laid an eye on! I always did say the Sioux knowed hossflesh, and this proves it. Reckon yore bread cast on the water shore come back to yuh, boss!"

Rafe studied the valley thoughtfully. They would have another month of good haying weather if there was no rain. Four men could not work much harder than they were, but the beaver were building their houses bigger and in deeper water, and from that and all other indications the winter was going to be hard.

He made his decision suddenly, and mentioned

it that night at the supper table. "I'm ridin' to Painted Rock. Want to go along, Tex?"

"Yeah." The Texan looked at him calculatingly. "Yeah, I'd like that."

"How about me?" Bo asked, grinning. "Johnny went last time. I could shore use a belt of that red-eye the National peddles, and mebbe a look around town."

"Take him along, boss," Johnny said. "I can hold this end. If he stays, he'll be ridin' me all the time, anyway."

"All right. Saddle up first thing in the mornin'."

"Boss . . ." Johnny threw one leg over the other, and lit his smoke. "One thing I better tell yuh. I hadn't said a word before, but two, three days ago, when I was down to the bend of the Crazy Man, I run into a couple fellers. One of 'em was Red Blazer, that big galoot who was with Boyne. Remember?"

Rafe turned around and looked down at the little, leather-faced cowhand. "Well," he said, "what about him?"

Gill took a long drag on his cigarette. "He told me he was carryin' a message from Trigger Boyne, and that Trigger was goin' to shoot on sight, next time yuh showed up in Painted Rock."

Rafe reached over on the table and picked up a piece of cold cornbread. "Then I reckon that's what he'll do," he said. "If he gets into action fast enough."

"Boss," Marsh pleaded, "if that redheaded Tom Blazer, brother to the one yuh had the run-in with . . . if he's there, I want him."

"That the one we saw on the National stoop?" Rafe asked Gill.

"Uhn-huh. There's five of them brothers. All gun-toters."

Gill got up and stretched. "Well, I'll have it purty lazy while you *hombres* are down there dustin' lead." He added: "It would be a good idea to sort of keep an eye out. Gee Bonaro's probably in town and could be feelin' mighty mad."

Rafe walked outside, strolling toward the corral. Behind him, Marsh turned to Gill. "Reckon he can sling a gun?"

Tex chuckled. "Mister, that *hombre* killed one of the fastest, slickest gun throwers that ever came out of Texas, and done it when he was no more'n sixteen, down on the C Bar. Also, while I've never seen him shoot, if he can shoot like he can fist-fight, Mister Trigger Boyne had better grab hisself an armful of hossflesh and start makin' tracks for the blackest part of the Black Hills . . . *fast!*"

VII

Nothing about the town of Painted Rock suggested drama or excitement. It lay sprawled comfortably in the morning sunlight in an elbow of Rock Creek. A normally roaring and plunging stream, the creek had decided here to loiter a while, enjoying the warm sun and the graceful willows that lined the banks. Behind and among the willows the white, slender trunks of the birch trees marched in neat ranks, each tree so like its neighbor that it was almost impossible to distinguish between them. Clumps of mountain alder, yellow rose, puffed clematis, and antelope bush were scattered along the far bank of the stream and advanced up the hill beyond in skirmishing formation. In a few weeks now the aspen leaves would be changing, and Painted Rock would take on a background of flaming color—a bank of trees, rising toward the darker growth of spruce and fir along the higher mountainside.

Painted Rock's one street was the only thing about the town that was ordered. It lay between two neat rows of buildings that stared at each other down across a long lane of dust and, during the rainy periods, of mud. At any time of day or night a dozen saddle horses would be standing three-legged at the hitching rails, usually in front of Joe Benson's National Saloon. A buckboard or a spring wagon would also be present, usually driven by some small rancher in for his supplies. The two big outfits sent two wagons together, drawn by mules.

Bruce Barkow sat in front of the sheriff's office this morning, deep in conversation with Pod Gomer. It was a conversation that had begun over an hour before. Gomer was a short, thick-set man, almost as deep from chest to spine as from shoulder to shoulder. He was not fat and was considered a tough man to tangle with. He was also a man who liked to play on the winning side, and long ago he had decided there was only one side to consider in this light—the side of Dan Shute and Bruce Barkow. Yet he was a man who was sensitive to the way the wind blew, and he frequently found himself puzzled when he considered his two bosses. There was no good feeling between them. They met on business or pleasure, saw things through much the same eyes, but each wanted to be kingpin. Sooner or later, Gomer knew, he must make a choice between them.

Barkow was shrewd, cunning. He was a planner and a conniver. He was a man who would use any method to win, but in most cases he kept himself in the background of anything smacking of crime or wrongdoing. Otherwise, he was much in the foreground. Dan Shute was another type of man. He was tall and broad of shoulder. Normally he was sullen, hard-eyed, and surly. He had little to say to anyone and was more inclined to settle matters with a blow or a gun than with words. He was utterly cold-blooded, felt slightly about anything, and would kill a man as quickly and with as little excitement as he would brand a calf.

Barkow might carve a notch on his gun butt. Shute wouldn't even understand such a thing. Shute was a man who seemed to be without vanity, and such men are dangerous. For the vanity is there, only submerged, and the slow-burning, deep fires of hatred for the vain smolder within them until suddenly they burst into flame and end in sudden, dramatic climax and ugly violence.

Pod Gomer understood little of Dan Shute. He understood the man's complex character just enough to know that he was dangerous, that as long as Shute rode along, Barkow would be top dog, but that if ever Barkow incurred Shute's resentment, the deep-seated fury of the gunman would brush his partner aside as he would swat a fly. In a sense, both men were using each other, but of the two Dan Shute was the man to be reckoned with. Yet Gomer had seen Barkow at work. He had seen how deviously the big rancher planned, how carefully he made friends. At the fort, they knew and liked him, and what little law there was outside the town of Painted Rock was in the hands of the commanding officer at the fort. Knowing this, Bruce Barkow had made it a point to know the personnel there, and to plan accordingly.

The big black that Rafe was riding was a powerful horse, and he let the animal have its head. Behind him in single file trailed Tex Brisco and Bo Marsh. Rafe Caradec was thinking as he rode. He had seen too much of violence and struggle to fail to understand men who lived lives along the frontier. He had correctly gauged the kind of courage Gee Bonaro possessed, yet he knew the man was dangerous and, if the opportunity offered, would shoot and shoot instantly.

Trigger Boyne was another proposition. Boyne was reckless, wickedly fast with a gun, and the type of man who would fight at the drop of a hat, and had his own ready to drop on the slightest pretext. Boyne liked the name of being a gunman, and he liked being top dog. If Boyne had sent a warning to Caradec, it would be only because he intended to back up that warning.

Rafe took the black along the mountain trail, riding swiftly. The big horse was the finest he had ever had between his knees. When a Sioux gave gifts, he apparently went all the way. A gift had been sent to each of the men on the Crazy Man, which was evidence that the Sioux had looked them over at the cabin. The black had a long, space-eating stride that seemed to put no strain on his endurance. The horses given to the others were almost as good. There were not four men in the mountains mounted as well, Rafe knew.

He rounded the big horse into the dusty street of Painted Rock and rode down toward the hitching rail at a spanking trot. He pulled up and swung down, and the other men swung down alongside him.

"Just keep your eyes open," Rafe said guardedly. "I don't want trouble. But if Boyne starts anything, he's my meat."

Marsh nodded, and walked up on the boardwalk alongside of Brisco, who was sweeping the street with quick, observant eyes.

"Have a drink?" Rafe suggested, and led the way inside the National.

Joe Benson was behind the bar. He looked up warily as the three men entered. He spoke to Bo, then glanced at Tex Brisco. He placed Tex as a stranger, and his mind leaped ahead. It took no long study to see that Tex was a hard character and a fighting man.

Joe was cautious and shrewd. Unless he was mistaken, Barkow and Shute had their work cut out for them. These men didn't look like the sort to backwater for anything or anyone. The town's saloonkeeper-mayor had an uncomfortable feeling that a change was in the offing, yet he pushed the feeling aside with irritation. That must not happen. His own failure and his own interests were too closely allied to those of Barkow and Shute. Of course, when Barkow married the Rodney girl that would give them complete title to the ranch. That would leave them in the clear, and these men, if alive, could be run off the ranch with every claim to legal process.

Caradec tossed off his whiskey and looked up sharply. His glance pinned Joe Benson to the spot. "Trigger Boyne sent word he was looking for me," he said abruptly. "Tell him I'm in town . . . ready,"

"How should I know Trigger better'n any other man who comes into this bar?" Benson demanded.

"You know him. Tell him."

Rafe hitched his guns into a comfortable position and strode through the swinging doors. There were a dozen men in sight, but none of them resembled Boyne or either of the Blazers he had seen.

He started for the Emporium. Behind him, Tex

stopped by one of the posts that supported the wooden awning over the walk, and leaned a negligent shoulder against it, a cigarette drooping from the corner of his mouth.

Bo Marsh sat back in a chair against the wall, his interested eyes sweeping the street. Several men who passed spoke to him and glanced at Tex Brisco's tall, lean figure.

Rafe opened the door of the Emporium and strode inside. Gene Baker looked up, frowning when he saw him. He was not glad to see Rafe, for the man's words on his previous visit had been responsible for some doubts and speculations.

"Is Ann Rodney in?"

Baker hesitated. "Yes," he said finally. "She's back there."

Rafe went around the counter toward the door, hat in his left hand.

"I don't think she wants to see yuh," Baker advised.

"All right," Rafe said, "we'll see."

He pushed past the screen, and stepped into the living room beyond.

Ann Rodney was sewing, and, when the quick step sounded, she glanced up. Her eyes changed. Something inside her seemed to turn over slowly. This big man who had brought such disturbing news affected her as no man ever had. Considering her engagement to Bruce Barkow, she didn't like to feel that way about any man. Since he had last been here, she had worried a good deal about what he had said and her reaction to it. Why would he come with such a tale? Shouldn't she have heard him out?

Bruce said no, that the man was an imposter and someone who hoped to get money from her. Yet she knew something of Johnny Gill, and she had danced with Bo Marsh, and knew that these men were honest and had been so as long as she had known of them. They were liked and respected in Painted Rock.

"Oh," she said, rising. "It's you?"

Rafe stopped in the center of the room, a tall, picturesque figure in his buckskin coat and with his waving black hair. He was, she thought, a handsome man. He wore his guns low and tied down, and she knew what that meant.

"I was goin' to wait," he said abruptly, "and let you come to me and ask questions, if you ever did, but when I thought it over, rememberin' what I'd promised your father, I decided I must come back now, lay all my cards on the table, and tell you what happened."

She started to speak, and he lifted his hand. "Wait. I'm goin' to talk quick, because in a few minutes I have an appointment outside that I must keep. Your father did not die on the trail back from California. He was shanghaied in San Francisco, taken aboard a ship while unconscious, and forced to work as a seaman. I was shanghaied at the same time and place. Your father and I in the months that followed were together a lot. He asked me to come here, to take care of you and his wife, and to protect you. He died of beatin's he got aboard ship, just before the rest of us got away from the ship. I was with him when he died, settin' beside his bed. Almost his last words were about you."

Ann Rodney stood very still, staring at him. There was a ring of truth in the rapidly spoken words, yet how could she believe this? Three men had told her they saw her father die, and one of them was the man she was to marry, the man who had befriended her, who had refused to foreclose on the mortgage he held and take from her the last thing she possessed in the world.

"What was my father like?" she asked.

"Like?" Rafe's brow furrowed. "How can anybody say what any man is like? I'd say he was about five feet eight or nine. When he died, his hair was almost white, but when I first saw him, he had only a few gray hairs. His face was a heap like yours. So were his eyes, except they weren't so large nor so beautiful. He was a kind man who wasn't used to violence, I think, and he didn't like it. He planned well, and thought well, but the West was not the country for him, yet. Ten years from now, when it has settled more, he'd have been a leadin' citizen. He was a good man, and a sincere man."

"It sounds like him," Ann said hesitantly, "but there is nothing you could not have learned here, or from someone who knew him."

"No," he said frankly. "That's so. But there's somethin' else you should know. The mortgage your father had against his place was paid."

"What?" Ann stiffened. "Paid? How can you say that?"

"He borrowed the money in Frisco and paid Barkow with it. He got a receipt for it."

"Oh, I can't believe that! Why, Bruce would have . . ."

"Would he?" Rafe asked gently. "You shore?"

She looked at him. "What was the other thing?"

"I have a deed," he said, "to the ranch made out to you and to me."

Her eyes widened, then hardened with suspicion. "So? Now things become clearer. A deed to my father's ranch made out to you and to me! In other words, you are laying claim to half of my ranch?"

"Please . . . ," Rafe said. "I . . ."

She smiled. "You needn't say anything more, Mister Caradec. I admit I was almost coming to believe there was something in your story. At least, I was wondering about it, for I couldn't understand how you hoped to profit from any such tale. Now it becomes clear. You are trying to get half my ranch. You have even moved into my house without asking permission." She stepped to one side of the door and pulled back the curtain. "I'm sorry, but I must ask you to leave. I must also ask you to vacate the house on Crazy Man at once. I must ask you to refrain from calling on me again, or from approaching me."

"Please," Rafe said, "you're jumping to conclusions. I never aimed to claim any part of the ranch. I came here only because your father asked me to."

"Good day, Mister Caradec!" Ann still held the curtain.

He looked at her, and for an instant their eyes held. She was first to look away. He turned abruptly and stepped through the curtain, and, as he did, the door opened and he saw Bo Marsh.

Marsh's eyes were excited and anxious. "Rafe," he said, "that Boyne *hombre*'s in front of the National. He wants yuh!"

"Why, shore," Rafe said quietly. "I'm ready."

He walked to the front door, hitching his guns into place. Behind him, he heard Ann Rodney asking Baker: "What did he mean? That Boyne was waiting for him?"

Baker's reply came to Rafe as he stepped out into the morning light. "Trigger Boyne's goin' to kill him, Ann. Yuh'd better go back inside."

Rafe smiled slightly. Kill him? Would that be it? No man knew better than he the tricks that Destiny plays on a man, or how often the right man dies at the wrong time and place. A man never wore a gun without inviting trouble; he never stepped into a street and began the gunman's walk without the full knowledge that he might be a shade too slow, that some small thing might disturb him just long enough.

VIII

Morning sun was bright, and the street lay empty of horses or vehicles. A few idlers loafed in front of the stage station, but all of them were on their feet.

Rafe Caradec saw his black horse switch his tail at a fly, and he stepped down into the street. Trigger Boyne stepped off the boardwalk to face him, some distance off. Rafe did not walk slowly; he made no measured, quiet approach. He started to walk toward Boyne, going fast.

Trigger walked down the street easily, casually. He was smiling. Inside, his heart was throbbing, and there was a wild reckless eagerness within him. This one he would finish off fast. This would be simple, easy. He squared in the street, and suddenly the smile was wiped from his face. Caradec was coming toward him, shortening the distance at a fast walk. That rapid approach did something to the calm on Boyne's face and in his mind. It was wrong. Caradec should have come slowly; he should have come poised and ready to draw. Knowing his own deadly marksmanship, Boyne felt sure he could kill this man at any distance. But as soon as he saw that walk, he knew that Caradec was going to be so close in a few more steps that he himself would be killed. It is one thing to know you are to kill another man, quite a different thing to know you are to die yourself. Why, if Caradec walked that way, he would be so close he couldn't miss!

Boyne's legs spread and the wolf sprang into his eyes, but there was panic there, too. He had to stop his man, get him now. His hand swept down for his gun. Yet something was wrong. For all his speed he seemed incredibly slow, because that other man, that tall, moving figure in the buckskin coat and black hat, was already shooting.

Trigger's own hand moved first, his own hand gripped the gun butt first, and then he was staring into a smashing, blossoming rose of flame that seemed to bloom beyond the muzzle of that big black gun in the hand of Rafe Caradec. Something stabbed at his stomach, and he went numb to his toes. Stupidly he swung his gun up, staring over it. The gun seemed awfully heavy. He must get a smaller one. That gun opposite him blossomed with rose again, and something struck him again in the stomach. He started to speak, half-turning toward the men in front of the stage station, his mouth opening and closing.

Something was wrong with him, he tried to say. Why, everyone knew he was the fastest man in Wyoming, unless it was Shute! Everyone knew that! The heavy gun in his hand bucked, and he saw the flame stab at the ground. He dropped the gun, swayed, then fell flat on his face.

He would have to get up. He was going to kill that stranger, that Rafe Caradec. He would have to get up. The numbness from his stomach climbed higher, and he suddenly felt himself in the saddle of a bucking horse, a monstrous and awful horse that leaped and plunged, and it was going up! Up! Up! Then it came down hard, and he felt himself leave the saddle, all sprawled out. The horse had thrown him. Bucked off into the dust. He closed his hands spasmodically.

Rafe Caradec stood tall in the middle of the gunman's walk, the black, walnut-stocked pistol in his right hand. He glanced once at the still figure sprawled in the street, then his eyes lifted, sweeping the walks in swift, accurate, appraisal. Only then, some instinct prodded his unconscious and warned him. The merest flicker of a curtain, and in the space between the curtain and the edge of the window the black muzzle of a rifle! His .44 lifted, and the heavy gun bucked in his hand just as flame leaped from the rifle barrel, and he felt quick, urgent fingers pluck at his sleeve. The .44 jolted again, and a rifle rattled on the shingled porch roof. The curtain made a tearing sound, and the head and shoulders of a man fell through, toppling over the sill. Overbalanced, the heels came up, and the man's body rolled over slowly, seemed to hesitate, then rolled over again, poised an instant on the edge of the roof, and dropped suddenly into the street. Dust lifted from around the body, settled back. Gee Bonaro thrust hard with one leg, and his face twisted a little. In the quiet street there was no sound, no movement.

For the space of a full half minute the watchers held themselves, shocked by the sudden climax, stunned with disbelief. Trigger Boyne had been beaten to the draw and killed; Gee Bonaro had made his try, and died.

Rafe Caradec turned slowly and walked back to

his horse. Without a word he swung into the saddle. He turned the horse and, sitting tall in the saddle, swept the street with a cold, hard eye that seemed to stare at each man there. Then, as if by his own wish, the black horse turned. Walking slowly, his head held proudly, he carried his rider down the street and out of town.

Behind him, coolly and without smiles, Bo Marsh and Tex Brisco followed. Like him, they rode slowly; like him they rode proudly. Something in their bearing seemed to say: *We were challenged. We came. You see the result.*

In the window of the National, Joe Benson chewed his mustache. He stared at the figure of Trigger Boyne with vague disquiet, then irritation. "Cuss it!" he muttered under his breath. "You was supposed to be a gunman? What in thunder was wrong with yuh?"

A bullet from Boyne's gun, or from Bonaro's, for that matter, could have ended it all. A bullet now could settle the whole thing, quiet the gossip, remove the doubts, and leave Barkow free to marry Ann, and the whole business could go forward. Instead, they had failed. It would be a long time now, Benson knew, before it was all over. A long time. Barkow was slipping. The man had better think fast and get something done. Rafe Caradec must die.

The Fort Laramie Treaty of 1868 had forbidden white men to enter the Powder River country, yet gold discoveries had brought prospectors north in increasing numbers. Small villages and mining camps had come into existence. Following them, cattlemen discovered the rich grasses of northern

Wyoming, and a few herds came over what later was to be known as the Texas Trail.

Indian attacks and general hostility caused many of these pioneers to retreat to more stable localities, but a few of the more courageous had stayed on. Prospectors had entered the Black Hills, following the Custer expedition in 1874, and the Sioux, always resentful of any incursion upon their hunting grounds or any flaunting of their rights, were preparing to do something more than talk.

The names of such chiefs as Red Cloud, Dull Knife, Crazy Horse, and the medicine man, Sitting Bull, came more and more into frontier gossip. A steamboat was reported to be *en route* up the turbulent Yellowstone, and river traffic on the upper Mississippi was an accepted fact. There were increasing reports of gatherings of Indians in the hills, and white men rode warily, never without arms.

Cut off from contact with the few scattered ranchers, Rafe Caradec and his riders heard little of the gossip except what they gleaned from an occasional prospector or wandering hunter. Yet no gossip was needed to tell them how the land lay.

Twice they heard sounds of rifle fire, and once the Sioux ran off a number of cattle from Shute's ranch, taking them from a herd kept not far from Long Valley. Two of Shute's riders were killed. None of Caradec's men was molested. He was left strictly alone. Indians avoided his place, no matter what their mission.

Twice, riders from the ranch went to Painted Rock. Each time they returned, they brought stories of an impending Indian outbreak. A few of the less courageous ranchers sold out and left the country. In all this time, Rafe Caradec lived in the saddle, riding often from dawn until dusk, avoiding the tangled brakes, but studying the lay of the land with care. There was, he knew, some particular reason for Bruce Barkow's interest in the ranch that belonged to Ann Rodney. What that reason was, he must know. Without it, he knew he could offer no real reason why Barkow would go to the lengths he had gone to get a ranch that was on the face of things of no more value than any piece of land in the country, most of which could be had for the taking. . . .

Ann spent much of her time alone. Business at the store was thriving, and Gene Baker and his wife, and often Ann as well, were busy. In her spare time the thought kept returning to her that Rafe Caradec might be honest. Yet she dismissed the thought as unworthy. If she admitted even for an instant that he was honest, she must also admit that Bruce Barkow was dishonest, a thief, and possibly a killer. Yet somehow the picture of her father kept returning to her mind. It was present there on one of the occasions when Bruce Barkow came to call.

A handsome man, Barkow understood how to appeal to a woman. He carried himself well, and his clothes were always the best in Painted Rock. He called this evening, looking even better than he had on the last occasion, his black suit neatly pressed, his mustache carefully trimmed.

They had been talking for some time when Ann mentioned Rafe Caradec. "His story sounded so sincere!" she said, after a minute. "He said he had been shanghaied in San Francisco with Father, and that they had become acquainted on the ship."

"He's a careful man," Barkow commented, "and a dangerous one. He showed that when he killed Trigger Boyne and Bonaro. He met Boyne on the range, and they had some trouble over an Indian girl."

"An Indian girl?" Ann looked at him questioningly.

"Yes." Barkow frowned as if the subject was distasteful to him. "You know how some of the cowhands are . . . always running after some squaw. They have stolen squaws, kept them for a while, then turned them loose or killed them. Caradec had a young squaw, and Boyne tried to argue with him to let her go. They had words, and there'd have been a shooting then if one of Caradec's other men hadn't come up with a rifle, and Shute's boys went away."

Ann was shocked. She had heard of such things happening and was well aware of how much trouble they caused. That Rafe Caradec would be a man like that was hard to believe. Yet, what did she know of the man? He disturbed her more than she allowed herself to believe. Despite the fact that he seemed to be trying to work some scheme to get all or part of her ranch, and despite all she had heard of him at one time or another from Bruce, she couldn't make herself believe that all she heard was true.

That he appealed to her, she refused to admit. Yet when with him, she felt drawn to him. She liked his rugged masculinity, his looks, his voice, and was impressed with his sincerity. Yet the killing of Boyne and Bonaro was the talk of the town. The

Bonaro phase of the incident she could understand from the previous episode in the store. But no one had any idea of why Boyne should be looking for Caradec. The solution now offered by Barkow was the only one. A fight over a squaw! Without understanding why, Ann felt vaguely resentful.

For days a dozen of Shute's riders had hung around town. There had been talk of lynching Caradec, but nothing came of it. Ann had heard the talk, and asked Baker about it.

The old storekeeper looked up, nodding.

"There's talk, but it'll come to nothin'. None of these boys aim to ride out there to Crazy Man and tackle that crowd. You know what Gill and Marsh are like. They'll fight, and they can. Well, Caradec's showed what he could do with a gun when he killed those two in the street. I don't know whether yuh saw that other feller with Caradec or not. The one from Texas. Well, if he ain't tougher than either Marsh or Gill, I'll pay off! Notice how he wore his guns? Nope, nobody'll go looking for them. If they got their hands on Caradec, that would be somethin' else."

Baker rubbed his jaw thoughtfully. "Unless they are powerful lucky, they won't last long, anyway. That's Injun country, and Red Cloud or Man-Afraid-Of-His-Hoss won't take kindly to white men livin' there. They liked yore pa, and he was friendly to 'em."

As a result of his conversations with Barkow, Sheriff Pod Gomer had sent messages south by stage to Cheyenne and the telegraph. Rafe Caradec had come from San Francisco, and Bruce Barkow wanted to know who and what he was.

More than that, he wanted to find out how he had been allowed to escape the *Mary S*. With that in mind he wrote to Bully Borger.

Barkow had known nothing about Caradec when the deal was made, but Borger had agreed to take Charles Rodney to sea and let him die there, silencing the truth forever. Allowing Rafe Caradec to come ashore with his story was not keeping the terms of the bargain. If Caradec had actually been aboard the ship and left it, there might be something in that to make him liable to the law. Barkow intended to leave no stone unturned, and in the meanwhile he spread his stories around about Caradec's reason for killing Boyne.

IX

Caradec went on with his haying. The nights were already growing chillier. At odd times, when not haying or handling cattle, he and the boys built another room onto the cabin, and banked the house against the wind. Fortunately its position was sheltered. Wind would not bother them greatly where they were, but there would be snow and lots of it.

Rafe rode out each day, and several times brought back deer or elk. The meat was jerked and stored away. Gill got the old wagon Rodney had brought from Missouri and made some repairs. It would be the easiest way to get supplies out from Painted Rock. He worked over it and soon had it in excellent shape.

On the last morning of the month, Rafe walked out to where Gill was hitching a team to the wagon.

"Looks good," he agreed. "You've done a job on it, Johnny."

Gill looked pleased. He nodded at the hubs of the wheels. "Notice 'em? No squeak!"

"Well, I'll be hanged." Rafe looked at the grease on the hubs. "Where'd you get the grease?"

"Sort of a spring back over in the hills. I brung back a bucket of it."

Rafe Caradec looked up sharply. "Johnny, where'd you find that spring?"

"Why,"—Gil looked puzzled—"it's just a sort of hole, back over next to that mound. You know, in that bad range. Ain't much account down there, but I was down there once and found this here spring. This stuff works as well as the grease yuh buy."

"It should," Rafe said dryly. "It's the same stuff!"

He caught up the black and threw a saddle on it. Within an hour he was riding down toward the barren knoll Gill had mentioned. What he found was not a spring, but a hole among some sparse rushes, dead and sick-looking. It was an oil seepage.

Oil! Swiftly his mind leaped ahead. This, then, could be the reason why Barkow and Shute were so anxious to acquire title to this piece of land, so anxious that they would have a man shanghaied and killed. Caradec recalled that Bonneville had reported oil seepages on his trip through the state some forty years or so before, and there had been a well drilled in the previous decade. One of the largest markets for oil was the patent medicine business, for it was the main ingredient in so-called British Oil.

The hole in which the oil was seeping in a thick stream might be shallow, but sounding with a six-foot stick found no bottom. Rafe doubted if it was much deeper. Still, there would be several barrels here, and he seemed to recall some talk of selling oil for twenty dollars the barrel.

Swinging into the saddle, he turned the big black down the draw and rode rapidly toward the hills. This could be the reason, for certainly it was reason enough. The medicine business was only one possible market, for machinery of all kinds needed lubricants. There was every chance that the oil industry might really mean something in time. If the hole was emptied, how fast would it refill? How constant was the supply? On one point he could soon find out.

He swung the horse up out of the draw, forded the Crazy Man, and cantered up the hill to the cabin. As he reined in and swung down at the door, he noticed two strange horses.

Tex Brisco stepped to the door, his face hard. "Watch it, boss!" he said sharply.

Pod Gomer's thick-set body thrust into the doorway. "Caradec," he said calmly, "yuh're under arrest."

Rafe swung down, facing him. Two horses. Who had ridden the other one?

"For what?" he demanded.

His mind was racing. *The mutiny? Have they found out about that?*

"For killin'. Shootin' Bonaro."

"Bonaro?" Rafe laughed. "You mean for defendin' myself? Bonaro had a rifle in that window. He was all set to shoot me."

Gomer nodded coolly. "That was most folks' opinion, but it seems nobody *saw* him aim any gun at yuh. We've only got yore say-so. When we got to askin' around, it begun to look sort of funnylike. It appears to a lot of folks that yuh just took that chance to shoot him and get away with it. Anyway, yuh'd be better off to stand trial."

"Don't go, boss," Brisco said. "They don't ever aim to have a trial."

"Yuh'd better not resist," Gomer replied calmly. "I've got twenty Shute riders down in the valley. I made 'em stay back. The minute any shootin' starts, they'll come a-runnin', and yuh all know what that would mean."

Rafe knew. It would mean the death of all four of them and the end to any opposition to Barkow's plans. Probably that was what the rancher hoped would happen.

"Why, shore, Gomer," Caradec said calmly, "I'll go."

Tex started to protest, and Rafe saw Gill hurl his hat into the dust.

"Give me yore guns, then," Gomer said, "and mount up."

"No." Rafe's voice was flat. "I keep my guns till I get to town. If that bunch of Shute's starts anything, the first one I'll kill will be you, Gomer."

Pod Gomer's face turned sullen. "Yuh ain't goin' to be bothered. I'm the law here. Let's go!"

"Gomer," Tex Brisco said viciously, "if anything happens to him, I'll kill you and Barkow both!"

"That goes for me, too!" Gill said harshly.

"And me," Marsh put in. "I'll get you if I have to dry-gulch yuh, Gomer."

"Well, all right!" Gomer said angrily. "It's just a trial. I told 'em I didn't think much of it, but the judge issued this warrant."

He was scowling blackly. It was all right for them to issue warrants, but if they thought he was going to get killed for them, they were bloody well wrong. Pod Gomer jammed his hat down on his head. This was a far cry from the coal mines of Lancashire, but sometimes he wished he was back in England. There was a look in Brisco's eyes he didn't like. *No,* he told himself, *he'll be turned loose before I take a chance. Let Barkow kill his own pigeons. I don't want these Bar M hands gunnin' for me!*

The man who had ridden the other horse stepped out of the cabin, followed closely by Bo Marsh. There was no smile on the young cowhand's face. The man was Bruce Barkow. For an instant, his eyes met Caradec's. "This is just a formality," Barkow said smoothly. "There's been some talk around Painted Rock, and a trial will clear the air a lot, and, of course, if yuh're innocent, Caradec, yuh'll be freed."

"You shore of that?" Rafe's eyes smiled cynically. "Barkow, you hate me and you know it. If I ever leave that jail alive, it won't be your fault."

Barkow shrugged. "Think what you want," he said indifferently. "I believe in law and order. We've got a nice little community at Painted Rock, and we want to keep it that way. Boyne had challenged yuh, and that was different. Bonaro had no part in the fight."

"No use arguin' that here," Gomer protested. "Court's the place for that. Let's go."

Tex Brisco lounged down the steps, his thumbs hooked in his belt. He stared at Gomer. "I don't like you," he said coolly. "I don't like you a bit. I think yuh're yeller as a coyote. I think yuh bob ever' time this here Barkow says bob."

Gomer's face whitened, and his eyes shifted. "Yuh've got no call to start trouble," he said. "I'm doin' my duty."

"Let it ride," Caradec told Tex. "There's plenty of time."

"Yeah," Tex drawled, his hard eyes on Gomer, "but just for luck I'm goin' to mount and trail yuh into town, keepin' to the hills. If that bunch of Shute riders gets fancy, I'm goin' to get myself a sheriff, and"—his eyes shifted—"mebbe another *hombre*."

"Is that a threat?" Barkow asked contemptuously. "Talk is cheap."

"Want to see how cheap?" Tex prodded. His eyes were ugly, and he was itching for a fight. It showed in every line of him. "Want to make it expensive?"

Bruce Barkow was no fool. He had not seen Tex Brisco in action, yet there was something chill and deadly about the tall Texan. Barkow shrugged. "We came here to enforce the law. Is this resistance, Caradec?"

"No," Rafe said. "Let's go."

The three men turned their horses and walked them down the trail toward Long Valley. Tex Brisco threw a saddle on his horse, then mounted. Glancing back, Pod Gomer saw the Texan turn his horse up a trail into the trees. He swore viciously.

Caradec sat his horse easily. The trouble would not come now. He was quite sure the plan had been to get him away, then claim the Shute riders had taken him from the law. Yet he was sure it would not come to that now. Pod Gomer would know that Brisco's Winchester was within range. Also, Rafe was still wearing his guns.

Rafe rode warily, lagging a trifle behind the sheriff. He glanced at Barkow, but the rancher's face was expressionless. Ahead of them, in a tight bunch, waited the Shute riders. The first he recognized were the Blazers. There was another man, known as Joe Gorman, whom he also recognized.

Red Blazer started forward abruptly. "He come, did he?" he shouted. "Now we'll show him!"

"Get back!" Gomer ordered sharply.

"Huh?" Red glared at Gomer. "Who says I'll get back! I'm stringin' this *hombre* to the first tree we get to."

"You stay back!" Gomer ordered. "We're takin' this man in for trial!"

Red Blazer laughed. "Come on, boys!" he yelled. "Let's hang the skunk!"

"I wouldn't, Red," Rafe Caradec said calmly. "You've overlooked somethin'. I'm wearin' my guns. Are you faster than Trigger Boyne?"

Blazer jerked his horse's head around, his face pale but furious. "Hey!" he yelled. "What the devil is this? I thought . . ."

"That you'd have an easy time of it?" Rafe shoved the black horse between Gomer and Barkow, pushing ahead of them. He rode right up to Blazer and let the big black shove into the other horse. "Well, get this, Blazer, any time you kill me, you'll do it with a gun in your hand, savvy? You're nothin' but a lot of lynch-crazy coyotes! Try it, damn it! Try it now, and I'll blow you out of that saddle so full of lead you'll sink a foot into the ground!" Rafe's eyes swept the crowd. "Think this is a joke? That goes for any of you. As for Gomer, he knows that if you *hombres* want any trouble, he gets it, too. There's a man up in the hills with a Winchester, and, if you don't think he can empty saddles, start somethin'. That Winchester carries sixteen shots, and I've seen him empty it and get that many rabbits! I'm packing two guns. I'm askin' you now so, if you want any of what I've got, start the ball rollin'. Mebbe you'd get me, but I'm tellin' you there'll be more dead men around here than you can shake a stick at."

Joe Gorman spoke quickly. "Watch it, boys! There is an *hombre* up on the mountain with a rifle. I seen him."

"What the hell is this?" Red Blazer repeated.

"The fun's over," Rafe replied shortly. "You might as well head for home and tell Dan Shute to kill his own wolves. I'm wearin' my guns, and I'm goin' to keep 'em. I'll stand trial, but you know and I know that Bonaro got what he was askin' for." Caradec turned his eyes on Blazer. "As for you, stay out of my sight. You're too blasted willin' to throw your hemp over a man you think is helpless. I don't like skunks and never did."

"Yuh can't call me a skunk!" Blazer bellowed.

Rafe stared at him. "I just did," he said calmly.

X

For a full minute their eyes held. Rafe's hand was on his thigh within inches of his gun. If it came to gun play now, he would be killed, but Blazer and Barkow would go down, too, and there would be others. He had not exaggerated when he spoke of Tex Brisco's shooting. The man was a wizard with the rifle.

Red Blazer was trapped. White to the lips, he stared at Rafe and could see cold, certain death looking back at him. He could stand it no longer. "Why don't some of yuh do somethin'?" he bellowed.

Joe Gorman spat: "You done the talkin', Red."

"Tarnation with it!"

Blazer swung his horse around, touched spurs to the animal, and raced off at top speed.

Bruce Barkow's hand hovered close to his gun. A quick draw, a shot, and the man would be dead. Just like that. His lips tightened, and his elbow crooked.

Gomer grabbed his wrist. "Don't, Bruce! Don't! That *hombre* up there . . . look!"

Barkow's head swung. Brisco was in plain sight,

his rifle resting over the limb of a tree. At that distance, he could not miss. Yet he was beyond pistol range, and, while some of the riders had rifles, they were out in the open without a bit of cover.

Barkow jerked his arm away and turned his horse toward town. Rafe turned the black and rode beside him. He said nothing, but Barkow was seething at the big man's obvious contempt. Rafe Caradec had outfaced the lot of them. He had made them look fools. Yet Barkow remembered as well as each of the riders remembered that Rafe had fired but three shots in the street battle, that all the shots had scored, and two men had died.

When the cavalcade reached the National, Rafe turned to Pod Gomer. "Get your court goin'," he said calmly. "We'll have this trial now."

"Listen here!" Gomer burst out, infuriated. "Yuh can do things like that too often! We'll have our court when we get blamed good and ready!"

"No," Rafe said, "you'll hold court this afternoon . . . now. You haven't got any calendar to interfere. I have business to attend to that can't wait, and I won't. You'll have yore trial today, or I'll leave, and you can come and get me."

"Who you tellin' what to do?" Gomer said angrily. "I'll have you know . . ."

"Then you tell him, Barkow . . . or does he take his orders from Shute? Call that judge of yours and let's get this over."

Bruce Barkow's lips tightened. He could see that Gene Baker and Ann Rodney were standing in the doorway of the store, listening.

"All right," Barkow said savagely. "Call him down here."

Not much later Judge Roy Gargan walked into the stage station and looked around. He was a tall, slightly stooped man with a lean, hangdog face and round eyes. He walked up to the table and sat down in the chair behind it. Bruce Barkow took a chair to one side where he could see the judge.

Noting the move, Rafe Caradec sat down where both men were visible. Barkow, nettled, shifted his chair irritably. He glanced up and saw Ann Rodney come in, accompanied by Baker and Pat Higley. He scowled again. *Why couldn't they stay out of this?*

Slowly the hangers-on around town filed in. Joe Benson came in and sat down close to Barkow. They exchanged looks. Benson's questioning glance made Barkow furious. If they wanted so much done, why didn't someone do something besides him?

"I'll watch from here," drawled a voice.

Barkow's head came up. Standing in the window behind and to the right of the judge was Tex Brisco. At the same instant Barkow noted him, the Texan lifted a hand.

"Hi, Johnny! Glad to see you."

Bruce Barkow's face went hard. Johnny Gill and, beside him, Bo Marsh. If anything rusty was pulled in this courtroom, the place would be a shambles. Maybe Dan Shute was right, after all. If they were going to be crooked, why not dry-gulch the fellow and get it over? All Barkow's carefully worked-out plans to get Caradec had failed.

There had been three good chances. Resistance, that would warrant killing in attempting an arrest; attempted escape, if he so much as made a wrong move; or lynching by the Shute riders. At every point they had been outguessed.

Judge Gargan slammed a six-shooter on the table.

"Order!" he proclaimed. "Court's in session! Reckon I'll appoint a jury. Six men will do. I'll have Joe Benson, Tom Blazer, Sam Mawson, Doc Otto, and . . ."

"Joe Benson's not eligible," Caradec interrupted.

Gargan frowned. "Who's runnin' this court?"

"Supposedly," Rafe said quietly, "the law, supposedly the interests of justice. Joe Benson was a witness to the shootin', so he'll be called on to give testimony."

"Who yuh tellin' how to run this court?" Gargan demanded belligerently.

"Doesn't the defendant even have a chance to defend himself?" Caradec asked gently. He glanced around at the crowd. "I think you'll all agree that a man on trial for his life should have a chance to defend himself, that he should be allowed to call and question witnesses, and that he should have an attorney. But since this court hasn't provided an attorney, and because I want to, I'll act for myself. Now,"—he looked around—"the judge picked out three members of the jury. I'd like to pick out three more. I'd like Pat Higley, Gene Baker, and Ann Rodney as members of the jury."

"What?" Gargan roared. "I'll have no woman settin' on the jury in my court! Why, of all the . . ."

Rafe said smoothly: "It kind of looks like Your Honor does not know the law in Wyomin'. By an act approved in December Eighteen Sixty-Nine, the first Territorial Legislature granted equal rights to women. Women served on juries in Laramie in Eighteen Seventy, and one was servin' as justice of the peace that year."

Gargan swallowed and looked uncomfortable. Barkow sat up, started to say something, but before he could open his mouth, Caradec was speaking again.

"As I understand, the attorney for the State and the defense attorney usually select a jury. As the Court has taken it upon himself to appoint a jury, I was just suggestin' the names of three responsible citizens I respect. I'm shore none of these three can be considered friends of mine, sorry as I am to say it. Of course," he added, "if the court objects to these three people . . . if there's somethin' about their characters I don't know, or if they are not good citizens . . . then I take back my suggestion." He turned to look at Bruce Barkow. "Or mebbe Mister Barkow objects to Ann Rodney servin' on the jury?"

Barkow sat up, flushing. Suddenly he was burning with rage. This whole thing had got out of hand. What had happened to bring this about? He was acutely conscious that Ann was staring at him, her eyes wide, a flush mounting in her cheeks at his hesitation. "No!" he said violently. "No, of course, no. Let her sit, but let's get this business started."

Pod Gomer was slumped in his chair, watching cynically. His eyes shifted to Barkow with a faintly curious expression. The planner and schemer had missed out on this trial. It had been his idea to condemn the man in public, then see to it that he was hanged.

"Yuh're actin' as prosecutin' attorney?" Gargan asked Barkow.

The rancher got to his feet, cursing the thought

that had given rise to this situation. That Rafe Caradec had won the first round he was unpleasantly aware. Somehow they had never contemplated any trouble on the score of the jury. In the few trials held thus far the judge had appointed the jury, and there had been no complaint. All the cases had gone off as planned.

"Yore Honor," he began, "and gentlemen of the jury. Yuh all know none of us here are lawyers. This court is bein' held only so's we can keep law and order in this community, and that's the way it will be till the county is organized. This prisoner was in a gunfight with Lemuel Boyne, known as Trigger. Boyne challenged him . . . some of yuh know the reason for that . . . and Caradec accepted. In the fight out in the street, Caradec shot Boyne and killed him. In almost the same instant, he lifted his gun and shot Gee Bonaro, who was innocently watchin' the battle from his window. If a thing like this isn't punished, any gunfighter is apt to shoot anybody he don't like at any time, and nothin' done about it. We've all heard that Caradec claims Bonaro had a rifle and was about to shoot at him, which was a plumb good excuse, but a right weak one. We know this Caradec had words with Bonaro at the Emporium, and almost got into a fight then and there. I say Caradec is guilty of murder in the first degree, and should be hung." Barkow turned his head and motioned to Red Blazer. "Red, you get up there and tell the jury what yuh know."

Red strode up to the chair that was doing duty for a witness stand and slouched down in the seat. He was unshaven, and his hair was uncombed. He sprawled his legs out and stuck his thumbs in his belt. He rolled his quid in his jaws, and spat.

"I seen this here Caradec shoot Boyne," he said, "then he ups with his pistol and cut down on Bonaro, who was a-standin' in the window, just a-lookin'."

"Did Bonaro make any threatening moves toward Caradec?"

"Him?" Red's eyes opened wide. "Shucks, no. Gee was just a-standin' there. Caradec was afeerd of him, an' seen a chance to kill him and get plumb away."

Rafe looked thoughtfully at Barkow. "Is the fact that the witness was not sworn in the regular way in this court? Or is his conscience delicate on the subject of perjury?"

"Huh?" Blazer sat up. "What'd he say?"

Barkow flushed. "It hasn't usually been the way here, but . . ."

"Swear him in," Caradec said calmly, "and have him say under oath what he's just said."

He waited until this was done, and then, as Red started to get up, Rafe motioned him back. "I've got a few questions," he said.

"Huh?" Red demanded belligerently. "I don't have to answer no more questions."

"Yes, you do." Rafe's voice was quiet. "Get back on that witness stand."

"Do I have to?" Blazer demanded of Barkow, who nodded.

If there had been any easy way out, he would have taken it, but there was none. He was beginning to look at Rafe Caradec with new eyes.

Rafe got up and walked over to the jury. "Gentlemen," he said, "none of you know me well. None of us, as Barkow said, knows much about how court business should be handled. All we want to do is get at the truth. I know that all of you here are busy men. You're willin' and anxious to help along justice and the beginnin's of law hereabouts, and all of you are honest men. You want to do the right thing. Red Blazer has just testified that I shot a man who was makin' no threatenin' moves, that Bonaro was standing in a window, just watching."

Caradec turned around and looked at Blazer thoughtfully. He walked over to him, squatted on his haunches, and peered into his eyes, shifting first to one side, then the other.

Red Blazer's face flamed. "What's the matter?" he blared. "Yuh gone crazy?"

"No," Caradec said, "just lookin' at your eyes. I was curious to see what kind of eyes a man had who could see through a shingle roof and a ceilin'."

"Huh?" Blazer glared.

The jury sat up, and Barkow's eyes narrowed. The courtroom crowd leaned forward.

"Why, Red, you must have forgot," Rafe said. "You were in the National when I killed Boyne. You were standin' behind Joe Benson. You were the first person I saw when I looked around. You could see me, and you could see Boyne . . . but you couldn't see the second-story window across the street."

Somebody whooped, and Pat Higley grinned.

"I reckon he's right," Pat said coolly. "I was standin' right alongside of Red."

"That's right!" somebody from back in the courtroom shouted. "Blazer tried to duck out without payin' for his drink, and Joe Benson stopped him!"

Everybody laughed, and Blazer turned fiery red, glaring back into the room to see who the speaker was, and not finding him.

Rafe turned to Barkow, and smiled. "Have you got another witness?"

XI

Despite herself, Ann Rodney found herself admiring Rafe Caradec's composure, his easy manner. Her curiosity was stirred. What manner of man was he? Where was he from? What background had he? Was he only a wanderer, or was he something different? His language, aside from his characteristic Texas drawl, and his manner spoke of refinement, yet she knew of his gun skill as exhibited in the Boyne fight.

"Tom Blazer's my next witness," Barkow said. "Swear him in."

Tom Blazer, a hulking redhead even bigger than Red, took the stand. Animosity glared from his eyes.

"Did you see the shootin'?" Barkow asked.

"Yuh're darned right I did!" Tom declared, staring at Rafe. "I seen it, and I wasn't inside no saloon! I was right out in the street!"

"Was Bonaro where yuh could see him?"

"He shore was!"

"Did he make any threatenin' moves?"

"Not any!"

"Did he lift a gun?"

"He shore didn't!"

"Did he make any move that would give an idea he was goin' to shoot?"

"Nope. Not any." As Tom Blazer answered each question, he glared triumphantly at Caradec.

Barkow turned to the jury. "Well, there yuh are. I think that's enough evidence. I think . . ."

"Let's hear Caradec ask his questions," Pat Higley said. "I want both sides of this yarn."

Rafe got up and walked over to Tom Blazer, then looked at the judge. "Your Honor, I'd like permission to ask one question of a man in the audience. He can be sworn or not, just as you say."

Gargan hesitated uncertainly. Always before things had gone smoothly. Trials had been railroaded through, objections swept aside, and the wordless little ranchers or other objectors to the rule of Barkow and Shute had been helpless. This time preparations should have been more complete. He didn't know what to do. "All right," he said, his misgiving showing in his expression and tone.

Caradec turned to look at a short, stocky man with a brown mustache streaked with gray. "Grant," he said, "what kind of a curtain have you got over that window above your harness and saddle shop?"

Grant looked up. "Why, it ain't rightly no curtain," he said frankly. "It's a blanket."

"You keep it down all the time? The window covered?"

"Uhn-huh. Shore do. Sun gets in there otherwise and makes the floor hot and she heats up the store thataway. Keepin' that window covered keeps her cooler."

"It was covered the day of the shooting?"

"Shore was."

"Where did you find the blanket after the shootin'?"

"Well, she laid over the sill, partly inside, partly outside."

Rafe turned to the jury. "Miss Rodney and gentlemen, I believe the evidence is clear. The window was covered by a blanket. When Bonaro fell after I shot him, he tumbled across the sill, tearin' down the blanket. Do you agree?"

"Shore!" Gene Baker found his voice. The whole case was only too obviously a frame-up to get Caradec. It was like Bonaro to try a sneak killing, anyway. "If that blanket hadn't been over the window, then he couldn't have fallen against it and carried part out with him."

"That's right." Rafe turned on Tom Blazer. "Your eyes seem to be as amazin' as your brother's. You can see through a wool blanket!"

Blazer sat up with a jerk, his face dark with sullen rage. "Listen!" he said, "I'll tell yuh . . ."

"Wait a minute!" Rafe whirled on him and thrust a finger in his face. "You're not only a perjurer but a thief! What did you do with that Winchester Bonaro dropped out of the window?"

"It wa'n't no Winchester!" Blazer blared furiously. "It was a Henry!" Then, seeing the expression on Barkow's face, and hearing the low murmur that swept the court, he realized what he had said. He started to get up, then sat back, angry and confused.

Rafe Caradec turned toward the jury. "The witness swore that Bonaro had no gun, yet he testified that the rifle Bonaro dropped was a Henry. Gentlemen and Miss Rodney, I'm goin' to ask that you recommend the case be dismissed, and also that Red and Tom Blazer be held in jail to answer charges of perjury."

"What?" Tom Blazer came out of the witness chair with a lunge. "Jail? Me? Why, you . . ."

He leaped, hurling a huge red-haired fist in a roundhouse swing. Rafe Caradec stepped in with a left that smashed Blazer's lips, then a solid right that sent him crashing to the floor.

He glanced at the judge. "And that, I think," he said quietly "is contempt of court."

Pat Higley got up abruptly. "Gargan, I reckon yuh better dismiss this case. Yuh haven't got any evidence or anything that sounds like evidence, and I guess ever'body here heard about Caradec facin' Bonaro down in the store. If he wanted to shoot him, there was his chance."

Gargan swallowed. "Case dismissed," he said.

He looked up at Bruce Barkow, but the rancher was walking toward Ann Rodney. She glanced at him, then her eyes lifted, and beyond him she saw Rafe Caradec. How fine his face was! It was a rugged, strong face. There was character in it, and sincerity. She came to with a start. Bruce was speaking to her.

"Gomer told me he had a case," Barkow said, "or I'd never have been a party to this. He's guilty as can be, but he's smooth."

Ann looked down at Bruce Barkow, and suddenly his eyes looked different to her than they ever had before. "He may be guilty of a lot of things," she said tartly, "but if ever there was a cooked-up, dishonest case, it was this one. And everyone in town knew it. If I were you, Bruce Barkow, I'd be ashamed of myself."

Abruptly she turned her back on him and started for the door, yet, as she went, she glanced up, and for a brief instant her eyes met those of Rafe Caradec's, and something within her leaped. Her throat seemed to catch. Head high, she hurried past him into the street. The store seemed a long distance away.

When Bruce Barkow walked into Pod Gomer's office, the sheriff was sitting in his swivel chair. In the big leather armchair across the room Dan Shute was waiting. He was a big man, with massive shoulders, powerfully muscled arms, and great hands. A shock of dusky blond hair covered the top of his head, and his eyebrows were the color of corn silk. He looked up as Barkow came in, and, when he spoke, his voice was rough. "You shore played hob!"

"The man's smart, that's all," Barkow said. "Next time we'll have a better case."

"Next time?" Dan Shute lounged back in the big chair, the contempt in his eyes unconcealed. "There ain't goin' to be a next time. Yuh're through, Barkow. From now on, this is my show, and we run it my way. Caradec needs killin', and we'll kill him. Also, yuh're goin' to foreclose that mortgage on the Rodney place." He held up a hand as Barkow started to speak. "No, you wait. Yuh was all for pullin' this slick stuff. Winnin' the girl, gettin' the property the easy way, the legal way. To blazes with that! This Caradec is makin' a monkey of yuh! Yuh're not slick! Yuh're just a country boy playin' with a real smooth lad! To blazes with that smooth stuff! You foreclose on that mortgage and do it plumb quick. I'll take care of Mister Rafe

Caradec! With my own hands, or guns if necessary. We'll clean that country down there so slick of his hands and cattle they won't know what happened."

"That won't get it," Barkow protested. "You let me handle this. I'll take care of things."

Dan Shute looked up at Barkow, his eyes sardonic. "I'll run this show. You're takin' the back seat, Barkow, from now on. All yuh've done is make us out fumblin' fools. Also," he added calmly, "I'm takin' over that girl."

"What?" Barkow whirled, his face livid. In his wildest doubts of Shute, and he had had many of them, this was one thing that had never entered his mind.

"You heard me," Shute replied. "She's a neat little lady, and I can make a place for her out to my ranch. You messed up all around, so I'm takin' over."

Barkow laughed, but his laugh was hollow with something of fear in it. Always before Dan Shute had been big, silent, and surly, saying little, letting Barkow plan and plot and take the lead. Bruce Barkow had always thought of the man as a sort of strong-arm squad to use in a pinch. Suddenly he was shockingly aware that this big man was completely sure of himself, that he held him, Barkow, in contempt. He would ride roughshod over everything. "Dan," Barkow protested, trying to keep his thoughts ordered, "yuh can't play with a girl's affections. She's in love with me. Yuh can't do anything about that. Yuh think she'd fall out of love with one man, and . . . ?"

Dan Shute grinned. "Who said anything about love? You talk about that all yuh want. Talk it to yoreself. I want the girl, and I'm goin' to have her. It doesn't make any difference who says no, and that goes for Gene Baker, her, or you."

Bruce Barkow stood flat-footed and pale. Suddenly he felt sick and empty. Here it was, then. He was through. Dan Shute had told him off, and in front of Pod Gomer. Out of the tail of his eye he could see the calm, yet cynical, expression on Gomer's face. He looked up, and he felt small under the flat, ironic gaze of Shute's eyes. "All right, Dan, if that's the way yuh feel. I expect we'd better part company."

Shute chuckled, and his voice was rough when he spoke. "No," he said, "we don't part company. You sit tight. Yuh're holdin' that mortgage, and I want that land. Yuh had a good idea there, Barkow, but yuh're too weak-kneed to swing it. I'll swing it, and mebbe, if yuh're quiet and obey orders, I'll see yuh get some of it."

Bruce Barkow glared at Shute. For the first time he knew what hatred was. Here, in a few minutes, he had been destroyed. This story would go the rounds, and before nightfall everyone in town would know it. Dan Shute, big, slow-talking Dan Shute with his hard fists and his guns had crushed Barkow. He stared at Shute with hatred livid in his eyes. "Yuh'll go too far!" he said viciously.

Shute shrugged. "Yuh can live, an' come out of this with a few dollars," he said calmly, "or yuh can die. I'd just as soon kill yuh, Barkow, as look at yuh." He picked up his hat. "We had a nice thing. That shanghaiin' idea was yores. Why yuh didn't shoot him, I'll never know. If yuh had, this Caradec would never have run into him at all and would never have come in here, stirrin' things up.

Yuh could have foreclosed that mortgage, and we could be makin' a deal on that oil now."

"Caradec don't know anything about that," Barkow protested.

"Like sin he don't!" Dan Shute sneered. "Caradec's been watched by my men for days. He's been wise there was somethin' in the wind, and he's scouted all over that place. Well, he was down to the knob the other day, and he took a long look at that oil seepage. He's no fool, Barkow."

Bruce Barkow looked up. "No," he replied suddenly, "he's not, and he's a hand with a gun, too, Dan. He's a hand with a gun. He took Boyne."

Shute shrugged. "Boyne was nothin'. I could have spanked him with his own gun. I'll kill Caradec someday, but first I want to beat him, to beat him with my own hands."

He heaved himself out of the chair and stalked outside. For an instant, Barkow stared after him, then his gaze shifted to Pod Gomer.

The sheriff was absently whittling a small stick. "Well," he said, "he told yuh."

XII

Hard and grim, Barkow's mouth tightened. So Gomer was in it, too. He started to speak, then hesitated. Like Caradec, Gomer was no fool, and he, too, was a good hand with a gun. Barkow shrugged. "Dan sees things wrong," he said. "I've still got an ace in the hole." He looked at Gomer. "I'd like it better if you were on my side."

Pod Gomer shrugged. "I'm with the winner. My health is good. All I need is more money."

"Yuh think Shute's the winner?"

"Don't you?" Gomer asked. "He told yuh plenty, and yuh took it."

"Yes, I did, because I know I'm no match for him with a gun. Nor for you." He studied the sheriff thoughtfully. "This is goin' to be a nice thing, Pod. It would split well, two ways."

Gomer got up and snapped his knife shut. "You show me the color of some money," he said, "and how Dan Shute's out, and we might talk. Also," he added, "if yuh mention this to Dan, I'll call yuh a liar in the street or in the National. I'll make you use that gun."

"I won't talk," Barkow said. "Only I've been

learnin' a few things. When we get answers to some of the messages yuh sent, and some I sent, we should know more. Borger wouldn't let Caradec off that ship willin'ly after he knew Rodney. I think he deserted. I think we can get something on him for mutiny, and that means hangin'."

"Mebbe yuh can," Gomer agreed. "You show me yuh're holdin' good cards, and I'll back yuh to the limit."

Bruce Barkow walked out on the street. Gomer, at least, he understood. He knew the man had no use for him, but if he could show evidence that he was to win, then Gomer would be a powerful ally. Judge Gargan would go as Gomer went, and would always adopt the less violent means. The cards were on the table now. Dan Shute was running things. What he could do, Barkow was not sure. He realized suddenly, with no little trepidation, that after all his association with Shute he knew little of what went on behind the hard brutality of the rancher's face. Yet he was not a man to lag or linger. What he did would be sudden, brutal, and thorough, but it would make a perfect shield under which he, Barkow, could operate and carry to fulfillment his own plans.

Dan Shute's abrupt statement of his purpose in regard to Ann Rodney had jolted Barkow. Somehow, he had taken Ann for granted. He had always planned a marriage. That he wanted her land was true. Perhaps better than Shute he knew what oil might mean in the future, and Barkow was a farsighted man. But Ann Rodney was lovely and interesting. She would be a good wife for him. There was one way he could defeat Dan Shute on that score. To marry Ann at once.

True, it might precipitate a killing, but already Bruce Barkow was getting ideas on that score. He was suddenly less disturbed about Rafe Caradec than Dan Shute. The rancher loomed large and formidable in his mind. He knew the brutality of the man, had seen him kill, and knew with what coldness he regarded people or animals. Bruce Barkow made up his mind. Come what may, he was going to marry Ann Rodney.

He could, he realized, marry her and get her clear away from here. His mind leaped ahead. Flight to the northwest to the gold camps would be foolhardy. To the Utah country would be as bad. In either case, Shute might and probably would overtake him. There remained another way out, and one that Shute probably would never suspect—he could strike for Fort Phil Kearney not far distant, and then, with or without a scouting party for escort, could head across country and reach the Yellowstone. Or he might even try the nearer Powder River. A steamer had ascended the Yellowstone earlier that year, and there was every chance that another would come. If not, with a canoe or barge they could head downstream until they encountered such a boat, and buy passage to St. Louis.

Ann and full title to her land would be in his hands then, and he could negotiate a sale or the leasing of the land from a safe distance. The more he thought of this, the more he was positive it remained the only solution for him.

Let Gomer think what he would. Let Dan Shute believe him content with a minor rôle. He would go ahead with his plans, then strike suddenly and swiftly and be well on his way before Shute realized what had happened. Once he made the fort, he would be in the clear. Knowing the officers as well as he did, he was sure he could get an escort to the river. He had never seen the Yellowstone, nor did he know much about either that river or Powder River. But they had been used by many men as a high road to the West, and he could use a river as an escape to the East.

Carefully he considered the plan. There were preparations to be made. Every angle must be considered. At his ranch were horses enough. He would borrow Baker's buckboard to take Ann for a ride, then at his ranch they would mount and be off. With luck they would be well on their way before anyone so much as guessed what had happened.

Stopping by the store, he bought ammunition from Baker. He glanced up to find the storekeeper's eyes studying him, and he didn't like the expression.

"Is Ann in?" he asked.

Baker nodded, and jerked a thumb toward the curtain. Turning, Barkow walked behind the curtain and looked at Ann, who arose as he entered. Quickly he sensed a coolness that had not been there before. This was no time to talk of marriage. First things first.

He shrugged shamefacedly. "I suppose yuh're thinkin' pretty bad of me," he suggested ruefully. "I know now I shouldn't have listened to Dan Shute or to Gomer. Pod swore he had a case, and Shute claims Caradec is a crook and a rustler. If I had realized, I wouldn't have had any hand in it."

"It was pretty bad," Ann agreed as she sat down and began knitting. "What will happen now?"

"I don't know," he admitted, "but I wish I could spare you all this. Before it's over I'm afraid there'll be more killin's and trouble. Dan Shute is plenty roused up. He'll kill Caradec."

She looked at him. "You think that will be easy?"

Surprised, he nodded. "Yes. Dan's a dangerous man, and a cruel and brutal one. He's fast with a gun, too."

"I thought you were a friend to Dan Shute?" she asked, looking at him hard. "What's changed you, Bruce?"

He shrugged. "Oh, little things. He showed himself up today. He's brutal, unfeelin'. He'll stop at nothin' to gain his ends."

"I think he will," Ann said composedly. "I think he'll stop at Rafe Caradec."

Barkow stared at her. "He seems to have impressed yuh. What makes yuh think that?"

"I never really saw him until today, Bruce," she admitted. "Whatever his motives, he is shrewd and capable. I think he is a much more dangerous man than Dan Shute. There's something behind him, too. He has background. I could see it in his manner more than his words. I wish I knew more about him."

Nettled at her defense of the man, and her apparent respect for him, Bruce shrugged his shoulders. "Don't forget, he probably killed your father."

She looked up. "Did he, Bruce?"

Her question struck fear into him. Veiling his eyes, he shrugged again. "Yuh never know. I'm worried about you, Ann. This country's going to be flamin' within a few days or weeks. If it ain't the fight here, it'll be the Indians. I wish I could get yuh out of it."

"But this is my home," Ann protested. "It is all I have."

"Not quite all." Her eyes fell before his gaze. "Ann, how would yuh like to go to Saint Louis?"

She looked up, startled. "To Saint Louis? But how . . . ?"

"Not so loud." He glanced apprehensively at the door. There was no telling who might be listening. "I don't want anybody to know about it unless yuh decide, and nobody to know till after we're gone. But Ann, we *could* go. I've always wanted to marry yuh, and there's no time better than now."

She got up and walked to the window. St. Louis. It was another world. She hadn't seen a city in six years, and, after all, they had been engaged for several months now. "How would we get there?" she asked, turning to face him.

"That's a secret." He laughed. "Don't tell anybody about it, but I've got a wonderful trip planned for yuh. I always wanted to do things for yuh, Ann. We could go away and be married within a few hours."

"Where?"

"By the chaplain, at the fort. One of the officers would stand up with me, and there are a couple of officers' wives there, too."

"I don't know, Bruce," she said hesitantly. "I'll have to think about it."

He smiled and kissed her lightly. "Then think fast, honey. I want to get yuh away from all this trouble, and quick."

When he got outside in the street, he paused,

smiling with satisfaction. *I'll show that Dan Shute a thing or two*, he told himself grimly. *I'll leave him standin' here flat-footed, holdin' the bag. I'll have the girl and the ranch, and won't be within miles of this place.* Abruptly he turned toward the cabin where he lived.

Dan Shute stood on the boardwalk, staring into the dust, big hands on his hips above the heavy guns, his gray hat pulled low, a stubble of corn-white beard along his hard jaws. *I think*, he said to himself, looking up, *that I'll kill Bruce Barkow. And I'm goin' to like the doin' of it.*

XIII

Gene Baker was sweeping his store and the stoop in front of it when he saw a tight little cavalcade of horsemen trot around the corner into the street. It was the morning after the fiasco of the trial, and he had been worried and irritated while wondering what the reaction would be from Barkow and Shute. Then word had come to him of the break between the two at Gomer's office.

Dan Shute, riding a powerful gray, was in the van of the bunch of horsemen. He rode up to the stoop of Baker's store, and reined in. Behind him were Red and Tom Blazer, Joe Gorman, Fritz Handl, Fats McCabe, and others of the hard bunch that trailed with Shute.

"Gene," Shute said abruptly, resting his big hands on the pommel of the saddle, "don't sell any more supplies to Caradec or any of his crowd." He added harshly: "I'm not askin' yuh. I'm tellin' yuh. And if yuh do, I'll put you out of business and run you out of the country. You know I don't make threats. The chances are Caradec won't be alive by daybreak, anyway, but, just in case, yuh've been told."

Without giving Baker a chance to reply, Dan

Shute touched spurs to his horse and led off down the south trail toward the Crazy Man. The door slammed behind Baker.

"Where are they going?" Ann wanted to know, her eyes wide. "What are they going to do?"

Gene stared after them bleakly. This was the end of something.

"They are goin' after Caradec and his crowd, Ann."

"What will they do to him?" Something inside her went sick and frightened. She had always been afraid of Dan Shute. The way he looked at her made her shrink. He was the only human being of whom she had ever been afraid. He seemed without feeling, without decency, without regard for anything but his own immediate desires.

"Kill him," Baker said. "They'll kill him. Shute's a hard man, and with him that's a mighty wicked lot of men."

"But can't someone warn him?" Ann protested.

Baker glanced at her. "So far as we know, that Caradec is a crook, and mebbe a killer, Ann. You ain't gettin' soft on him, are yuh?"

"No!" she exclaimed, startled. "Of course not! What an idea! Why, I've scarcely talked to him."

Yet there was a heavy, sinking feeling in her heart as she watched the riders disappear in the dust along the southward trail. If there were only something she could do! If she could warn them!

Suddenly she remembered the bay horse her father had given her. Because of the Indians, she had not been riding in a long time, but if she took the mountain trail . . . Hurrying through the door, she swiftly saddled the bay. There was no thought in her mind. She was acting strictly on impulse, prompted by some memory of the way the hair swept back from Rafe's brow, and the look in his eyes when he met her gaze. She told herself she wanted to see no man killed, that Bo Marsh and Johnny Gill were her friends. Yet even in her heart she knew the excuse would not do. She was thinking of Rafe, and only of Rafe.

The bay was in fine shape and impatient after his long restraint in the corral. He started for the trail, eagerly, and his ears pricked up at every sound. The leaves had turned to red and gold now, and in the air there was a hint of frost. Winter was coming. Soon the country would be blanketed, inches deep, under a thick covering of snow.

Hastily Ann's mind leaped ahead. The prairie trail, which the Shute riders had taken, swept wide into the valley, then crossed the Crazy Man, and turned to follow the stream up the cañon. By cutting across over the mountain trail, there was every chance she could beat them to the ranch. In any case, her lead would be slight due to the start the bunch had had.

The trail crossed the mountainside through a long grove of quaking aspens, their leaves shimmering in the cool wind, dark green above, a gray below. Now with oncoming autumn, most of the leaves had turned to bright yellow intermixed with crimson, and here and there among the forest of mounting color were the darker arrowheads of spruce and lodgepole pine.

Once, coming out in a small clearing, she got a view of the valley below. She had gained a little, but only a little. Frightened, she touched spurs to the bay, and the little horse leaped ahead and swept down through the woods at a rapid gallop. Ahead, there was a ledge. It was a good six miles off yet, but from there she would be able to see the cañon of the Crazy Man and the upper cañon. A rider had told her that Caradec had been putting up hay in the wind-sheltered upper cañon and was obviously planning on feeding his stock there near the warm spring.

She recalled it because she remembered it was something her father had spoken of doing. There was room in the upper valley for many cattle, and, if there was hay enough for them, the warm water would be a help, and with only that little help the cattle should survive even the coldest weather.

Fording the stream where Caradec had encountered the young squaw, she rode higher on the mountain, angling across the slope under a magnificent stand of lodgepole pine. It was a splendid avenue of trees, all seemingly of the same size and shape as though cast from a mold. Once she glimpsed a deer, and another time in the distance in a small, branching valley she saw a small bunch of elk. This was her country. No wonder her father had loved it, wanted it, worked to get and to keep it.

Had her father paid the mortgage? Wouldn't Bruce have told her if he had? She could not believe Bruce dishonest or deceitful, and certainly he had made no effort to foreclose, but had been most patient and thoughtful with her. What would he think of this ride? To warn a man he regarded as an enemy. But she could never forgive herself if Rafe Caradec were killed, and she had made no effort to avert it.

Too often she had listened to her father discourse on the necessity for peace and consideration of the problems of others. She believed in that policy wholeheartedly, and the fact that occasionally violence was necessary did not alter her convictions one whit. No system of philosophy or ethics, no growth of government, no improvement in living came without trial and struggle. Struggle, she had often heard her father say, quoting Hegel, was the law of growth.

Without giving too much thought to it, she understood that such men as Rafe Caradec, Tex Brisco, and others of their ilk were needed. For all their violence, their occasional heedlessness and the desire to go their own way, they were men building a new world in a rough and violent land where everything tended to extremes. Mountains were high, the prairies wide, the streams roaring, the buffalo by the thousand and tens of thousands. It was a land where nothing was small, nothing was simple. Everything, the lives of men and the stories they told, ran to extremes.

The bay pony trotted down the trail, then around a stand of lodgepole. Ann brought him up sharply on the lip of the ledge that had been her first goal. Below her, a vast and magnificent panorama, lay the ranch her father had pioneered. The silver curve of the Crazy Man lay below and east of her, and opposite the ledge was the mighty wall of the cañon. From below, a faint thread of smoke among the trees marked the cabin.

Turning her head, she looked west and south into the upper cañon. Far away, she seemed to see a horseman moving, and the black dot of a herd. Turning the bay, she started west, riding fast. If they were working the upper cañon, she still had a chance.

An hour later, the little bay showing signs of his rough traveling, she came down to the floor of the cañon. Not far away, she could see Rafe Caradec, moving a bunch of cattle into the trees.

He looked around at her approach, and the black, flat-crowned hat came off his head. His dark, wavy hair was plastered to his brow with sweat, and his eyes were gray and curious.

"Good mornin'!" he said. "This is a surprise!"

"Please!" she burst out. "This isn't a social call! Dan Shute's riding this way with twenty men or more. He's going to wipe you out!"

"You shore?" She could see the quick wonder in his eyes at her warning, then he wheeled his horse and yelled: "Johnny! Johnny Gill! Come a-runnin'!"

Jerking his rifle from his boot, he looked at her again. He put his hand over hers suddenly, and she started at his touch. "Thanks, Ann," he said simply. "You're regular."

Then he was gone, and Johnny Gill was streaking after him. As Gill swept by, he lifted a hand and waved.

There they went, and below were twenty men, all armed. Would they come through alive? She turned the bay and, letting the pony take his own time, started him back over the mountain trail.

Rafe Caradec gave no thought to Ann's reason for warning him. There was no time for that. Tex Brisco and Bo Marsh were at the cabin. They were probably working outside, and their rifles would probably be in the cabin and beyond them. If they were cut off from their guns, the Shute riders would mow them down and kill them one by one at long range with rifle fire.

Rafe heard Gill coming up, and slacked off a little to let the little cowhand draw alongside.

"Shute!" he said. "And about twenty men. I guess this is the pay-off!"

"Yeah!" Gill yelled.

Rifle fire came to them suddenly. A burst of shots, then a shot that might have been from a pistol. Yet that was sheer guesswork, Rafe knew, for distinguishing the two was not easy and especially at this distance.

Their horses rounded the entrance and raced down the main cañon toward the cabin on the Crazy Man, running neck and neck. A column of smoke greeted them, and they could see riders circling and firing.

"The trees on the slope!" Rafe yelled, and raced for them.

He reached the trees with the black at a dead run and hit the ground before the animal had ceased to move. He raced to the rocks at the edge of the trees. His rifle lifted, settled, his breath steadied. Then the rifle spoke.

A man shouted and waved an arm, and at the same moment Gill fired. A horse went down. Two men, or possibly three, lay sprawled in the clearing before the cabin. Were Tex and Bo already down? Rafe steadied himself and squeezed off another shot. A saddle emptied. He saw the fallen man lunge to his feet, then spill over on his face. Coolly then, and taking their time, he and Gill began to fire. Another man went down, and rifles began to smoke in their direction. A bullet clipped the leaves overhead, but too high.

Rafe knocked the hat from a man's head and, as the fellow sprinted for shelter, dropped him.

Suddenly the attack broke, and he saw the horses sweeping away from them in a ragged line. Mounting, Rafe and Gill rode cautiously toward the cabin.

There was no cabin. There was only a roaring inferno of flames. There were five sprawled bodies now, and Rafe ran toward them. A Shute rider—another. Then he saw Bo. The boy was lying on his face with a dark, spreading stain on the back of his shirt. There was no sign of Tex.

Rafe dropped to his knees and put a hand over the young cowhand's heart. It was still beating! Gently, with Johnny lending a hand, he turned the boy over. Then, working with the crude but efficient skill picked up in war and struggle in a half dozen countries, he examined the wounds.

"Four times," he said grimly. He felt something mount and swell within him, a tide of fierce, uncontrollable anger. Around one bullet hole in the stomach the cloth of the cowhand's shirt was still smoldering!

"I seen that!" It was Tex Brisco, his face haggard and smoke-grimed. "I saw it! I know who done it! He walked up where the kid was laying, stuck a gun against his stomach, and shot! He didn't want the kid to go quick. He wanted him to die slow and hard!"

"Who done it?" Gill demanded fiercely. "I'll git him now! Right now!"

Brisco's eyes were red and inflamed. "Nobody gets him but me. This kid was your pard, but I *seen* it!" He turned abruptly on Rafe. "Boss, let me go to town. I want to kill a man!"

"It won't do, Tex," Caradec said quietly. "I know how you feel, but the town will be full of 'em.

They'll be celebratin'. They burned our cabin, ran off some cattle, and they got Bo. It wouldn't do."

"Yeah." Tex spat. "I know. But they won't be expectin' any trouble now. We've been together a long time, boss, and if yuh don't let me go, I'll quit."

Rafe looked up from the wounded man. "All right, Tex. I told you I know how you feel. But if somethin' should happen . . . who did it?"

"Tom Blazer. That big redhead. He always hated the kid. The kid was shot down and left lay. I was out back in the woods, lookin' for a pole to cut. They rode up so fast the kid never had a chance. He was hit twice before he knew what was goin' on. Then, again, when he started toward the house. After the house was afire, Tom Blazer walked up, and the kid was conscious. Tom said somethin' to Bo, shoved the gun against him, and pulled the trigger." He stared miserably at Bo. "I was out of pistol range. Took me a few minutes to get closer, then I got me two men before you rode up."

Wheeling, he headed toward the corral.

Rafe had stopped the flow of blood, and Johnny had returned with a blanket from a line back of the house.

"Reckon we better get him over in the trees, boss," Gill said.

Easing the cowboy to the blanket with care, Rafe and Johnny carried Bo into the shade in a quiet place under the pines. Caradec glanced up as they put him down. Tex Brisco was riding out of the cañon. Johnny Gill watched him go.

"Boss," Gill said, "I wanted like blazes to go, but I ain't the man Brisco is. Rightly I'm a quiet man, but that Texan is a wolf on the prowl. I'm some glad I'm not Tom Blazer right now." He looked down at Bo Marsh. The young cowhand's face was flushed, his breathing hoarse. "Will he live, Rafe?" Johnny asked softly.

Caradec shrugged. "I don't know," he said hoarsely. "He needs better care than I can give him." He studied the situation thoughtfully. "Johnny," he said, "you stay with him. Better take time to build a lean-to for cover in case of rain or snow. Get some fuel, too."

"What about you?" Johnny asked. "Where you goin'?"

"To the fort. There's an Army doctor there, and I'll go get him."

"Reckon he'll come this far?" Johnny asked doubtingly.

"He'll come."

Rafe Caradec mounted the black and rode slowly away into the dusk. It was a long ride to the fort, and, even if he got the doctor, it might be too late. That was the chance he would have to take. There was small danger of an attack now. Yet it was not really a return of Dan Shute's riders that disturbed him, but a subtle coolness in the air, a chill that was of more than autumn. Winters in this country could be bitterly cold, and all the signs gave evidence this one would be the worst in years, and they were without a cabin. He rode on toward the fort, with a thought that Tex Brisco now must be nearing town.

XIV

It was growing late, and Painted Rock was swathed in velvety darkness when Tex Brisco walked his horse to the edge of town. He stopped across the bend of the stream from town and planned to leave his horse among the trees there. He would have a better chance of escape from across the stream than from the street, and by leaving town on foot he could create some doubt as to his whereabouts. He was under no misapprehension as to the problem he faced. Painted Rock would be filled to overflowing with Shute and Barkow riders, many of whom knew him by sight. Yet, although he could envision their certainty of victory, their numbers, and was well aware of the reckless task he had chosen, he knew they would not be expecting him, or any riders from Crazy Man.

He tied his horse loosely to a bush among the trees, and crossed the stream on a log. Once across, he thought of his spurs. Kneeling down, he unfastened them from his boots and hung them over a root near the end of the log. He wanted no jingling spurs to give his presence away at an inopportune moment.

Carefully avoiding any dwellings with lights, he made his way through the scattered houses to the back of the row of buildings across the street. He was wearing the gun he usually wore, and for luck he had taken another from his saddlebags and thrust it into his waistband.

Tex Brisco was a man of the frontier. From riding the range in South and West Texas, he had drifted north with trail herds. He had seen some of the days around the beginning of Dodge and Ellsworth, and some hard fighting down in the Nations, and with rustlers along the Mexican border. He was an honest man, a sincere man. He had a quality to be found in many men of his kind and period—a quality of deep-seated loyalty that was his outstanding trait. Hard and reckless in demeanor, he rode with dash and acted with a flair. He had at times been called a hardcase. Yet no man lived long in a dangerous country, if he were reckless. There was a place always for courage, but intelligent courage, not the heedlessness of a harebrained youngster. Tex Brisco was twenty-five years old, but he had been doing a man's work since he was eleven. He had walked with men, ridden with men, fought with men as one of them. He had asked no favors and had been granted none. Now, at twenty-five, he was a seasoned veteran. He was a man who knew the plains and the mountains, knew cattle, horses, and guns. He possessed a fierce loyalty to his outfit and to his friends.

Shanghaied, he had quickly seen that the sea was not his element. He had concealed his resentment and gone to work, realizing that safety lay along that route. He had known his time would come. It had come when Rafe Caradec came aboard, and all his need for friendship, for loyalty, and for a cause had been tied to the big, soft-spoken stranger.

Now Painted Rock was vibrant with danger. The men who did not hate him in Painted Rock were men who would not speak for him, or act for him. It was like Tex Brisco that he did not think in terms of help. He had his job, he knew his problem, and he knew he was the man to do it.

The National Saloon was booming with sound. The tinny jangle of an out-of-tune piano mingled with hoarse laughter, shouts, and the rattle of glasses. The hitching rail was lined with horses.

Tex walked between the buildings to the edge of the dark and empty street. Then he walked up to the horses and, speaking softly, made his way along the hitching rail, turning every slipknot into a hard knot.

The Emporium was dark, except for a light in Baker's living quarters where he sat with his wife and Ann Rodney. The stage station was lit by a feeble glow of a light over a desk as a station agent worked late over his books.

It was a moonless night, and the stars were bright. Tex lit a cigarette, loosened his guns in his holsters, and studied the situation. The National was full. To step into that saloon was suicide, and Tex had no such idea in mind. It was early, and he would have to wait. Yet might it be the best way, if he stepped in? There would be a moment of confusion. In that instant he could act.

Working his way back to a window, he studied the interior. It took him several minutes to locate Tom Blazer. The big man was standing by the bar

with Fats McCabe. Slipping to the other end of the
window, Tex could see that no one was between
them and the rear door. He stepped back into the
darkest shadows and, leaning against the building,
finished his cigarette. When it was down to a stub,
he threw it on the ground and carefully rubbed it
out with the toe of his boot. Then he pulled his hat
low, and walked around to the rear of the saloon.

There was some scrap lumber there, and he
skirted the rough pile, avoiding some bottles. It
was cool out here, and he rubbed his fingers a little,
working his hands to keep the circulation going.
Then he stepped up to the door and turned the
knob. It opened under his hand, and, if it made a
sound, it went unheard. Stepping inside, he closed
the door after him, pleased that it opened outward.

In the hurly-burly of the interior one more cowhand went unseen. Nobody even glanced his way.
He sidled up to the bar, then reached over under
Tom Blazer's nose, drew the whiskey bottle toward
him, and poured a drink into a glass just rinsed by
the bartender.

Tom Blazer scarcely glanced at the bottle, for
other bottles were being passed back and forth.
Fats McCabe stood beside Tom and, without
noticing Tex, went on talking.

"That blasted Marsh!" Tom said thickly. "I got
him! I been wantin' him a long time! Yuh should
have seen the look in his eyes when I shoved that
pistol against him and pulled the trigger!"

Tex's lips tightened, and he poured his glass full
once more. He left it sitting on the bar in front of
him. His eyes swept the room. Bruce Barkow was
here, and Pod Gomer. Tex moved over a little
closer to McCabe.

"That'll finish 'em off," McCabe was saying. "When Shute took over, I knew they wouldn't last long. If they get out of the country, they'll be lucky. They've no supplies now, and it will be snowin' within a few days. The winter will get 'em, if we don't, or the Injuns."

Tex Brisco smiled grimly. *Not before I get you!* he thought. *That comes first.*

The piano was banging away with "Oh, Susanna!" and a bunch of cowhands were trying to sing it. Joe Benson leaned on his bar talking to Pod Gomer. Barkow sat at a table in the corner, staring morosely into a glass. Joe Gorman and Fritz Handl were watching a poker game.

Tex glanced again at the back door. No one stood between the door and himself. Well, why wait?

Just then Tom Blazer reached for the bottle in front of Tex, and Tex pulled it away from his hand. Tom stared. "Hey, what yuh tryin' to do?" he demanded belligerently.

"I've come for yuh, Blazer," Tex said. "I've come to kill a skunk that shoots a helpless man when he's on his back. How are yuh against standin' men, Blazer?"

"Huh?" Tom Blazer said stupidly. Then he realized what had been said, and he thrust his big face forward for a closer look. The gray eyes he saw were icy, the lantern-jawed Texan's face was chill as death, and Tom Blazer jerked back. Slowly, his face white, Fats McCabe drew aside.

To neither man came the realization that Tex Brisco was alone. All they felt was the shock of his sudden appearance, here, among them. Brisco turned, stepping one pace away from the bar. "Well, Tom," he said quietly, his voice just loud enough to carry over the sound of the music, "I've come for yuh."

Riveted to the spot, Tom Blazer felt an instant of panic. Brisco's presence here had the air of magic, and Tom was half-frightened by the sheer unexpectedness of it. Sounds in the saloon seemed to die out, although they still went full blast, and Tom stared across that short space like a man in a trance, trapped and faced with a fight to the death. There would be no escaping this issue, he knew. He might win, and he might lose, but it was here, now, and he had to face it. He realized suddenly that it was a chance he had no desire to make. Wouldn't anyone notice? Why didn't Fats say something? Tex Brisco stood there, staring at him.

"Yuh've had yore chance," Tex said gently. "Now I'm goin' to kill yuh!"

The shock of the word *kill* snapped Tom Blazer out of it. He dropped into a half crouch, and his lips curled in a snarl of mingled rage and fear. His clawed hand swept back for his gun.

In the throbbing and rattle of the room the guns boomed like a crash of thunder. Heads whirled, and liquor-befuddled brains tried to focus eyes. All they saw was Tom Blazer, sagging back against the bar, his shirt darkening with blood, and the strained, foolish expression on his face like that of a man who had been shocked beyond reason.

Facing the room was a lean, broad-shouldered man with two guns, and, as they looked, he swung a gun at Fats McCabe. Instinctively, at the *boom* of guns, McCabe's brain had reacted, but a shade slow. His hand started for his gun. It was an involuntary movement that, had he had but a moment's thought, would never have been made. He had no intention of drawing. All he wanted was out, but the movement of his hand was enough. It was too much.

Tex Brisco's gun *boomed* again, and Fats toppled over on his face. Then Tex opened up, and three shots, blasting into the brightly lit room, brought it to complete darkness. Brisco faded into that darkness, swung the door open, and vanished as a shot clipped the air over his head.

He ran hard for fifty feet, then ducked into the shadow of a barn, threw himself over a low corral fence, and ran across the corral in a low crouch. Shouts and orders, then the *crash* of glass, came from the saloon.

The door burst open again, and he could have got another man, but only by betraying his position. He crawled through the fence and, keeping close to a dark house, ran swiftly to its far corner. He paused there, breathing heavily. So far, so good.

From here on he would be in comparative light, but the distance was enough now. He ran on swiftly for the river. Behind him he heard curses and yells as men found their knotted bridle reins. At the end of the log, Tex retrieved his spurs. Then, gasping for breath from his hard run, he ran across the log and started for his horse. He saw it suddenly, and then he saw something else.

XV

In the dim light, Tex recognized Joe Gorman by his hat. Joe wore his hat brim rolled to a point in front.

"Hi, Texas!" Gorman said. Tex could see the gun in his hand, waist high and leveled on him.

"Hi, Joe. Looks like yuh smelled somethin'."

"Yeah"—Joe nodded—"I did at that. Happened to see somebody ride up here in the dark, and got curious. When yuh headed for the saloon, I got around yuh and went in. Then I saw yuh come in the back door. I slipped out just before the shootin' started, so's I could beat yuh back here in case yuh got away."

"Too bad yuh missed the fun," Brisco said quietly.

Behind Tex the pursuit seemed to have gained no direction as yet. His mind was on a hair trigger, watching for a break. Which of his guns was still loaded? He had forgotten whether he put the loaded gun in the holster or in his belt.

"Who'd yuh get?" asked Gorman.

"Tom Blazer. Fats McCabe, too."

"I figgered Tom. I told him he shouldn't have shot the kid. That was a low-down trick. But why shoot Fats?"

"He acted like he was reachin' for a gun."

"Huh. Don't take a lot to get a man killed, does it?"

Brisco could see in the dark enough to realize that Gorman was smiling a little.

"How do yuh want it, Tex? Should I let yuh have it now, or save yuh for Shute? He's a bad man, Tex."

"I think yuh'd better slip yore gun in yore holster and go back home, Joe," Tex said. "Yuh're the most decent one of a bad lot."

"Mebbe I want the money I'd get for you, Tex. I can use some."

"Think yuh'd live to collect?"

"Yuh mean Caradec? He's through, Brisco. Through. We got Bo. Now we got you. That leaves only Caradec and Johnny Gill. They won't be so tough."

"Yuh're wrong, Joe," Tex said quietly. "Rafe could take the lot of yuh, and he will. But you bought into my game yoreself. I wouldn't ask for help, Joe. I'd kill yuh myself."

"You?" Gorman chuckled with real humor. "And me with the drop on yuh? Not a chance! Why, Tex, *one* of these slugs would get yuh, and, if I have to start blastin', I'm goin' to empty the gun before I quit."

"Uhn-huh," Tex agreed, "yuh mean, get me before I could shoot?" He repeated: "Not a chance."

The sounds of pursuit were coming now. The men had a light and had found his tracks.

"Toward the river, I'll be a 'coon!" a voice yelled. "Let's go!"

Here it was! Joe Gorman started to yell, then saw the black figure ahead of him move, and his gun blazed. Tex felt the shocking jolt of a slug, and his knees buckled, but his gun was out, and he triggered two shots, fast. Joe started to fall, and he fired again, but the hammer fell on an empty chamber.

Tex jerked the slipknot in his reins loose and dragged himself into the saddle. He was bleeding badly. His mind felt hazy, but he saw Joe Gorman move on the ground, and heard him say: "Yuh did it, damn yuh! Yuh did it!"

"So long, Joe," Tex whispered hoarsely.

He walked the horse for twenty feet, then started moving faster. His brain was singing with a strange noise, and his blood seemed to drum in his brain. He headed up the tree-covered slope, and the numbness crawled up his legs. He fought like a cornered wolf against the darkness that crept over him. *I can't die . . . I can't!* he kept saying in his brain. *Rafe'll need help! I can't!*

Fighting the blackness and numbness, he tied the bridle reins to the saddle horn, and thrust both feet clear through the stirrups. Sagging in the saddle, he got his handkerchief out and fumbled a knot, tying his wrists to the saddle horn.

The light glowed and died, and the horse walked on, weaving in the awful darkness, weaving through a world of agony and the soft, clutching hands that seemed to be pulling Tex down, pulling him down. The darkness closed in around him, but under him he seemed still to feel the slow plodding of the horse. . . .

Roughly, the distance to the fort was seventy miles, a shade less, perhaps. Rafe Caradec rode steadily into the increasing cold of the wind. There was no mistaking the seriousness of Bo's condition. The young cowhand was badly shot up, weak from loss of blood, and despite the amazing vitality of frontier men, his chance was slight unless his wounds had proper care.

Bowing his head to the wind, Rafe headed the horse down a draw and its partial shelter. There was no use thinking of Tex. Whatever had happened in Painted Rock had happened now, or was happening. Brisco might be dead. He might be alive and safe, even now heading back to the Crazy Man, or he might be wounded and in need of help. Tex Brisco was an uncertainty, but Bo Marsh hung between life and death, hence there was no choice. The friendship and understanding between the lean, hard-faced Texan and Rafe Caradec had grown aboard ship. Rafe was not one to take lightly the Texan's loyalty in joining him in his foray into Wyoming. Now Brisco might be dead, killed in a fight he would never have known but for Rafe. Yet Tex would have had it no other way. His destinies were guided by his loyalties. Those loyalties were his life, his religion, his reason for living.

Yet despite his worries over Marsh and Brisco, Rafe found his thoughts returning again and again to Ann Rodney. Why had she ridden to warn them of the impending attack? Had it not been for that warning the riders would have wiped out Brisco at the same time they got Marsh, and would have followed it up to find Rafe and Johnny back in the cañon. It would have been, or could have been, a clean sweep.

Why had Ann warned them? Was it because of

her dislike of violence and killing? Or was there some other, some deeper, feeling? Yet how could that be? What feeling could Ann have for any of them, believing as she seemed to believe that he was a thief, or worse? The fact remained that she had come, that she had warned them. Remembering her, he recalled the flash of her eyes, the proud lift of her chin, the way she walked. He stared grimly into the night and swore softly. Was he in love?

"Who knows?" he demanded viciously of the night. "And what good would it do if I was?"

He had never been to the fort, yet knew it lay between the forks of the Piney and its approximate location. His way led across the billowing hills and through a country marked by small streams lined with cottonwood, box elder, willow, chokeberry, and wild plum. That this was the Indian country, he knew. The unrest of the tribes was about to break into open warfare, and already there had been sporadic attacks on haying or wood-cutting parties, and constant attacks were being made on the Missouri steamboats far to the north.

Red Cloud, most influential chieftain among the Sioux, had tried to hold the tribes together and, despite the continued betrayal of treaties by the white man, had sought to abide by the code he had laid down for his people. With Man-Afraid-Of-His-Horse, the Oglala chief, Red Cloud was the strongest of all the Sioux leaders, or had been. With Custer's march into the Black Hills and the increasing travel over the Laramie and Bozeman trails, the Sioux were growing restless. The Sioux medicine man, Sitting Bull, was indulging in war talk, and he was aided and abetted by two powerful warriors—Crazy Horse and Gall. No one in the West but understood that an outbreak of serious nature was overdue.

Rafe Caradec was aware of all this. He was aware, too, that it would not be an easy thing to prevail upon the doctor to leave the fort, or upon the commander to allow him to leave. In the face of impending trouble, his place was with the Army. . . .

News of the battle on the Crazy Man, after Ann's warning, reached her that evening. The return of the triumphant Shute riders was enough to tell her what had happened. She heard them ride into the street, heard their yells and their shouts. She heard that Bo Marsh was definitely dead, even though some of the Shute riders were harsh in their criticism of Tom Blazer for that action.

While the Shute outfit had ridden away, following their attack, fearful of the effects of sharpshooting from the timber, they were satisfied. Winter was coming on, and they had destroyed the cabin on the Crazy Man and killed Bo Marsh. Mistakenly they also believed they had killed Brisco and wounded at least one other man.

Sick at heart, Ann had walked back into her room and stood by the window. Suddenly she was overwhelmed by the desire to get away, to escape all this sickening violence, the guns, the killings, the problems of frontier life. Back East there were lovely homes along quiet streets, slow-running streams, men who walked quietly on Sunday mornings. There were parties, theaters, friends, homes.

Her long ride had tired her. The touch of Rafe Caradec's hand, the look in his eyes, had given her a lift. Something had sparked within her, and she felt herself drawn to him, yearning toward him with everything feminine that was in her. Riding away, she had heard the crash of guns, shouts, and yells. Had she been too late?

There had been no turning back. She had known there was nothing she could do. Her natural good sense had told her that she would only complicate matters if she tried to stay. Nor did she know now what she would have done if she had stayed. Where was her sympathy? With Shute's riders, or with this strange, tall young man who had come to claim half her ranch and tell fantastic stories of knowing her father aboard a ship? Every iota of intelligence she had told her the man was all wrong, that his story could not be true. Bruce Barkow's story of her father's death had been the true one. What reason for him to lie? Why would he want to claim her land when there was so much more to be had for the taking? Her father had told her, and Gene Baker agreed, that soon all this country would be open to settlement, and there would be towns and railroads here. Why choose one piece of land, a large section of it worthless, when the hills lay bare for the taking?

Standing by the window and looking out into the darkness, Ann knew suddenly she was sick of it all. She would get away, go back East. Bruce was right. It was time she left here, and, when he came again, she would tell him she was ready. He had been thoughtful and considerate. He had protected her, been attentive and affectionate. He was a man of intelligence. He was handsome. She could be proud of him.

She stifled her misgivings with a sudden resolution, and hurriedly began to pack.

XVI

Vaguely Ann had sensed Barkow's fear of something, but she believed it was fear of an attack by Indians. Word had come earlier that day that the Oglalas were gathering in the hills, and there was much war talk among them. That it could be Dan Shute whom Barkow feared Ann had no idea.

She had completed the packing of the few items she would need for the trip when she heard the sound of gunfire from the National. The shots brought her to her feet with a start, her face pale. Running into the living room, she found that Gene Baker had caught up his rifle. She ran to Mrs. Baker, and the two women stood together, listening.

Baker looked at them. "Can't be Indians," he said after a moment. "Mebbe some wild cow-hand celebratin'."

They heard excited voices, yells. Baker went to the door, hesitated, then went out. He was gone several minutes before he returned. His face was grave.

"It was that Texas rider from the Crazy Man," he said. "He stepped into the back door of the National and shot it out with Tom Blazer and Fats McCabe. They're both dead."

"Was he alone?" Ann asked quickly.

Baker nodded, looking at her somberly. "They're huntin' him now. He won't get away, I'm afeerd."

"You're *afraid* he won't?"

"Yes, Ann," Baker said, "I am. That Blazer outfit's poison. All of the Shute bunch, far's that goes. Tom killed young Bo Marsh by stickin' a pistol against him whilst he was lyin' down."

The flat bark of a shot cut across the night air, and they went rigid. Two more shots rang out.

"Guess they got him," Baker said. "There's so many of them, I figgered they would."

Before the news reached them of what had actually happened, daylight had come. Ann Rodney was awake after an almost sleepless night. Tex Brisco, she heard, had killed Joe Gorman when Gorman had caught him at his horse. Tex had escaped, but from all the evidence he was badly wounded. They were trailing him by the blood from his wounds. Bo Marsh, now Brisco. Was Johnny Gill alive? Was Rafe? If Rafe were alive, then he must be alone, harried like a rabbit by hounds.

Restless, Ann paced the floor. Shute riders came and went in the store. They were buying supplies and going out in groups of four and five, scouring the hills for Brisco or any of the others of the Crazy Man crowd.

Bruce Barkow came shortly after breakfast. He walked into the store. He looked tired, worried.

"Ann," he said abruptly, "if we're goin', it'll

have to be today. This country is goin' to the
wolves. All they think about now is killin'. Let's
get out."

She hesitated only an instant. Something inside
her seemed lost and dead. "All right, Bruce. We've
planned it for a long time. It might as well be now."

There was no fire in her, no spark. Barkow
scarcely heeded that. She would go, and, once
away from here and married, he would have title
to the land, and Dan Shute for all his talk and
harsh ways would be helpless. "All right," he said.
"We'll leave in an hour. Don't tell anybody. We'll
take the buckboard like we were goin' for a drive,
as we often do."

She was ready, so there was nothing to do after
he had gone.

Baker seemed older, worried. Twice riders came
in, and each time Ann heard that Tex Brisco was
still at large. His horse had been trailed, seemingly wandering without guidance, to a place on a
mountain creek. There the horse had walked into
the water, and no trail had been found to show
where he had left it. He was apparently headed for
the high ridges, south by west, nor had anything
been found of Marsh or Gill. Shute riders had returned to the Crazy Man, torn down the corral,
and hunted through the woods, but no sign had
been found beyond a crude lean-to where the
wounded man had evidently been sheltered.
Marsh, if dead, had been buried, and the grave
concealed. Nothing had been found of any of
them, although one horse had ridden off to the
northeast, mostly east.

One horse had gone east! Ann Rodney's heart
gave a queer leap. East would mean toward the

fort! Perhaps. . . . But she was being foolish. Why should it be Caradec rather than Gill, and why to the fort? She expressed the thought, and Baker looked at her.

"Likely enough one of 'em's gone there. If Marsh ain't dead, and the riders didn't find his body, chances are he's mighty bad off. The only doctor around is at the fort."

The door to the store opened, and Baker went in, leaving the living room. There was a brief altercation, then the curtain was pushed aside, and Ann looked up. A start of fear went through her.

Dan Shute was standing in the door. For a wonder, he was clean-shaven except for his mustache. He looked at her with his queer, gray-white eyes. "Don't you do nothin' foolish," he said, "like tryin' to leave here. I don't aim to let yuh."

Ann got up, amazed and angry. "You don't aim to let me?" she flared. "What business is it of yours?"

Shute stood there with his big hands on his hips, staring at her insolently. "Because I want to make it my business," he said. "I've told Barkow where he stands with you. If he don't like it, he can say so and die. I ain't particular. I just wanted yuh should know that from here on yuh're my woman."

"Listen here, Shute," Baker flared. "You can't talk to a decent woman that way!"

"Shut yore mouth," Shute said, staring at Baker. "I talk the way I please. I'm tellin' her. If she tries to get away from here, I'll take her out to the ranch now. If she waits . . ."—he looked her up and down coolly—"I may marry her. Don't know why I should." He added, glaring at Baker: "You butt into this and I'll smash yuh. She ain't no woman for a weak sister like Barkow. I guess she'll come to like me all right. Anyway, she'd better." He turned toward the door. "Don't get any ideas. I'm the law here, and the only law."

"I'll appeal to the Army," Baker declared.

"You do," Shute said, "and I'll kill yuh. Anyway, the Army's goin' to be some busy. A bunch of Sioux raided a stage station way south of here last night and killed three men, then ran off the stock. Two men were killed hayin' over on Otter last night. A bunch of soldiers hayin' not far from the Piney were fired on and one man wounded. The Army's too busy to bother with the likes of you. Besides," he added, grinning, "the commandin' officer said that in case of Injun trouble, I was to take command at Painted Rock and make all preparations for defense."

He turned and walked out of the room. They heard the front door slam, and Ann sat down suddenly.

Gene Baker walked to the desk and got out his gun. His face was stiff and old.

"No, not that," Ann said. "I'm leaving, Uncle Gene."

"Leavin'? How?" He turned on her, his eyes alert.

"With Bruce. He's asked me several times. I was going to tell you, but nobody else. I'm all packed."

"Barkow, eh?" Gene Baker stared at her. "Well, why not? He's half a gentleman, anyway. Shute is an animal and a brute."

The back door opened gently. Bruce Barkow stepped in.

"Was Dan here?"

Baker explained quickly. "Better forget that buckboard idea," he said, once Barkow had outlined the plan. "Take the hosses and go by the river trail. Leave at noon when everybody will be eatin'. Take the Bannock Trail, then swing north and east and cut around toward the fort. They'll think yuh're tryin' for the gold fields."

Barkow nodded. He looked stiff and pale, and he was wearing a gun. It was almost noon.

When the streets were empty, Bruce Barkow went out back to the barn and saddled the horses. There was no one in sight. The woods along the creek were only a hundred yards away.

Walking outside, the two got into their saddles and rode at a walk to the trees, the dust muffling the beat of horses' hoofs, then they took the Bannock Trail. Two miles out, Barkow rode into a stream, then led the way north.

Once away from the trail they rode swiftly, keeping the horses at a rapid trot. Barkow was silent, and his eyes kept straying to the back trail. Twice they saw Indian sign, but their escape had evidently been made successfully, for there was no immediate sound of pursuit.

Bruce Barkow kept moving, and, as he rode, his irritation, doubt, and fear began to grow more and more obvious. He rode like a man in the grip of deadly terror. Ann, watching him, wondered. Before, Shute had tolerated Barkow. Now a definite break had been made, and with each mile of their escape Barkow became more frightened. There was no way back now. He would be killed on sight, for Dan Shute was not a man to forgive or tolerate such a thing.

It was only on the girl's insistence that he stopped for a rest, and to give the horses a much needed blow. They took it, while Ann sat on the grass, and Bruce paced the ground, his eyes searching the trail over which they had come. When they were in the saddle again, he seemed to relax, to come to himself. Then he looked at her. "Yuh must think I'm a coward," he said, "but it's just that I'm afraid of what Shute would do if he got his hands on you, and I'm no gunfighter. He'd kill us both."

"I know." She nodded gravely.

This man who was to be her husband impressed her less at every moment. Somehow, his claim that he was thinking of her failed to ring with sincerity. Yet with all his faults, he was probably only a weak man, a man cut out for civilization, and not for the frontier. They rode on, and the miles piled up behind them. . . .

Rafe Caradec awakened with a start to the sound of a bugle. It took him several seconds to realize that he was in bed at the fort. Then he remembered. The commanding officer had refused to allow the surgeon to leave before morning, and then only with an escort. With Lieutenant Bryson and eight men they would form a scouting patrol, would circle around by Crazy Man, then cut back toward the fort.

The party at the fort was small, for the place had been abandoned several years before, and had been utilized only for a few weeks as a base for scouting parties when fear of an Indian outbreak began to grow. It was no longer an established post but merely a camp. Further to the south there was a post at Fort Fetterman, named for the leader of the troops trapped in the Fetterman Massacre. A wagon train had been attacked within a short distance of Fort Phil Kearney, and a group of seventy-nine soldiers and two civilians were to march out to relieve them under command of Major James Powell, a skilled Indian fighter. However, Brevet Lieutenant Colonel Fetterman had used his rank to take over command, and had ridden out. Holding the fighting ability of the Indians in contempt, Fetterman had pursued some of them beyond a ridge. Firing had been heard, and, when other troops were sent out from the fort, they had discovered Fetterman and his entire command wiped out, about halfway down the ridge. The wagon train they had gone to relieve had reached the fort later, unaware of the encounter on the ridge.

Getting into his clothes, Rafe hurried outside. The first person he met was Bryson.

"Good morning, Caradec!" Bryson said, grinning. "Bugle wake you up?"

Caradec nodded. "It isn't the first time."

"You've been in the service, then?" Bryson asked, glancing at him quickly.

"Yes." Rafe glanced around the stockade. "I was with Sully. In Mexico for a while, too, and Guatemala."

Bryson glanced at him. "Then you're *that* Caradec? Man, I've heard of you! Major Skehan will be pleased to know. He's an admirer of yours, sir." He nodded toward two weary, dust-covered horses. "You're not the only arrival from Painted Rock," Bryson said. "Those horses came in last night, almost daylight, in fact, with two riders. A chap named Barkow, and a girl. Pretty, too, the lucky dog."

Rafe turned on him, his eyes sharp. "A woman? A girl?"

Bryson looked surprised. "Why, yes! Her name's Rodney. She . . ."

"Where is she?" Rafe snapped. "Where is she now?"

Bryson smiled slightly. "Why, that's her over there! A friend of yours?"

But Rafe was gone.

Ann was standing in the door of one of the partly reconstructed buildings, and, when she saw him, her eyes widened.

"Rafe! You, here? Then you got away!"

"I came after a doctor for Marsh. He's in a bad way." He tossed the remark aside, studying her face. "Ann, what are you doing here with Barkow?"

His tone nettled her. "Why? How does it concern you?"

"Your father asked me to take care of you," he said, "and, if you married Bruce Barkow, I certainly wouldn't be doin' it."

"Oh?" Her voice was icy. "Still claiming you knew my father? Well, Mister Caradec, I think you'd be much better off to forget that story. I don't know where you got the idea, or how, or what made you believe you could get away with it, but it won't do. I've been engaged to Bruce for months. I intend to marry him now. There's a chaplain here. Then we'll go on to the river and down to Saint Louis. There's a steamer on the way up that we can meet."

"I won't let you do it, Ann," Rafe said harshly.

Her weariness, her irritation, and something

else brought quick anger to her face and lips. "You won't let me? You have nothing to do with it! It simply isn't any of your business! Now, if you please, I'm waiting for Bruce. Will you go?"

"No," he said violently, "I won't. I'll say again what I said before. I knew your father. He gave me a deed givin' us the ranch. He asked me to care for you. He also gave me the receipt that Bruce Barkow gave him for the mortgage money. I wanted things to be different, Ann. I . . ."

"Caradec!" Bryson called. "We're ready!"

He glanced around. The small column awaited him, and his horse was ready. For an instant he glanced back at the girl. Her jaw was set, her eyes blazing. "Oh, what's the use?" he flared. "Marry who you blasted well please!"

Wheeling, he walked to his horse and swung into the saddle, riding away without a backward glance.

XVII

L ips parted to speak, Ann Rodney stared after the disappearing riders. Suddenly all her anger was gone. She found herself gazing at the closing gate of the stockade and fighting a mounting sense of panic. What had she done? Suppose what Rafe had said was the truth? What had he ever done to make her doubt him?

Confused, puzzled by her own feelings for this stranger of whom she knew so little, yet who stirred her so deeply, she was standing there, one hand partly upraised when she saw two men come around the corner of the building. Both wore the rough clothing of miners. They paused near her, one a stocky, thick-set man with a broad, hard jaw, the other a slender blond young man.

"Miss," the younger man said, "we just come in from the river. The major was tellin' us you were goin' back that way?"

She nodded dumbly, then forced herself to speak. "Yes, we are going to the river with some of the troops. Or that has been our plan."

"We come up the Powder from the Yellowstone, miss," the young man said, "and, if yuh could tell us where to find yore husband, we might sell him our boats."

She shook her head. "I'm not married yet. You will have to see my fiancé, Bruce Barkow. He's in the mess hall."

The fellow hesitated, turning his hat in his hand. "Miss, they said yuh was from Painted Rock. Ever hear tell of a man named Rafe Caradec over there?"

She stiffened. "Rafe Caradec?" She looked at him quickly. "You know him?"

He nodded, pleased by her sudden interest. "Yes, miss. We were shipmates of his. Me and my partner over there, Rock Mullaney. My name is Penn, miss . . . Roy Penn."

Suddenly her heart was pounding. She looked at him and bit her lip. Then she said carefully: "You were on a ship with him?"

"That's right."

Penn was puzzled, and he was growing wary. After all, there was the manner of their leaving. Of course, that was months ago, and they were far from the sea now, but that still hung over them.

"Was there . . . aboard that ship . . . a man named Rodney?"

Ann couldn't look at them now. She stared at the stockade, almost afraid to hear their reply. Vaguely she realized that Bruce Barkow was approaching.

"Rodney? Shorest thing yuh know! Charles Rodney. Nice feller, too. He died off the California coast after . . ." He hesitated. "Miss, you ain't no relation of his now?"

"I'm Charles Rodney's daughter."

"Oh?" Then Penn's eyes brightened. "Say, then

you're the girl Rafe came here to see! You know, Charlie's daughter!"

Bruce Barkow stopped dead still. His dark face was suddenly wary.

"What was that?" he said sharply. "What did yuh say?"

Penn stared at him. "No reason to get excited, mister. Yeah, we knew this young lady's father aboard ship. He was shanghaied out of San Francisco."

Bruce Barkow's face was cold. Here it was, at the last minute. He could see in Ann's face the growing realization of how he had lied, how he had betrayed her, and even—he could see that coming into her eyes, too—the idea that he had killed her father. Veins swelled in his forehead and throat. He glared at Penn, half-crouching, like some cornered animal. "Yuh're a liar," he snarled.

"Don't call me that," Penn said fiercely. "I'm not wearing a gun, mister."

If Barkow heard the last words, they made no impression. His hand was already sweeping down. Penn stepped back, throwing his arms wide, and Bruce Barkow, his face livid with the fury of frustration, whipped up a gun and shot him twice through the body. Penn staggered back, uncomprehending, staring.

"No . . . gun!" he gasped. "I don't . . . gun."

He staggered into an Army wagon, reeled, and fell headlong.

Bruce Barkow stared at the fallen man, then his contorted face turned upward. On the verge of escape and success he had been trapped, and now he had become a killer. Wheeling, he sprang into the saddle. The gate was open for a wood wagon, and he whipped the horse through it, shouting hoarsely.

Men had rushed from everywhere, and Rock Mullaney, staring in shocked surprise, could only fumble at his belt. He wore no gun, either. He looked up at Ann. "We carried rifles," he muttered. "We never figgered on no trouble!" Then he rubbed his face, sense returning to his eyes. "Miss, what did he shoot him for?"

She stared at him, humbled by the grief written on the man's hard, lonely face. "That man, Barkow, killed my father," she said.

"No, miss. If yuh're Charlie Rodney's daughter, Charlie died aboard ship with us."

She nodded. "I know, but Barkow was responsible. Oh, I've been a fool! An awful fool!"

An officer was kneeling over Penn's body. He got up, glanced at Mullaney, then at Ann. "This man is dead," he said.

Resolution came suddenly to Ann. "Major," she sad, "I'm going to catch the patrol. Will you lend me a fresh horse? Ours will still be badly worn out after last night."

"It wouldn't be safe, Miss Rodney," he protested. "It wouldn't at all. There's Indians out there. How Caradec got through, or you and Barkow, is beyond me." He gestured to the body. "What you know about this?"

Briefly, concisely she explained, telling all. She made no attempt to spare herself or to leave anything out. She outlined the entire affair, taking only a few minutes.

"I see." He looked thoughtfully at the gate. "If I could give you an escort, I would, but . . ."

"If she knows the way," Mullaney said, "I'll go

with her. We came down the river from Fort Benton, then up the Yellowstone and the Powder. We thought we would come and see how Rafe was getting along. If we'd knowed there was trouble, we'd have come before."

"It's as much as your life is worth, man," the major warned.

Mullaney shrugged. "Like as not, but my life has had chances taken with it before. Besides,"—he ran his fingers over his bald head—"there's no scalp here to attract Indians."

Well-mounted, Ann and Mullaney rode swiftly. The patrol would be hurrying because of Bo Marsh's serious condition, but they should overtake them, and following was no immediate problem. Mullaney knew the West and had fought before in his life as a wandering jack-of-all-trades, and he was not upset by the chance they were taking. He glanced from time to time at Ann, then, rambling along, he began to give her an account of their life aboard ship, of the friendship that had grown between her father and Rafe Caradec, and all Rafe had done to spare the older man work and trouble. He told her how Rafe had treated Rodney's wounds when he had been beaten, how he had saved food for him, and how close the two had grown. Twice, noting her grief and shame, he ceased talking, but each time she insisted on his continuing.

"Caradec?" Mullaney said finally. "Well, I'd say he was one of the finest men I've known. A fighter, he is. The lad's a fighter from 'way back. Yuh should have seen the beatin' he gave that Borger! I got only a glimpse, but Penn told me about it.

And if it hadn't been for Rafe, none us would have got away. He planned it, and he carried it out. He planned it before yore father's last trouble . . . the trouble that killed him . . . but when he saw yore father would die, he carried on with it."

They rode on in silence. All the time, Ann knew now, she should have trusted her instincts. Always they had warned her about Bruce Barkow, always they had been sure of Rafe Caradec. As she had sat in the jury box and watched him talk, handling his case, it had been his sincerity that had impressed her, even more than his shrewd handling of questions. He had killed men, yes. But what men! Bonaro and Trigger Boyne, both acknowledged and boastful killers of men themselves, men unfit to walk in the tracks of such as Rafe. She had to find him! She must!

The wind was chill, and she glanced at Mullaney. "It's cold!" she said. "It feels like snow!"

He nodded grimly. "It does that," he said. "Early for it, but it's happened before. If we get a norther now . . ." He shook his head.

They made camp while it was still light, and Mullaney built a fire of dry sticks that gave off almost no smoke. Water was heated, and they made coffee. While Ann was fixing the little food they had, he rubbed the horses down with handfuls of dry grass.

"Can yuh find yore way in the dark?" he asked her.

"Yes, I think so. It is fairly easy from here, for we have the mountains. That highest peak will serve as a landmark unless there are too many clouds."

"All right," he said, "we'll try to keep movin'."

She found herself liking the burly seaman and cowhand. He helped her smother the fire and wipe out traces of it.

"If we stick to the trail of the soldiers," he said, "it'll confuse the Injuns. They'll think we're with their party."

They started on. Ann led off, keeping the horses at a fast walk. Dusk came, and with it the wind grew stronger. After an hour of travel, Ann reined in.

Mullaney rode up beside her. "What's the matter?"

She indicated the tracks of a single horse crossing the route of the soldiers.

"Yuh think this is Barkow?" He nodded as an idea came. "It could be. The soldiers don't know what happened back there. He might ride with 'em for protection."

Another thought came to him. He looked at Ann keenly. "Suppose he'd try to kill Caradec?"

Her heart jumped. "Oh, no!" She was saying no to the thought, not to the possibility. She knew it was a possibility. What did Bruce have to lose? He was already a fugitive, and another killing would make it no worse. And Rafe Caradec had been the cause of it all.

"He might," she agreed. "He might, at that. . . ."

Miles to the west, Bruce Barkow, his rifle across his saddle, leaned into the wind. He had followed the soldiers for a way, and the idea of a snipe shot at Caradec stayed in his mind. He could do it, and they would think the Indians had done it. But there was a better way, a way to get at them all. If he could ride on ahead, reach Gill and Marsh before the patrol did, he might kill them, then get Caradec when he approached. If then he could get rid of Shute, Gomer would have to swing with him to save something from the mess. Maybe Dan Shute's idea was right, after all! Maybe killing was the solution.

Absorbed by the possibilities of the idea, Barkow turned off the route followed by the soldiers. There was a way that could make it safer, and somewhat faster. He headed for the old Bozeman Trail, now abandoned.

He gathered his coat around him to protect him from the increasing cold. His mind was fevered with worry, doubt of himself, and mingled with it was hatred of Caradec, Shute, Ann Rodney, and everyone and everything. He drove on into the night.

Twice, he stopped to rest. The second time he started on, it was turning gray with morning, and, as he swung into the saddle, a snowflake touched his cheek. He thought little of it. His horse was uneasy, though, and anxious for the trail. Snow was not a new thing, and Barkow scarcely noticed as the flakes began to come down thicker and faster.

Gill and the wounded man had disappeared, he knew. Shute's searchers had not found them near the house. Bruce Barkow had visited that house many times before the coming of Caradec, and he knew the surrounding hills well. About a half mile back from the house, sheltered by a thick growth of lodgepole pine, was a deep cave among some rocks. If Johnny Gill had found that cave, he might have moved Marsh there. It was, at least, a chance. Bruce Barkow was not worried about the tracks he was leaving. Few Indians would be moving in this inclement weather, nor would the party from the fort have come this far north. From the route they had taken, he knew they were keeping to the low country. He was nearing the first range of foothills now, the hills that divided Long Valley from the open plain that sloped gradually away to the Powder and the old Bozeman Trail. He rode into the pines and started up the trail, intent upon death. His mind was sharpened like that of a hungry coyote. Cornered and defeated for the prize himself, his only way out, either for victory or revenge, lay in massacre, wholesale killing.

It was like him that having killed once, he did not hesitate to accept the idea of killing again. He did not see the big man on the gray horse who fell in behind him. He did not glance back over his trail, although by now the thickening snow obscured the background so much the rider, gaining slowly on him through the storm, would have been no more than a shadow.

To the right, behind the once bald and now snow-covered dome, was the black smear of seeping oil. Drawing abreast of it, Bruce Barkow reined in and glanced down. Here it was, the cause of it all. The key to wealth, to everything a man could want. Men had killed for less; he could kill for this. He knew where there were four other such seepages, and the oil sold from twenty dollars to thirty dollars a barrel.

He got down and stirred it with a stick. It was thick now, thickened by cold. Well, he still might win. Then he heard a shuffle of hoofs in the snow, and looked up. Dan Shute's figure was gigantic in the heavy coat he wore, sitting astride the big horse. He looked down at Barkow, and his lips parted.

"Tried to get away with her, did yuh? I knew yuh had coyote in yuh, Barkow."

His hand came up, and in the gloved hand was a pistol. In a sort of shocked disbelief, Bruce Barkow saw the gun lift. His own gun was under his short, thick coat.

"No!" he gasped hoarsely. "Not that! *Dan!*"

The last word was a scream, cut sharply off by the hard *bark* of the gun. Bruce Barkow folded slowly and, clutching his stomach, toppled across the black seepage, staining it with a slow shading of red.

For a minute, Dan Shute sat his horse, staring down. Then he turned the horse and moved on. He had an idea of his own. Before the storm began, from a mountain ridge he had picked out the moving patrol. Behind it were two figures. He had a hunch about those two riders, striving to overtake the patrol. He would see.

XVIII

Pushing rapidly ahead through the falling snow, the patrol came up to the ruins of the cabin on the Crazy Man on the morning of the second day out from the fort. Steam rose from the horses, and the breath of horses and men fogged the air. There was no sign of life. Rafe swung down, and stared about. The smooth surface of the snow was unbroken, yet he could see that much had happened since he started his trek to the fort for help. The lean-to, not quite complete, was abandoned.

Lieutenant Bryson surveyed the scene thoughtfully. "Are we too late?" he asked.

Caradec hesitated, staring around. There was no hope in what he saw. "I don't think so," he said. "Johnny Gill was a smart hand. He would figger out somethin', and, besides, I don't see any bodies."

In his mind, he surveyed the cañon. Certainly Gill could not have gone far with the wounded man. Also, it would have to be in the direction of possible shelter. The grove of lodgepoles offered the best chance. Turning, he walked toward them. Bryson dismounted his men, and they started fires.

Milton Waitt, the surgeon, stared after Rafe, then walked in his tracks. When he came up with him, he suggested: "Any caves around?"

Caradec paused, considering that. "There may be. None that I know of, though. Still, Johnny prowled in these rocks a lot and may have found one. Let's have a look." Then a thought occurred to him. "They'd have to have water, Doc. Let's go to the spring."

There was ice over it, but the ice had been broken and had frozen again. Rafe indicated it.

"Somebody drank here after the cold set in."

He knelt and felt of the snow with his fingers, working his way slowly around the spring. Suddenly he stopped.

"Found something?" Waitt watched curiously. This made no sense to him.

"Yes. Whoever got water from the spring splashed some on this side. It froze. I can feel the ice it made. That's a fair indication that whoever got water came from that side of the spring." Moving around, he kept feeling of the snow. "Here." He felt again. "There's an icy ring where he set the bucket for a minute. Water left on the bottom froze." He straightened, studying the mountainside. "He's up here, somewheres. He's got a bucket, and he's able to come down here for water, but findin' him'll be the devil's own job. He'll need fuel, though. Somewhere he's been breakin' sticks and collectin' wood, but wherever he does, it won't be close to his shelter. Gill's too smart for that."

Studying the hillside, Rafe indicated the nearest clump of trees.

"He wouldn't want to be out in the open on this

snow any longer than he had to," he said thoughtfully, "and the chances are he'd head for the shelter of those trees. When he got there, he would
probably set the bucket down while he studied the
back trail and made shore he hadn't been seen."

Waitt nodded, his interest aroused. "Good rea-
soning, man. Let's see."

They walked to the clump of trees, and, after a
few minutes' search, Waitt found the same icy
frozen place just under the thin skimming of
snow. "Where do we go from here?" he asked.

Rafe hesitated, studying the trees. A man would
automatically follow the line of easiest travel, and
there was an opening between the trees. He started
on, then stopped. "This is right. See? There's not so
much snow on this branch. There's a good chance
he brushed it off in passin'."

It was mostly guesswork, he knew. Yet, after
they had gone three hundred yards, Rafe looked
up and saw the cliff pushing its rocky shoulder in
among the trees. At its base was a tumbled cluster
of gigantic boulders and broken slabs. He led off
for the rocks, and almost the first thing he saw
was a fragment of loose bark lying on the snow,
and a few crumbs of dust such as is sometimes
found between the bark and tree. He pointed it
out to Waitt.

"He carried wood this way."

They paused there, and Rafe sniffed the air.
There was no smell of wood smoke. Were they
dead? Had cold done what rifle bullets couldn't
do? No, he decided, Johnny Gill knew too well
how to take care of himself.

Rafe walked between the rocks, turning where it
felt natural to turn. Suddenly he saw a tipped-up

slab of granite leaning against a larger boulder. It looked dry underneath. He stooped and glanced in. It was dark and silent, yet some instinct seemed to tell him it was not so empty as it appeared.

He crouched in the opening, leaving light from outside to come in first along one wall, then another. His keen eyes picked out a damp spot on the leaves. There was no place for a leak, and the wind had been in the wrong direction to blow in here.

"Snow," he said. "Probably fell off a boot."

They moved into the cave, bending over to walk. Yet it was not really a cave at first, merely a slab of rock offering partial shelter. About fifteen feet farther along the slab ended under a thick growth of pine boughs and brush that formed a canopy overhead, offering almost as solid shelter as the stone itself. Then, in the rock face of the cliff, they saw a cave, a place gouged by wind and water long since and completely obscured behind the boulders and brush from any view but from where they stood.

They walked up to the entrance. The overhang of the cliff offered a shelter that was all of fifty feet deep, running along one wall of a diagonal gash in the cliff that was invisible from outside. They stepped in on the dry sand, and had taken only a step when they smelled wood smoke. At almost the same instant, Johnny Gill spoke.

"Hi, Rafe!" He stepped down from behind a heap of débris against one wall of the rock fissure. "I couldn't see who yuh were till now. I had my rifle ready so's if yuh was the wrong one, I could plumb discourage yuh." His face looked drawn and tired. "He's over here, Doc," Gill continued, "and he's been delirious all night."

While Waitt was busy over the wounded man, Gill walked back up the cave with Rafe.

"What's happened," Gill asked. "I thought they'd got yuh."

"No, they haven't, but I don't know much of what's been goin' on. Ann's at the fort with Barkow, says she's goin' to marry him."

"What about Tex?" Gill asked quickly.

Rafe shook his head, scowling. "No sign of him. I don't know what's come off at Painted Rock. I'm leavin' for there as soon as I've told the lieutenant and his patrol where Doc is. You'll have to stick here because the Doc has to get back to the fort."

"You goin' to Painted Rock?"

"Yes. I'm goin' to kill Dan Shute."

"I'd like to see that," Gill said grimly, "but watch yoreself!" The little cowhand looked at him seriously. "Boss, what about that girl?"

Rafe's lips tightened, and he stared at the bare wall of the cave. "I don't know," he said grimly. "I tried to talk her out of it, but I guess I wasn't what you'd call tactful."

Gill stuck his thumbs in his belt. "Tell her yuh're in love with her yoreself?"

Caradec stared at him. "Where'd yuh get that idea?"

"Readin' signs. Yuh ain't been the same since yuh ran into her the first time. She's yore kind of people, boss."

"Mebbe. But looks like she reckoned she wasn't. Never would listen to me give the straight story on her father. Both of us flew off the handle this time."

"Well, I ain't no hand at ridin' herd on women folks, but I've seen a thing or two, boss. The chances are, if yuh'd 'a' told her yuh're in love with her, she'd never have gone with Bruce Barkow."

Rafe was remembering those words when he rode down the trail toward Painted Rock. What lay ahead of him could not be planned. He had no idea when or where he would encounter Dan Shute. He knew only that he must find him.

After reporting to Bryson so he wouldn't worry about the doctor, Rafe had hit the trail for Painted Rock alone. By now he knew that mountain trail well, and even the steady fall of snow failed to make him change his mind about making the ride.

He was burning up inside. The old, driving recklessness was in him, the urge to be in and shooting. His enemies were in the clear, and all the cards were on the table in plain sight. Barkow he discounted. Dan Shute was the man to get, and Pod Gomer the man to watch. What he intended to do was as high-handed in its way as what Shute and Barkow had attempted, but in Rafe's case the cause was just.

Mullaney stopped in a wooded draw short of the hills. The pause was for a short rest just before daybreak on that fatal second morning. The single rider had turned off from the trail and was no longer with the patrol. Both he and the girl needed rest, aside from the horses.

He kicked snow away from the grass, then swept some of it clear with a branch. In most places it was already much too thick for that. After he made coffee, and they had eaten, he got up.

"Get ready," he said, "and I'll get the hosses."

All night he had been thinking of what he would do when he found Barkow. He had seen the man draw on Penn, and he was not fast. That made it an even break, for Mullaney knew that he was not fast himself.

When he found the horses missing, he stopped. Evidently they had pulled their picket pins and wandered off. He started on, keeping in their tracks. He did not see the big man in the heavy coat who stood in the brush and watched him go.

Dan Shute threaded his way down to the campfire. When Ann looked up at his approach, she thought it was Mullaney, and then she saw Shute. Eyes wide, she came to her feet. "Why, hello! What are you doing here?"

He smiled at her, his eyes sleepy and yet wary. "Huntin' you. Reckoned this was you. When I seen Barkow, I reckoned somethin' had gone wrong."

"You saw Bruce? Where?"

"North a ways. He won't bother yuh none." Shute smiled. "Barkow was spineless. Thought he was smart. He never was half as smart as that Caradec, nor as tough as me."

"What happened?" Ann's heart was pounding. Mullaney should be coming now. He would hear their voices and be warned.

"I killed him." Shute was grinning cynically. "He wasn't much good. Don't be wonderin' about that *hombre* with yuh. I led the hosses off and turned his adrift. He'll be hours catchin' it, if he ever does. However, he might come back, so we'd better drift."

"No," Ann said, "I'll wait."

He smiled. "Better come quiet. If he came back, I'd have to kill him. Yuh don't want him killed, do yuh?"

She hesitated only a moment. This man would stop at nothing. He was going to take her if he had to knock her out and tie her. Better anything than that. If she appeared to play along, she might have a chance. "I'll go," she said simply. "You have a horse?"

"I kept yores," he said. "Mount up."

XIX

By the time Rafe Caradec was *en route* to
Painted Rock, Dan Shute was riding with his
prisoner into the ranch yard of his place near
Painted Rock. Far to the south and west, Rock
Mullaney long since had come up to the place
where Shute had finally turned his horse loose
and ridden on, leading the other. Mullaney kept
on the trail of the lone horse and came up with it
almost a mile farther.

Lost and alone in the thickly falling snow, the
animal hesitated at his call, then waited for him to
catch up. When he was mounted once more, he
turned back to his camp, and the tracks, nearly
covered, told him little. The girl, accompanied by
another rider, had ridden away. She would never
have gone willingly.

Mullaney was worried. During the travel they
had talked little, yet Ann had supplied a few of the
details, and he knew vaguely about Dan Shute,
about Bruce Barkow. He also knew, having heard
all about it long before reaching the fort, that an
Indian outbreak was feared.

Mullaney knew something about Indians, and
doubted any trouble until spring or summer.

There might be occasional shootings, but Indians were not as a rule cold-weather fighters. For that, he didn't blame them. Yet any wandering, hunting, or foraging parties must be avoided, and it was probable that any warrior or group of them coming along a fresh trail would fail to follow it and count coup on an enemy if possible.

He knew roughly the direction of Painted Rock, yet instinct told him he'd better stick to the tangible and near, so he swung back to the trail of the Army patrol and headed for the pass into Lone Valley.

Painted Rock lay still under the falling snow when Rafe Caradec drifted down the street in front of the Emporium, and went in. Baker looked up, and his eyes grew alert when he saw Rafe. At Caradec's question, he told him of what had happened to Tex Brisco so far as he knew, of the killing of Blazer, McCabe, and Gorman, and Brisco's escape while apparently wounded. He also told him of Dan Shute's arrival and threat to Ann, and her subsequent escape with Barkow. Baker was relieved to know they were at the fort.

A wind was beginning to moan around the eaves, and they listened a moment.

"Won't be good to be out in that," the storekeeper said gravely. "Sounds like a blizzard comin'. If Brisco's found shelter, he might be all right."

"Not in this cold," Caradec said, scowling. "No man with his resistance lowered by a wound is going to last in this. It's going to be worse before it's better."

Standing there at the counter, letting the warmth

of the big potbellied stove work through his system, Rafe assayed his position. Bo Marsh, while in bad shape, had been tended by a doctor and would have Gill's care. There was nothing more to be done there for the time being. Ann had made her choice. She had gone off with Barkow, and in his heart he knew that if there was any choice between the two—Barkow or Shute—she had made the better. Yet there had been another choice. Or had there? Yes, she could at least have listened to him.

The fort was not far away, and all he could do now was trust to Ann's innate good sense to change her mind before it was too late. In any event, he could not get back there in time to do anything about it.

"Where's Shute?" he demanded.

"Ain't seen him," Baker said worriedly. "Ain't seen hide nor hair of him. But I can promise yuh one thing, Caradec. He won't take Barkow's runnin' out with Ann lyin' down. He'll be on their trail."

The door opened in a flurry of snow, and Pat Higley pushed in. He pulled off his mittens and extended stiff fingers toward the red swell of the stove. He glanced at Rafe.

"Hear yuh askin' about Shute?" he asked. "I just seen him, headed for the ranch. He wasn't alone, neither." He rubbed his fingers. "Looked to me like a woman ridin' along."

Rafe looked around. "A woman?" he asked carefully. "Now who would that be?"

"He's found Ann!" Baker exclaimed.

"She was at the fort," Rafe said, "with Barkow. He couldn't take her away from the soldiers."

"No, he couldn't," Baker agreed, "but she might have left on her own. She's a stubborn girl when she takes a notion. After you left, she may have changed her mind."

Rafe pushed the thought away. The chance was too slight. And where was Tex Brisco? "Baker," he suggested, "you and Higley know this country. You know about Tex. Where do you reckon he'd wind up?"

Higley shrugged. "There's no tellin'. It ain't as if he knew the country, too. They trailed him for a while, and they said it looked like his hoss was wanderin' loose without no hand on the bridle. Then the hoss took to the water, so Brisco must have come to his senses somewhat. Anyway, they lost his trail when he was ridin' west along a fork of Clear Creek. If he held to that direction, it would take him over some plumb high, rough country south of the big peak. If he did get across, he'd wind up somewheres down along Tensleep Cañon, mebbe. But that's all guesswork."

"Any shelter that way?"

"Nary a mite. Not if yuh mean human shelter. There's plenty of shelter there, but wolves, too. There's also plenty of shelter in the rocks. The only humans over that way are the Sioux, and they ain't in what yuh'd call a friendly mood. That's where Man-Afraid-Of-His-Hoss has been holed up."

Finding Tex Brisco would be like hunting a needle in a haystack and worse, but it was what Rafe Caradec had to do. He had to make an effort, anyway. Yet the thought of Dan Shute and the girl returned to him. Suppose it was Ann? He shuddered to think of her in Shute's hands. The man was without a spark of decency or mercy. Not even his best friends would deny that.

"No use goin' out in this storm," Baker said. "Yuh can stay with us, Caradec."

"You've changed your tune some, Baker," Rafe suggested grimly.

"A man can be wrong, can't he?" Baker inquired testily. "Mebbe I was. I don't know. Things have gone to perdition around here fast, ever since you came in here with that story about Rodney."

"Well, I'm not stayin'," Rafe told him. "I'm going to look for Tex Brisco."

The door was pushed open, and they looked around. It was Pod Gomer. The sheriff looked even squarer and more bulky in a heavy buffalo coat. He cast a bleak look at Caradec, then walked to the fire, sliding out of his overcoat. "You still here?" he asked, glancing at Rafe out of the corners of his eyes.

"Yes, I'm still here, Gomer, but you're traveling."

"What?"

"You heard me. You can wait till the storm is over, then get out, and keep movin'."

Gomer turned, his square, hard face dark with angry blood. "You . . . tellin' me?" he said furiously. "I'm sheriff here!"

"You were," Caradec said calmly. "Ever since you've been hand in glove with Barkow and Shute, runnin' their dirty errands for them, pickin' up the scraps they tossed you. Well, the fun's over. You slope out of here when the storm's over. Barkow's gone, and within a few hours Shute will be, too."

"Shute?" Gomer was incredulous. "Yuh'd go up against Dan Shute? Why, man, yuh're insane!"

"Am I?" Rafe shrugged. "That's neither here nor there. I'm talkin' to you. Get out and stay out. You can take your tinhorn judge with you."

Gomer laughed. "You're the one who's through! Marsh dead, Brisco either dead or on the dodge, and Gill mebbe dead. What chance have you got?"

"Gill's in as good a shape as I am," Rafe said calmly, "and Bo Marsh is gettin' Army care, and he'll be out of the woods, too. As for Tex, I don't know. He got away, and I'm bankin' on that Texan to come out walkin'. How much stomach are your boys goin' to have for the fight when Gill and I ride in here? Tom Blazer's gone, and so are a half dozen more. Take your coat"—Rafe picked it up with his left hand—"and get out. If I see you after this storm, I'm shootin' on sight. Now, get!"

He heaved the heavy coat at Gomer, and the sheriff ducked, his face livid. Yet, surprisingly, he did not reach for a gun. He lunged and swung with his fist. A shorter man than Caradec, he was wider and thicker, a powerfully built man who was known in mining and trail camps as a rough-and-tumble fighter.

Caradec turned, catching Gomer's right on the cheekbone, but bringing up a solid punch to Gomer's midsection. The sheriff lunged close and tried to butt, and Rafe stabbed him in the face with a left, then smeared him with a hard right.

It was no match. Pod Gomer had fancied himself as a fighter, but Caradec had too much experience. He knocked Gomer back into a heap of sacks, then walked in on him, and slugged him wickedly in the middle with both hands. Gomer went to his knees.

"All right, Pod," Rafe said, panting, "I told you. Get goin'."

The sheriff stayed on his knees, breathing heavily, blood dripping from his smashed nose. Rafe Caradec slipped on his coat and walked to the door.

Outside, he took the horse to the livery stable, brushed him off, then gave him a rub-down and some oats.

He did not return to the store but, after a meal, saddled his horse and headed for Dan Shute's ranch. He couldn't escape the idea that the rider with Shute may have been Ann, despite the seeming impossibility of her being this far west. If she had left the fort within a short time after the patrol, then it might be, but there was small chance of that. Barkow would never return, having managed to get that far away. There was no one else at the fort to bring her. Scouts had said that a party of travelers was coming up from the river, but there would be small chance that any of them would push on to Painted Rock in this weather.

Dan Shute's ranch lay in a hollow of the hills near a curving stream. Not far away, the timber ran down to the plain's edge and dwindled away into a few scattered groves, blanketed now in snow. A thin trail of smoke lifted from the chimney of the house, and another from the bunkhouse. Rafe Caradec decided on boldness as the best course and his muffled, snow-covered appearance to disguise him until within gun range. He opened a button on the front of his coat so he could get at a gun thrust into his waistband. He removed his right hand from the glove and thrust it deeply in his pocket. There it would be warm and at the same time free to grasp the six-gun when he needed it.

No one showed. It was very cold, and, if there was anyone around and they noticed his approach, their curiosity did not extend to the point where they would come outside to investigate. Rafe strode directly to the house, walked up on the porch, and rapped on the door with his left hand. There was no response. He rapped again, much harder.

All was silence. The mounting wind made hearing difficult, but he put his ear to the door and listened. There was no sound.

He dropped his left hand to the door and turned the knob. The door opened easily, and he let it swing wide, standing well out of line. The wind howled in, and a few flakes of snow, but there was no sound. He stepped inside and closed the door after him.

His ears tingled with cold, and he resisted a desire to rub them, then let his eyes sweep the wide room. A fire burned on the huge stone fireplace, but there was no one in the long room. Two exits from the room were hung with blankets. There was a table, littered with odds and ends, and one end held some dirty dishes where a hasty meal had been eaten. Beneath that spot was a place showing dampness as though a pair of boots had shed melting snow.

There was no sound in the living room but the crackle of the fire and the low moan of the wind around the eaves. Walking warily, Rafe stepped over a saddle and some bits of harness and walked across to the opposite room. He pushed the blanket aside. Empty. There was an unmade bed of tumbled blankets and a lamp standing on a table by the bed.

Rafe turned and stared at the other door, then looked back into the bedroom. There was a pair of dirty socks lying there, and he stepped over and felt of them. They were damp. Someone, within the last hour or less, had changed socks here. Walking outside, he noticed something he had not seen before. Below a chair near the table was another spot of dampness. Apparently two people had been here.

He stepped back into the shadow of the bedroom door and put his hand in the front of his coat. He hadn't wanted to reach for that gun in case anyone was watching. Now, with his hand on the gun, he stepped out of the bedroom and walked to the other blanket-covered door. He pushed it aside.

A large kitchen. A fire glowed in the huge sheet-metal stove, and there was a coffeepot filled with boiling coffee. Seeing it, Rafe let go of his gun and picked up a cup. When he had filled it, he looked around the unkempt room. Like the rest of the house it was strongly built, but poorly kept inside. The floor was dirty, and dirty dishes and scraps of food were around.

He lifted the coffee cup, then his eyes saw a bit of white. He put down the cup and stepped over to the end of the woodpile. His heart jumped. It was a woman's handkerchief!

XX

Quickly Rafe Caradec glanced around. Again he looked at the handkerchief in his hand, and lifted it to his nostrils. There was a faint whiff of perfume—a perfume he remembered only too well. She had been here, then. The other rider with Dan Shute had been Ann Rodney. But where was she now? Where could she be? What had happened?

He gulped a mouthful of the hot coffee, and stared around again. The handkerchief had been near the back door. He put down the coffee, and eased the door open. Beyond were the barn and a corral. He walked outside and, pushing through the curtain of blowing snow, reached the corral, and then the barn.

Several horses were there. Hurrying along, he found two with dampness marking the places where their saddles had been. There were no saddles showing any evidence of having been ridden, and the saddles would be sweaty underneath if they had been. Evidently two horses had been saddled and ridden away from this barn.

Scowling, Rafe stared around. In the dust of the floor he found a small track, almost obliterated by a larger one. Had Shute saddled two horses and taken the girl away? If so, where would he take her, and why? He decided suddenly that Shute had not taken Ann from here. She must have slipped away, saddled a horse, and escaped. It was a far-fetched conclusion, but it offered not only the solution he wanted, but one that fitted with the few facts available or, at least, with the logic of the situation. Why would Shute take the girl away from his home ranch? There was no logical reason. Especially in such a storm as this when so far as Shute knew there would be no pursuit? Rafe himself would not have done it. Perhaps he had been overconfident, believing that Ann would rather share the warmth and security of the house than the mounting blizzard.

Only the bunkhouse remained unexplored. There was a chance they had gone there. Turning, Rafe walked to the bunkhouse. Shoving the door open, he stepped inside. Four men sat on bunks, and one, his boots off and his socks propped toward the stove, stared glumly at him from a chair made of a barrel. The faces of all the men were familiar, but he could put a name to none of them. They had seen the right hand in the front of his coat, and they sat quietly appreciating its significance.

"Where's Dan Shute?" he demanded.

"Ain't seen him," said the man in the barrel chair.

"That go for all of you?" Rafe's eyes swung from one to the other.

A lean, hard-faced man with a scar on his jaw-bone grinned, showing yellow teeth. He raised himself on his elbow. "Why, no. It shore don't, pilgrim. I seen him. He rode up here nigh onto an hour ago with that there girl from the store. They went inside. S'pose you want to get killed, you go to the house."

"I've been there. It's empty."

The lean-faced man sat up. "That right? That don't make sense. Why would a man with a filly like that go off into the storm?"

Rafe Caradec studied them coldly. "You men," he said, "had better get out of here when the storm's over. Dan Shute's through."

"Ain't yuh countin' unbranded stock, pardner?" the lean-faced man said, smiling tauntingly. "Dan Shute's able to handle his own troubles. He took care of Barkow."

This was news to Rafe. "He did! How'd you know that?"

"He done told me. Barkow was with this girl, and Shute trailed him. I didn't only see Shute come back, I talked some with him, and I unsaddled his hosses." He picked up a boot and pulled it on. "This here Rodney girl, she left the fort, runnin' away from Barkow and takin' after the Army patrol that rode out with you. Shute, he seen 'em. He also seen Barkow. He hunted Bruce down and shot him near that bare dome in your lower valley, and then he left Barkow and caught up with the girl and this strange *hombre* with her. Shute led their hosses off, then got the girl while this *hombre* was huntin' the hosses."

The explanation cleared up several points for Rafe. He stared thoughtfully around. "You didn't see 'em leave here?"

"Not us," the lean-faced 'puncher said dryly. "None of us hired on for punchin' cows or ridin' herd on women in blizzards. Come a storm, we

hole up and set her out. We aim to keep on doin'
just that."

Rafe backed to the door and stepped out. The
wind tore at his garments, and he backed away
from the building. Within twenty feet it was lost
behind a curtain of blowing snow. He stumbled
back to the house.

More than ever, he was convinced that somehow Ann had escaped. Yet where to look? In this
storm there was no direction, nothing. If she
headed for town, she might make it. However,
safety for her would more likely lie toward the
mountains, for there she could improvise shelter,
and probably could last the storm out. Knowing
the country, she would know how long such
storms lasted. It was rarely more than three days.

He had little hope of finding Ann, yet he knew
she would never return here. Seated in the ranch
house, he coolly ate a hastily picked-up meal and
drank more coffee. Then he returned to his horse
that he had led to the stable. Mounting, he rode
out into the storm on the way to town.

Gene Baker and Pat Higley looked up when Rafe
Caradec came in. Baker's face paled when he saw
that Rafe was alone. "Did yuh find out?" he asked.
"Was it Ann?"

Briefly Rafe explained, telling all he had learned
and his own speculations as to what had happened.

"She must have plumb got away," Higley
agreed. "Shute would never take her away from
his ranch in this storm. But where could she have
gone?"

Rafe explained his own theories on that. "She

probably took it for granted he would think she would head for town," he suggested, "so she may have taken to the mountains. After all, she would know that Shute would kill anybody who tried to stop him."

Gene Baker nodded miserably. "That's right, and what can a body do?"

"Wait," Higley said. "Just wait."

"I won't wait," Rafe said. "If she shows up here, hold her. Shoot Dan if you have to, dry-gulch him or anything. Get him out of the way. I'm goin' into the mountains. I can at least be lookin', and I might stumble onto some kind of a trail. . . ."

Two hours later, shivering with cold, Rafe Caradec acknowledged how foolhardy he had been. His black horse was walking steadily through a snow-covered avenue among the pines, weaving around fallen logs and clumps of brush. He had found nothing that resembled a trail, and twice he had crossed the stream. This, he knew, was also the direction that had been taken by the wounded Tex Brisco.

No track could last more than a minute in the whirling snow-filled world in which Rafe now rode. The wind howled and tore at his garments, even here, within the partial shelter of the lodge-poles. Yet he rode on, then dismounted, and walked ahead, resting the horse. It was growing worse instead of better, yet he pushed on, taking the line of least resistance, sure that this was what the fleeing Ann would have done.

The icy wind ripped at his clothing, at times faced him like a solid, moving wall. The black stumbled wearily, and Rafe was suddenly contrite.

The big horse had taken a brutal beating in these last few days, and even its great strength was weakening.

Squinting his eyes against the blowing snow, he remounted and stared ahead. He could see nothing, but he was aware that the wall of the mountain was on his left. Bearing in that direction, he came up to a thicker stand of trees and some scattered boulders. He rode on, alert for some possible shelter for himself and his horse.

Almost an hour later, he found it, a dry, sandy place under the overhang of the cliff, sheltered from the wind and protected from the snow by the overhang and by the trees and brush that fronted it. Swinging down, Rafe led the horse into the shelter and hastily built a fire.

From the underside of a log he got some bark, great sheets of it, and some fibrous, rotting wood. Then he broke some low branches on the trees, dead and dry. In a few minutes his fire was burning nicely. Then he stripped the saddle from the horse and rubbed him down with a handful of crushed bark. When that was done, he got out the nosebag and fed the horse some of the oats he had appropriated from Shute's barn.

The next hour he occupied himself in gathering fuel. Luckily there were a number of dead trees close by, débris left from some landslide from up the mountain. He settled down by the fire, made coffee. Dozing against the rock, he fed the blaze intermittently, his mind far away.

Somehow, sometime, he fell asleep. Around the rocks the wind, moaning and whining, sought with icy fingers for a grasp at his shoulder, at his hands. But the log burned well, and the big horse stood close, stamping in the sand and dozing beside the man on the ground.

Once, starting from his sleep, Rafe noticed that the log had burned until it was out of the fire, so he dragged it around, then laid another across it. Soon he was again asleep.

He awakened suddenly. It was daylight, and the storm was still raging. His fire blazed among the charred embers of his logs, and he lifted his eyes. Six Indians faced him beyond the fire, and their rifles and bows covered him. Their faces were hard and unreadable. Two stepped forward and jerked him to his feet, stripped his guns from him, and motioned for him to saddle his horse.

Numb with cold, he could scarcely realize what had happened to him. One of the Indians, wrapped in a worn red blanket, jabbered at the others and kept pointing to the horse, making threatening gestures. Yet when Rafe had the animal saddled, they motioned to him to mount. Two of the Indians rode up then, leading the horses of the others. So this was the way it ended. He was a prisoner.

XXI

Uncomprehending, Rafe Caradec opened his eyes to darkness. He sat up abruptly and stared around. Then, after a long minute, it came to him. He was a prisoner in a village of the Oglala Sioux, and he had just awakened. Two days before they had brought him here, bound him hand and foot, and left him in the teepee he now occupied. Several times squaws had entered the teepee and departed. They had given him food and water.

It was night, and his wrists were swollen from the tightness of the bonds. It was warm in the teepee, for there was a fire, but smoke filled the skin wigwam and filtered out at the top. He had a feeling it was almost morning.

What had happened at Painted Rock? Where was Ann? And where was Tex Brisco? Had Dan Shute returned?

He was rolling over toward the entrance to catch a breath of fresh air when the flap was drawn back and a squaw came in. She spoke rapidly in Sioux, then picked a brand from the fire, and, as it blazed up, held it close to his face. He drew back, thinking she meant to sear his eyes. Then, looking beyond the blaze, he saw that the squaw holding it was the Indian girl he had saved from Trigger Boyne!

With a burst of excited talk, she bent over him. A knife slid under his bonds, and they were cut. Chafing his ankles, he looked up. In the flare of the torchlight he could now see the face of a male Indian.

He spoke, gutturally, but in fair English. "My daughter say you man help her," he said.

"Yes," Rafe replied. "The Sioux are not my enemies, nor am I theirs."

"Your name Caradec." The Indian's statement was flat, not to be contradicted.

"Yes." Rafe stumbled to his feet, rubbing his wrists.

"We know your horse, also the horses of the others."

"Others?" Rafe asked quickly. "There are others here?"

"Yes, a woman and a man. The man is much better. He had been injured."

Ann and Tex! Rafe's heart leaped.

"May I see them?" he asked. "They are my friends."

The Indian nodded. He studied Rafe for a minute. "I think you are good man. My name Man-Afraid-Of-His-Horse."

The Oglala chief! Rafe looked again at the Indian. "I know the name. With Red Cloud you are the greatest of the Sioux."

The chief nodded. "There are others. John Grass, Gall, Crazy Horse, many others. The Sioux have many great men."

The girl led Rafe away to the tent where he found

Tex Brisco, lying on a pile of skins and blankets. Tex was pale, but he grinned when Rafe came in.

"Man," he said, "it's good to see yuh! And here's Ann?"

Rafe turned to look at her, and she smiled, then held out her hand. "I have learned how foolish I was. First from Penn, and then from Mullaney and Tex."

"Penn? Mullaney?" Rafe squinted his eyes. "Are they here?"

Quickly Ann explained about Barkow's killing of Penn, and her subsequent attempt to overtake Bruce, guided and helped by Rock Mullaney.

"Barkow's dead," Rafe said. "Shute killed him."

"Ann told me," Tex said. "He had it comin'. Where's Dan Shute now?"

Caradec shrugged. "I don't know, but I'm goin' to find out."

"Please." Ann came to him. "Don't fight with him, Rafe. There has been enough killing. You might be hurt, and I couldn't stand that."

He looked at her. "Does it matter so much?"

Her eyes fell. "Yes," she said simply, "it does. . . ."

Painted Rock lay quietly in a world of white, its shabbiness lost under the purity of freshly fallen snow. Escorted by a band of Oglalas, Ann, Rafe, and Tex rode to the edge of town, then said a quick good-bye to the friendly warriors. The street was empty, and the town seemed to have no word of their coming.

Tex Brisco, still weak from loss of blood and looking pale, brought up the rear. With Ann, he headed right for the Emporium. Rafe Caradec rode ahead until they neared the National Saloon, then swung toward the boardwalk, and waited until they had gone by.

Baker came rushing from the store and, with Ann's help, got Tex down from the horse and inside.

Rafe Caradec led his own horse down the street and tied it to the hitching rail. Then he glanced up and down the street, looking for Shute. Within a matter of minutes Dan would know he was back, and, once he was aware of it, there would be trouble.

Pat Higley was inside the store when Rafe entered. He nodded at Rafe's story of what had taken place.

"Shute's been back in town," Higley said. "I reckon after he lost Ann in the snowstorm he figgered she would circle around and come back here."

"Where's Pod Gomer?" Rafe inquired.

"If yuh mean has he taken out, why I can tell yuh he hasn't," Baker said. "He's been around with Shute, and he's wearin' double hardware right now."

Higley nodded. "They ain't goin' to give up without a fight," he warned. "They're keepin' some men in town, quite a bunch of 'em."

Rafe also nodded. "That will end as soon as Shute's out of the way."

He looked up as the door pushed open, and started to his feet when Johnny Gill walked in with Rock Mullaney.

"The soldiers rigged a sled," Gill announced at once. "They're takin' Bo back to the fort, so we reckoned it might be a good idea to come down here and stand by in case of trouble."

Ann came to the door, and stood there by the

curtain, watching them. Her eyes continually strayed to Rafe, and he looked up, meeting their glance. Ann flushed and looked away, then invited him to join her for coffee.

Excusing himself, he got up and went inside. Gravely Ann showed him to a chair, brought him a napkin, then poured coffee for him, and put sugar and cream beside his cup. He took the sugar, then looked up at her.

"Can you ever forgive me?" she asked.

"There's nothin' to forgive," he said. "I couldn't blame you. You were sure your father was dead."

"I didn't know why the property should cause all that trouble until I heard of the oil. Is it really worth so much?"

"Quite a lot. Shippin' is a problem now, but that will be taken care of soon. So it could be worth a great deal of money. I expect they knew more about that end of it than we did." Rafe looked at her. "I never aimed to claim my half of the ranch," he said, "and I don't now. I accepted it just to give me some kind of a legal basis for workin' with you, but now that the trouble is over, I'll give you the deed, the will your father made out, and the other papers."

"Oh, no!" she exclaimed quickly. "You mustn't! I'll need your help to handle things, and you must accept your part of the ranch and stay on. That is," she added, "if you don't think I'm too awful for the way I acted."

He flushed. "I don't think you're awful, Ann," he said clumsily, getting to his feet. "I think you're wonderful. I guess I always have, ever since that first day when I came into the store and saw you." His eyes strayed, and carried their glance out the window. He came to with a start and got to his feet. "There's Dan Shute," he said. "I got to go."

Ann arose with him, white to the lips. He avoided her glance, then turned abruptly toward the door. The girl made no protest, but as he started through the curtain, she said: "Come back, Rafe. I'll be waiting."

He walked to the street door, and the others saw him go, then something in his manner apprised them of what was about to happen. Mullaney caught up his rifle and started for the door, also, and Baker reached for a scattergun.

Rafe Caradec glanced quickly at the snow-covered street. One wagon had been down the center of the street about daybreak, and there had been no other traffic except for a few passing riders. Horses stood in front of the National and the Emporium and had kicked up the snow, but otherwise it was an even, unbroken expanse of pure white.

Rafe stepped out on the porch of the Emporium. Dan Shute's gray was tied at the National's hitching rail, but Shute was nowhere in sight. Rafe walked to the corner of the store, his feet crunching on the snow. The sun was coming out, and the snow might soon be gone. As he thought of that, a drop fell from the roof overhead and touched him on the neck.

Dan Shute would be in the National. Rafe walked slowly down the walk to the saloon and pushed open the door. Joe Benson looked up from behind his bar, and hastily moved down toward the other end. Pod Gomer, slumped in a chair at a table across the room, sat up abruptly, his eyes shifting to the big man at the bar.

Dan Shute's back was to the room. In his short, thick coat he looked enormous. His hat was off, and his shock of blond hair, coarse and uncombed, glinted in the sunlight.

Rafe stopped inside the door, his gaze sweeping the room in one all-encompassing glance. Then his eyes riveted on the big man at the bar.

"All right, Shute," he said calmly. "Turn around and take it."

Dan Shute turned, and he was grinning. He was grinning widely, but there was a wicked light dancing in his eyes. He stared at Caradec, letting his slow, insolent gaze go over him from head to foot.

"Killin' yuh would be too easy," he said. "I promised myself that when the time came I would take yuh apart with my hands, and then, if there was anything left, shoot it full of holes. I'm goin' to kill yuh, Caradec."

Out of the tail of his eye, Rafe saw that Johnny Gill was leaning against the jamb of the back door, and that Rock Mullaney was just inside of that same door.

"Take off your guns, Caradec, and I'll kill yuh," Shute said softly.

"It's their fight," Gill said suddenly. "Let 'em have it the way they want it!"

The voice startled Gomer so that he jerked, and he glanced over his shoulder, his face white. Then the front door pushed open, and Higley came in with Baker. Pod Gomer touched his lips with his tongue and shot a sidelong glance at Benson. The saloonkeeper looked unhappy.

Carefully Dan Shute reached for his belt buckle and unbuckled the twin belts, laying the big guns on the bar, butts toward him. At the opposite end of the bar, Rafe Caradec did the same. Then, as one man, they shed their coats.

Lithe and broad-shouldered, Rafe was an inch shorter and forty pounds lighter than the other man. Narrow-hipped and lean as a greyhound, he was built for speed, but the powerful shoulders and powerful hands and arms spoke of years of training as well as hard work with a double jack, axe, or heaving at heavy, wet lines of a ship.

Dan Shute's neck was thick, his chest broad and massive. His stomach was flat and hard. His hands were big, and he reeked of sheer animal strength and power. Licking his lips like a hungry wolf, he started forward. He was grinning, and the light was dancing in his hard gray-white eyes. He did not rush or leap. He walked right up to Rafe, with that grin on his lips, and Caradec stood flat-footed, waiting for him. But as Shute stepped in close, Rafe suddenly whipped up a left to the wind that beat the man to the punch. Shute winced at the blow, and his eyes narrowed. Then he smashed forward with his hard skull, trying for a butt. Rafe clipped him with an elbow and swung away, keeping out of the corner.

XXII

Still grinning, Dan Shute moved in. The big man was deceptively fast, and, as he moved in, suddenly he left his feet and hurled himself feet foremost at Rafe. Caradec sprang back, but too slowly. The legs jackknifed around him, and Rafe staggered and went to the floor. He hit hard, and Dan was the first to move. Throwing himself over, he caught his weight on his left hand and swung with his right. It was a wicked, half-arm blow, and it caught Rafe on the chin. Lights exploded in his brain, and he felt himself go down. Then Shute sprang for him.

Rafe rolled his head more by instinct than knowledge, and the blow clipped his ear. He threw his feet high, and tipped Dan over on his head and off his body. Both men came to their feet like cats and hurled themselves at each other. They struck like two charging bulls with an impact that shook the room.

Rafe slugged a right to the wind and took a smashing blow to the head. They backed off, then charged together, and both men started pitching them—short, wicked hooks thrown from the hips with everything they had in the world in every punch. Rafe's head was roaring, and he felt the smashing blows rocking his head from side to side. He smashed an inside right to the face, and saw a thin streak of blood on Shute's cheek. He fired his right down the same groove, and it might well have been on a track. The split in the skin widened, and a trickle of blood started. Rafe let go another one to the same spot, then whipped a wicked left uppercut to the wind.

Shute took it coming in and never lost stride. He ducked and lunged, knocking Rafe off balance with his shoulder, then swinging an overhand punch that caught Rafe on the cheekbone. Rafe tried to sidestep and failed, slipping on a wet spot on the floor. As he went down, Dan Shute aimed a terrific kick at his head that would have ended the fight right there but, half off balance, Rafe hurled himself at the pivot leg and knocked Dan sprawling.

Both men came up and walked into each other, slugging. Rafe evaded a kick aimed for his stomach and slapped a palm under the man's heel, lifting it high. Shute went over on his back, and Rafe left the floor in a dive and lit right in the middle of Dan Shute and knocked the wind out of him, but not enough so that Dan's thumb failed to stab him in the eye.

Blinded by pain, Rafe jerked his head away from that stabbing thumb and felt it rip along his cheek. Then he slammed two blows to the head before Shute heaved him off. They came up together.

Dan Shute was bleeding from the cut on his cheek, but he was still smiling. His gray shirt was torn, revealing bulging white muscles. He was not even breathing hard, and he walked into Rafe with a queer little bounce in his step. Rafe weaved right to left, then straightened suddenly and left-handed a stiff one into Shute's mouth. Dan went under a duplicate punch and slammed a right to the wind that lifted Rafe off the floor. They went into a clinch then, and Rafe was the faster, throwing Dan with a rolling hillock. He came off the floor fast, and the two went over like a pinwheel, gouging, slugging, ripping, and tearing at each other with fists, thumbs, and elbows.

Shute was up first, and Rafe followed, lunging in, but Dan stepped back and whipped a right uppercut that smashed every bit of sense in Rafe's head into a blinding pinwheel of white light. But he was moving fast and went on in with the impetus of his rush, and both men crashed to the floor.

Up again and swinging, they stood toe to toe and slugged viciously, wickedly, each punch a killing blow. Jaws set, they lashed at each other like madmen. Then Rafe let his right go down the groove to the cut cheek. He sidestepped and let go again, then again and again. Five times straight he hit that split cheek. It was cut deeply now and streaming blood.

Dan rushed and grabbed Rafe around the knees, heaving him clear of the floor. He brought him down with a thunderous crash that would have killed a lesser man. Rafe got up, panting, and was set for Shute as he rushed. He split Dan's lips with another left, then threw a right that missed and caught a punch in the middle that jerked his mouth open and brought his breath out of his lungs in one great gasp.

All reason gone, the two men fought like animals, yet worse than animals for in each man was the experience of years of accumulated brawling and slugging in the hard, tough, wild places of the world. They lived by their strength and their hands and the fierce animal drive that was within them, the drive of the fight for survival.

Rafe stepped in, punching Shute with a wicked, cutting, stabbing left, and his right went down the line again, and blood streamed from the cut cheek. They stood then, facing each other, shirts in ribbons, blood-streaked, with arms a-swing. They started to circle, and suddenly Shute lunged. Rafe took one step back and let go a kick from the hips. An inch or so lower down and he would have caught the bigger man in the solar plexus. As it was, the kick struck him on the chest and lifted him clear of the floor. He came down hard, but his powerful arms grabbed Rafe's leg as they swung down, and both men hit the floor together.

Shute sank his teeth into Rafe's leg, and Rafe stabbed at his eye with a thumb. Shute let go and got up, grabbing a chair. Rafe went under it, heard the chair splinter, and scarcely realized in the heat of battle that his back had taken the force of the blow. He shoved Dan back and smashed both hands into the big man's body, then rolled aside and spilled him with a rolling hillock.

Dan Shute came up, and Rafe walked in. He stabbed a left to the face, and Shute's teeth showed through his lip, broken and ugly. Rafe set himself and whipped an uppercut that stood Shute on his toes.

Tottering and punch-drunk, the light of battle still flamed in Shute's eyes. He grabbed at a bottle and lunged at Rafe, smashing it down on his shoulders. Rafe rolled with the blow and felt the bottle shatter over the compact mass of the deltoid at the end of his shoulder, then he hooked a left with that same numb arm, and felt the fist sink into Shute's body.

The strong muscles of that rock-ribbed stomach were yielding now. Rafe set himself and threw a right from the hip to the same place, and Shute staggered, his face greenish-white. Rafe walked in and stabbed three times with a powerful, cutting left that left Shute's lips in shreds. Then, suddenly calling on some hidden well of strength, Dan dived for Rafe's legs, got him around the knees, and jerked back. Rafe hit the floor on the side of his head, and his world splintered into fragments of broken glass and light, flickering and exploding in a flaming chain reaction. He rolled over, took a kick on the chest, then staggered up as Shute stepped in, drunk with a chance of victory. Heavy, brutal punches smashed him to his knees, but Rafe staggered up. A powerful blow brought him down again, and he lunged to his feet.

Again he went to his knees, and again, he came up. Then he uncorked one of his own, and Dan Shute staggered. But Dan had shot his bolt. Head ringing, Rafe Caradec walked in, grabbed the bigger man by the shirt collar and belt, right hand at the belt, then turned his back on him and jerked down with his left hand at the collar and heaved up with the right. He got his back under him, and then hurled the big man like a sack of wheat.

Dan Shute hit the table beside which Gene Baker was standing, and both went down in a heap. Suddenly Shute rolled over and came to his knees, his eyes blazing. Blood streamed from the gash in his cheek, open now from mouth to ear, his lips were shreds, and a huge blue lump concealed one eye. His face was scarcely human, yet in the remaining eye gleamed a wild, killing, insane light. And in his hands he held Gene Baker's double-barreled shotgun! He did not speak—just swept the gun up and squeezed down on both triggers.

Yet at the very instant that he squeezed those triggers, Rafe's left hand had dropped to the table near him, and with one terrific heave he spun it toward the kneeling man. The gun belched flame and thunder as Rafe hit the floor flat on his stomach, and rolled over to see an awful sight.

Joe Benson, crouched over the bar, took the full blast of buckshot in the face and went over backward with a queer, choking scream.

Rafe heaved himself erect, and suddenly the room was deathly still. Pod Gomer's face was a blank sheet of white horror as he stared at the spot where Benson had vanished.

Staggering, Caradec walked toward Dan Shute. The man lay on his back, arms outflung, head lying at a queer angle.

Mullaney pointed. "The table," he said. "It busted his neck."

Rafe turned and staggered toward the door. Johnny Gill caught him there. He slid an arm under Rafe's shoulders and strapped his guns to his waist.

"What about Gomer?" he asked.

Caradec shook his head. Pod Gomer was getting up to face him, and he lifted a hand. "Don't start anything. I've had enough. I'll go."

Somebody brought a bucket of water, and Rafe fell on his knees and began splashing the ice-cold water over his head and face. When he had dried himself on a towel someone had handed him, he started for a coat. Baker had come in with a clean shirt from the store.

"I'm sorry about that shotgun," he said. "It happened so fast I didn't know."

Rafe tried to smile, and couldn't. His face was stiff and swollen. "Forget it," he said. "Let's get out of here."

"Yuh ain't goin' to leave, are yuh?" Baker asked. "Ann said that she . . ."

"Leave? Shucks, no! We've got an oil business here, and there's a ranch. While I was at the fort, I had a wire sent to the C Bar down in Texas for some more cattle."

Ann was waiting for him, wide-eyed when she saw his face. He walked past her toward the bed and fell across it. "Don't let it get you, honey," he said. "We'll talk about it when I wake up next week."

She stared at him, started to speak, and a snore sounded in the room. Ma Baker smiled. "When a man wants to sleep, let him sleep, and I'd say he'd earned it."

ANDREW J. FENADY

Owen Wister Award-Winning Author of *Big Ike*

No mission is too dangerous as long as the cause—
and the money—are right. Four soldiers of fortune,
along with a beautiful woman, have crossed the
Mexican border to dig up five million dollars in
buried gold. But between the Trespassers and their
treasure lie a merciless comanchero guerilla band,
a tribe of hostile Yaqui Indians and Benito Juarez's
army. It's a journey no one with any sense would
hope to survive, or would even dare to try, except...

The Trespassers

Andrew J. Fenady is a Spur Award finalist and re-
cipient of the prestigious Owen Wister Award for
his lifelong contribution to Western literature, and
the Golden Boot Award, in recognition of his contri-
butions to the Western genre. He has written eleven
novels and numerous screenplays, including the
classic John Wayne film *Chisum*.

ISBN 13: 978-0-8439-6024-2

MAX BRAND®

Luck

Pierre Ryder is not your average Jesuit missionary. He's able to ride the meanest horse, run for miles without tiring, and put a bullet in just about any target. But now he's on a mission of vengeance to find the man who killed his father. The journey will test his endurance to its utmost—and so will the extraordinary woman he meets along the way. Jacqueline "Jack" Boone has all the curves of a lady but can shoot better than most men. In the epic tradition of *Riders of the Purple Sage*, their story is one for the ages.

ISBN 13: 978-0-8439-5875-1

FIRST TIME IN PAPERBACK!

Max Brand®

"Brand practices his art to something like perfection."
—*The New York Times*

Sequel to **LUCK**

CROSSROADS

"There's bad luck all around me."

Jacqueline "Jack" Boone couldn't say she didn't warn him. But Dix was a man who made his own luck. And he couldn't resist a beautiful woman who, according to tales told round the campfire, had bested one of the most notorious gunmen in decades. Except the people who were after Dix for a murder he didn't mean to commit are now after Jack too. Relentlessly stalked by a man known as El Tigre, the pair can only ride headlong into danger and hope that in the end their luck holds out.

ISBN 13: 978-0-8439-5876-8

"When you think of the West, you think of Zane Grey." —*American Cowboy*

ZANE GREY

THE RESTORED, FULL-LENGTH NOVEL,
IN PAPERBACK FOR THE FIRST TIME!

The Great Trek

terl Hazelton is no stranger to trouble. But the hooting that made him an outlaw was one he didn't o. Though it was his cousin who pulled the trigger, terl took the blame, and now he has to leave the ountry if he wants to stay healthy. Sterl and his loyal riend, Red Krehl, set out for the greatest adventure f their lives, signing on for a cattle drive across the ast northern desert of Australia to the gold fields f the Kimberley Mountains. But it seems no matter vhere Sterl goes, trouble is bound to follow!

"Grey stands alone in a class untouched by others." —*Tombstone Epitaph*

ISBN 13: 978-0-8439-6062-4

Cotton Smith

"Cotton Smith is one of the finest of a new breed o
writers of the American West."

—Don Coldsmith

Return of the
Spirit Rider

In the booming town of Denver, saloon owner Vir
Lockhart is known as a savvy businessman with a
quick gun. But he will never forget that he was raised
an Oglala Sioux. So when Vin's Oglala friends need
ed help dealing with untruthful, encroaching white
men, he swore he would do what he could. His dra
matic journey will include encounters with Wild Bill
Hickok and Buffalo Bill Cody. But when an ambush
leaves him on the brink of death, his only hope is
what an old Oglala shaman taught him long ago.

"Cotton Smith is one of the best new authors ou
there."

—Steven Law, Read Wes

ISBN 13: 978-0-8439-5854-6

☐ **YES!**

Sign me up for the Leisure Western Book Club and send my FREE BOOKS! If I choose to stay in the club, I will pay only $14.00* each month, a savings of $9.96!

NAME: _____

ADDRESS: _____

TELEPHONE: _____

EMAIL: _____

☐ I want to pay by credit card.

☐ VISA   ☐ MasterCard.   ☐ DISCOVER

ACCOUNT #: _____

EXPIRATION DATE: _____

SIGNATURE: _____

Mail this page along with $2.00 shipping and handling to:
Leisure Western Book Club
PO Box 6640
Wayne, PA 19087
Or fax (must include credit card information) to:
610-995-9274

You can also sign up online at **www.dorchesterpub.com**.